"Sugar, Cream or Murder"

Le Doux Mysteries #2

By Abigail Thornton

This is a work of fiction. Similarities to real people, places, or events are entirely coincidental.

SUGAR, CREAM OR MURDER

First edition. September 16, 2021.

Copyright © 2021 Abigail Thornton.

Written by Abigail Thornton.

DEDICATION

To my oldest.
You see life through a different lens
and I love you for it!
Never stop teaching me about life and love.

ACKNOWLEDGEMENTS

No author works alone. Thank you, Cathy.
Your cover work is beautiful!
And to Laura, for your timely and thorough editing!

NEWSLETTER

Stay up to date on all my new releases by joining my newsletter!
You can find it and other exciting news at
abigailthorntonbooks.com

CHAPTER 1

"What do you think, Vi?" Wynona set the new jar on the open shelf and stood back to admire her collection. Rows upon rows of tea mixtures decorated her shelves. They were all home-grown and custom made, and after everything Wynona Le Doux had been through, she was extremely proud of her accomplishment.

Violet, Wynona's purple mouse, chittered and ran circles on the workshop table. The creature had gotten its unusual color during a hex gone wrong from Wynona's sister, Celia. Wynona and Violet had become wonderful friends ever since the near-disaster and the tiny rodent was now a permanent fixture in Wynona's life.

Wynona smiled. "I know. It looks good, doesn't it?" She let her eyes scan the neat labels, which included lists of all the ailments the teas would help. Her mind continually churned with more ideas of how to mix herbs and tea leaves in order to help people, and Wynona looked forward to trying them all.

Violet skittered down the table leg and dashed across the room, diving into a dark corner.

Wynona frowned, but didn't stop the creature. It wasn't like Violet belonged to Wynona. They were friends, not master and pet. When Violet decided she was done with a situation, there was little Wynona could do about it, except hope that her small companion came back later to enjoy a meal together. Wynona was growing used to Violet's lavender color and had even decided the uniqueness of it fit the mouse's bold personality.

Wynona knew what it was like to be different, especially when that difference came because of a curse. Maybe that was why she had put such effort into drawing Violet out from her hidey hole behind the bookcase after Celia's attempted killing. Birds of a feather and all that...

The biggest difference between the two was the fact that while Violet's curse was visible to everyone, Wynona's was nearly invisible. She had had the unfortunate luck to be born into the most powerful witch family in all of Hex Haven. Her father and mother ruled the valley, with her father holding the title of President Le Doux.

At her birth, Wynona had more than likely been born with great powers, if her family line was anything to go by, but something had gone wrong. From the moment she had entered the world, her powers had been bound.

Her family had been completely unaware of the problem until it was too late and no amount of research had helped them find the culprit. As someone who had now become completely worthless to her family, Wynona spent all her growing up years isolated in the castle. Her family and even the servants either ignored her, or treated her like dirt.

The only bright spot in her life had been Granny Saffron Le Doux. She had refused to allow Wynona's unfortunate situation to color the way she treated her grandchild. Thus the older witch had taken Wynona under her wing and taught her everything she could that didn't require magic.

The large inventory of teas and spices were a testament to Granny's tutelage and why Wynona had named her tea shop Saffron's Tea House.

Without her grandmother, Wynona would never have escaped her family and never had a chance to live her own life.

"And despite dead bodies and grumpy vampire police chiefs...we made it, didn't we?" Wynona whispered to the empty room.

Violet must have decided to take a nap, since she didn't answer.

Brushing her fingers against her pants, Wynona began to put away all the tools she had used to create her latest tinctures. Her workspace smelled like someone had spilled incense on every surface, but she didn't mind.

Each smell only reminded her of her granny and the few good moments of her childhood. There were times when it was far too easy to dwell on the bad parts of her life. Like the fact that her family hated her, the fact that she had no magic, the fact that she'd been mentally abused as a child...

But Wynona didn't want to dwell on those things. She wanted freedom from it all. Freedom from pain and nightmares and heavy grudges. That's why she had decided to open the shop. When she was busy helping other paranormals, she was too busy to be angry at her family.

It was a win-win for everybody. Wynona got to use the skills Granny had taught her and her family could ignore a pest they hadn't wanted in the first place.

Wynona was just wiping down the last workcounter when her stomach growled. She automatically put a hand on it and grimaced. "Guess I should have eaten breakfast." Shaking her head, she quickly finished up, then hurried inside.

Her kitchen was just as neat and tidy as the rest of her house. There was something so wonderful about having a place for everything and everything being in its place. An unbidden smile pulled at Wynona's lips as she walked into her small, but cozy kitchen. She had bought the house from a dryad when she'd first escaped her family. It bordered on the Grove of Secrets. A magical forest that no sane person or creature ever entered willingly.

The isolation had been perfect for Wynona. The magic of the forest helped infuse the plants in her greenhouse with a little something extra, and nobody bothered her while she was working.

The pan she had placed on the stove started sizzling and Wynona pulled herself from her wandering thoughts and cracked a couple of eggs. A squeak from behind caught her attention and Wynona smiled over her shoulder. "Hungry?"

Violet stood on her back legs, nose twitching toward the stove.

"Grab a seat," Wynona said, waving toward the table. She grinned wider when she could hear the scuffling of tiny legs hurrying to their usual spot. Without missing a beat, Wynona stirred the eggs and gathered two plates. One large, one small. It only took a few moments to toss some bread in the toaster and begin to put the food on the plates.

"Here you go." Wynona added a few slices of strawberries to each serving, then set the tea saucer in front of Violet. The house was quiet as the two ate their simple meal, contentment thrumming through the air.

Wynona couldn't stop the smile on her face as she ate. It had taken her a long time to get to this point. Years of heartache, struggles, failures and now finally, she was seeing a rainbow at the end of the storm. She had her business, she loved what she did, and she had new friends. Including the little mouse at her side.

"Good?" Wynona asked.

Violet chattered, scrubbing her face with her tiny, purple paws.

Wynona's phone buzzed and she grabbed it from the farside of the table.

We still on for lunch?

Wynona glanced at the clock. She had promised her friends she would host a tea luncheon.

Yep. As long as you bring the flowers you promised.

Primrose was Wynona's best friend who happened to be a fairy, and was also one of the premiere flower growers in Hex Haven. Just like Wynona and Violet, Prim was a bit different from the rest of her species in that she didn't have any wings, but no one could talk to a rose the way Prim could.

Wynona had seen flowers move as Prim walked by, just because they felt her presence. Being born without wings definitely hadn't dampened Prim's magic at all, though many in the fairy community refused to acknowledge it. The flower farmer's own ostracization was part of the reason she and Wynona had become such good friends.

Wynona had learned very quickly after escaping her parents' castle that tragedy brought people together.

Oh, they're ready. It's the invitation to the wolf shifter that I'm worried about.

Wynona bit her bottom lip. Deputy Chief Strongclaw, otherwise known as Rascal, had been instrumental in not only saving Wynona's life when she was helping catch a killer a few months ago, but he had also seen to it that Chief Ligurio, a grumpy vampire who had a grudge against the Le Doux family, listened to Wynona and her ideas.

Along with that already impressive resume, Rascal was also very handsome and a strong flirt. Wynona had so little experience with men that she wasn't sure if his flirting was serious or not, but she would be the first to admit that she wanted to find out.

In an act of bravery, she had invited him to this Sunday's afternoon luncheon. It would be his first time attending one of her tea parties and Wynona was more than a little nervous. Though she wasn't exactly sure why. It wasn't a date and she didn't even know if Rascal was interested in her as more than a friend. But the sprites that took flight in Wynona's stomach whenever they were close to each other gave her hope.

You didn't chicken out, did you?

Wynona sighed and texted back.

No. I invited him. He said he'd come.

Wynona could practically hear the squeal that would be leaving Prim's mouth right now, and just knowing it was happening was enough to make Wynona smile...again.

She couldn't believe this was her life now. A year ago this was nothing but a dream and here she was, looking forward to many more days spent just like this.

"Come on, Vi," Wynona said, standing up and stuffing her phone in her pocket. "Let's go make sure those imps haven't burned down the kitchen." Wynona bent down and picked Violet up and put her on her shoulder. "And let's hope that their antics didn't drive Lusgu into giving his notice!"

CHAPTER 2

"Ouch!" Primrose cried, jumping to her feet and swatting at her back. "You ridiculous imps!"

Wynona pinched the bridge of her nose, shaking her head. "Kyoz and Gnuq!" she scolded. "Stop it right now!"

The twin imps, their blue faces nearly purple with laughter, danced through the air on their way back to the kitchen.

"If they weren't the best bakers in town now that Chef Droxon is dead..." Prim said through gritted teeth. Rubbing her shoulder, she sat back down.

"I'm sorry," Wynona moaned. "I wish I could tell them to get lost, but trying to keep up with the baking and the tea making was too much!" She shook her head. "At least they aren't here full time. They were dropping off tomorrow's pastries."

Violet chittered and nuzzled Wynona's neck in a comforting gesture.

Wynona's hand reached up, petting the creature in an almost unconscious gesture.

Prim made a point of looking around, then pinned Wynona with her bright pink stare. "I thought you said you invited him."

Wynona pinched her lips together and tapped the edge of her teacup. "I did. He said he'd come." She didn't want to admit to the heavy feeling in her stomach. She had been excited to see Rascal again, but now that he was ten minutes late, she was beginning to wonder if maybe he wasn't as excited to see her.

"Sorry I'm late!" Rascal came skidding into the dining room. The wolf shifter's hair, as usual, was standing up in messy piles all over his head. His chin had a couple days' growth on it, just tempting Wynona's fingers to touch.

She curled said fingers into fists. Handsome as Rascal might be, they didn't have that kind of relationship...yet. The Deputy Chief of the Hex Haven police station had become Wynona's friend, but so far that's all they were. She needed to remember that.

"Rascal!" Prim cried. "Finally! Someone to arrest those two troublemakers in the kitchen." She opened her pink eyes wide and waved toward the doorway behind her. "They're menaces to society."

Rascal grinned and sauntered to the table. Reaching down, he grabbed one of the mini pies and took a large bite. Groaning, he quickly swallowed and ate the rest of it. "No can do, Prim," he said, grabbing the napkin Wynona offered to wipe the blueberry off his mouth. "The only crime they've committed is making something too good to resist."

Wynona grinned, then blushed when Rascal winked at her.

He slid lazily into a seat.

"Let me get some more hot water," Wynona said, standing from her seat. "This is too cool to steep properly."

Rascal grabbed her hand as she started to walk away. He grinned at her with those golden eyes, his thumb rubbing her knuckles. "You don't have to go to that trouble."

"It's no trouble," she replied breathlessly. Blinking, Wynona straightened and slowly pulled her hand out of his. The feeling was entirely too warm and comforting. Turning, she practically fled to the kitchen.

"Messy, messy, messy..." Lusgu, the brownie who cleaned up the tea shop, shook his head and muttered. "Wolves shouldn't be allowed."

Wynona sighed. "How did you even know he's here?" she asked. Her hired janitor had hated Rascal from the start, though Wynona had no idea why.

Lusgu glared at her and tapped the side of his nose. "He's here." One side of the small man's mouth curled up in a sneer. "Messy."

Wynona had to pinch her lips to keep from laughing. One day she would get to the bottom of that mystery, but right now, she would simply keep Lusgu and Rascal away from each other as best she could. Focusing on the task in front of her, she turned on the stove top in order to heat the kettle.

Lusgu grumbled, then pointed a finger at the pot.

Steam began to pour out of the spout, whistling immediately. Wynona forced herself to keep smiling and say thank you to the cantankerous employee before picking up the kettle and taking it out front. She worked hard not to let it bother her, but watching others use their magic so easily always brought out a trickle of jealousy. There were many times in her life when that magic would have been more than useful. In fact, it could have saved her life not too long ago, but Rascal had saved it instead.

She owed her new friend more than she could say.

Pushing the door with her back, she went back into the dining room and her friends. "Lusgu didn't seem happy that you were here," Wynona teased. "I wouldn't recommend going inside the kitchen."

Rascal gave a dramatic shiver. "Good thing I have you to protect me."

Wynona chuckled. "I'm afraid I have very little control over the brownie."

Prim sniffed. "And that's why no one else wanted him on their staff." She held the teacup to her lips and raised her eyebrows.

Wynona rolled her eyes. "You seem to have a lot of opinions when it comes to my staff."

Prim pursed her lips, her shoulders straightening. If she had been born with wings, like the other fairies, Wynona was sure they would have been fluttering enough to pull her up in the air.

"Someone has to watch out for you," Prim said haughtily. She grinned, breaking the snooty persona she had put on. "Otherwise this place would be overrun with misfits."

"Speak for yourself," Rascal said as he set down his tea cup. "There's absolutely nothing weird about a wolf shifter being on the police force."

"Maybe not," Prim said wryly. "But there is something wrong with a man who doesn't know how to use napkins." She held one out on the end of a long finger.

Rascal snorted, but took it from her. Once again he wiped his mouth, only this time it was the powdered sugar leaving a mess.

Wynona tried to cover her grin with her cup, but she knew full well that Rascal could see it. When the tips of his ears turned red, she couldn't help but grin even wider. Her eyes dropped from his and she took a long sip of her tea. Mint and lavender was one of her favorite combinations. Just right to help her calm down before hosting a busy day tomorrow.

In fact, every day was a busy hosting day. Her calendar was wonderfully booked for the next several months. Sundays were just about the only day Wynona had to spend time with friends and loved ones.

"So tell me about these imps," Rascal said, setting his cup down. "When did you find them?" He reached for another pastry, then paused. "Don't get me wrong," he said quickly. "Your cookies and stuff were great, but these are..." He made a face as he trailed off, realizing that he had inadvertently insulted Wynona.

Prim put a hand over her mouth, trying to hold in her giggling, but the sound was completely audible.

Wynona smiled at Rascal. "Don't worry, I'm fully aware that I'm not as good as Kyoz and Gnuq." She leaned back in her seat. "If I was, I wouldn't have hired them."

"You needed to hire someone," Prim pointed out. "After that first week, you were worse than a wilted lily."

Wynona rolled her eyes. "Thanks. I think."

Prim preened. "You're welcome."

Wynona turned back to Rascal. "I called the HHCRCP."

Rascal blinked, but otherwise didn't appear to understand.

"The Hex Haven Career Resource Center for Paranormals?" Wynona raised her eyebrows in expectation.

"Ah, gotcha." Rascal nodded and took another sip of his tea. "Isn't that the same place you found good ole Lu?"

Wynona laughed softly and shook her head. "Don't let him hear you say that. He doesn't like nicknames."

Rascal shrugged. "Lu and I are destined to be buddies. You'll see."

Careful of Violet, who was still eating, Wynona leaned forward onto the table. "Just what did you do to make Lusgu hate you so much?"

Rascal met her across the table. "You really want to know?"

Wynona nodded.

"I walked into his kitchen."

Wynona huffed. "I go in there all the time."

"Yeah, but it was your kitchen first," Rascal pointed out.

"I've been in the kitchen," Prim added. "He doesn't chase me out with spoons."

Rascal shrugged, leaning back as if he hadn't a care in the world. "Guess you're not as lucky as I am. Or maybe he just has a thing for pretty ladies."

Wynona smiled and shook her head before picking up her tea. She was too happy with her situation to dig any more. How did life get to be so wonderful? She'd gone from one extreme to the other and there were days when she still struggled to believe it.

"Or..." Prim drew the word out. "He just doesn't like messy people."

Rascal put a hand on his chest. "You think I'm messy?"

Prim shrugged. "That's exactly what Lusgu says every time you're around." She made a grumpy face and dropped her voice. "Messy, messy, messy."

"Prim," Wynona scolded, though there was no heat in her tone. Lusgu was an usual character. But where else was she going to find someone who could make her kitchen shine like a crystal ball? The brownie might be grumpy and territorial, but he was an excellent janitor.

Rascal grinned. "Pretty good. Been practicing?"

Prim giggled. The sound of bells echoed through the room. She might not have wings, but Prim had definitely inherited most of the other fairy traits. Her pink eyes went up to the wall. "Ah, geez. I gotta get back." She jumped to her feet and leaned over to kiss Wynona's cheek. "Have a great week. I'll check on the flowers in a few days."

Wynona stood. "Let me walk you to the door."

"Oh, no!" Prim said, walking swiftly across the room and waving a hand over her back. She was in her human form at the moment, giving her long enough legs to outrun Wynona. "I know my way around. You just relax." She stopped at the room entrance. "You'll have to do enough running around tomorrow for guests. Don't worry about it now." With a pointed look at Rascal's back, Prim winked and disappeared.

Wynona plopped down in her seat, her cheeks flaming. She hoped Rascal hadn't noticed Prim's unvoiced insinuation. "How's your tea?" Wynona asked, desperate for a safe topic.

Rascal took another sip. "It's great. Thanks. You have a real knack for knowing what people like." His golden eyes never left hers and Wynona began to shift in her seat.

She both enjoyed and was uncomfortable with his attention. Having been stuck in her parents' house for thirty years, she had very little experience when it came to the opposite sex, at least any that wasn't contained in a book or a movie. Not to mention, when

Wynona had finally gotten free, the first man who had made a move toward her ended up being a killer. It made it difficult for Wynona to trust any of her instincts when it came to men, but there was just something about Rascal she couldn't quite ignore.

"Sorry I was late," he said abruptly.

Wynona jerked her head up to meet his gaze. "It's okay. I know you're busy."

Rascal snorted. "I was fixing Mama Reyna's television. She wouldn't let me go until she could watch *The Old and Haunted*."

Wynona barked a laugh, then covered her mouth. "I take it you managed to fix it?"

Rascal rolled his eyes. "For now. I'm sure there'll be something else for me to fix by the time I get home."

"I had no idea that you were such a handyman," Wynona said. She leaned one elbow onto the table and put her chin in it. "I mean, I remember you fixing Mrs. Reyna's clogged kitchen sink, but now you're doing electronics? You're just a jack-of-all-trades, aren't you?"

Rascal folded his arms over his chest. "Not really, but I try."

Wynona's smile felt like a permanent part of her face at this point, but she couldn't quite bring herself to care. "It's really sweet of you to help her out. Especially since you said Mrs. Reyna tends to be a bit..." She scrunched her nose and pursed her lips, looking for the right word. "Cantankerous?"

Rascal chuckled. The sound was deep and lovely. "That's a big word, and probably much nicer than the one I would have used."

"Still..." Wynona sat up straight. "I think it's great you help her out."

He nodded. "Thanks. That's nice of you to say."

The room felt far warmer than normal as their eyes locked. Wynona could practically feel the blush working its way up her neck and into her face. She really ought to look away. She really should.

Staring like this wasn't very ladylike. Even Granny Saffron, who *loved* instigating shenanigans, would tell Wynona this was too much...

"Would you like to take a walk?"

Wynona blinked, forcing her mind to catch up with the present. "I'm sorry. What?" she asked, shaking her head to clear it from whatever haze she had been caught in.

Rascal rubbed the back of his neck, looking almost as nervous as Wynona. "I was just thinking that it was kind of a nice afternoon and I was wondering if you'd like to, uh, maybe take a walk?" One side of his face was scrunched up in question, making him look like a young, insecure boy.

Wynona's lips twitched. Seeing him a bit uncomfortable helped her feel better about her own reaction to him. "I think that sounds great," she said softly.

Rascal smiled and stood up, starting to walk around to her side.

Wynona's smile was wide enough to split her face when her phone broke her concentration, buzzing wildly on the table. She looked at it and frowned at the number. "I'm sorry," she said to Rascal. "Just a moment." She answered the call. "Hello. This is Saffron's Tea House. Wynona speaking. How may I help you?"

The voice on the other side of the line immediately broke into a long-winded monologue concerning her upcoming tea party reservation later that week. Wynona tried to intervene several times in order to reassure the elderly witch that all would be well, but she was never able to break in.

"Wy," Rascal whispered, his face sporting a resigned smile. "I'll catch you another time."

Wynona put her hand up, trying to stop him, but he was gone before she could say anything, especially with Mrs. Maganti still moaning in her ear. Disappointed more than she could say, Wynona slumped in her seat, tuning out her customer's worries.

Violet whimpered and climbed up Wynona's arm, nuzzling her neck.

Reaching up, Wynona petted the furry animal, the soft fur soothing to her depressed emotions. "Me too," Wynona whispered. "Me too."

CHAPTER 3

Wynona flipped on yet another light switch as she glanced out the window. She was trying to close up for the day, but it was growing more difficult by the minute. A summer storm was moving in and the normally bright evening was growing unexpectedly dark.

Thunder rumbled as Wynona stared at the dark clouds. "We're in for a good one, Vi," Wynona said softly, still keeping an eye outside.

The sidewalks were quickly being cleared as people and creatures prepared for the rain that was sure to break at any moment.

Violet skittered across the floor and Wynona turned just in time to see her dive under the rodent's favorite bookcase.

"That bad, huh?" Wynona smiled. "I didn't take you for such a scaredy mouse."

Violet poked her nose out, only to duck back under the bookcase when another roll of thunder rumbled across the sky.

Wynona moved away from the window and went back to wiping down tables. It only took another two minutes before the window was being pounded with a fierce rain.

"Messy, messy, messy," Lusgu muttered as he walked through the room. The broom was trailing in his wake, sweeping back and forth with ease.

As far as Wynona could see, the tool wasn't actually picking anything up, since Lusgu never seemed to stop cleaning. There was never any time for dust to actually accumulate before the housekeeping janitor had removed it. But she never tired of watching the magic at work, no matter how hard it was not to be jealous.

"At least we don't have any more appointments tonight," Wynona ventured. "No mud will be coming in."

Lusgu gave her a heavy glare before disappearing into the kitchen, the broom slipping in just before the door closed.

Wynona chuckled to herself before sweeping the crumbs into her hand and taking them to the garbage. She jumped when a bright flash of lightning, followed quickly by a crash of thunder strong enough to shake the antique tea cup display, echoed through the room. "Oh, heavens." Wynona gasped. "Vi? Can I fit under that bookcase too?"

Violet chattered, but refused to appear.

There was a buzz in the air that Wynona recognized as natural magic. She might not be able to utilize it, but that didn't mean she was immune to it. The hum of nature's power resonated inside Wynona's chest, filling her with a strange desire to get closer to the source. Slowly, as if in a trance, Wynona walked back to the front window. The pull intensified the closer she came to the elements. The tea house had ceased to exist and Wynona felt as if she held no control over her body, but she was too caught up in the magic to be scared or upset. The closer she got, the stronger the pulse in her chest, urging, begging, pleading with her to join in the display. Without permission, her hand came up, gently coming into contact with the cool glass.

Wynona's reflection looked back at her, since outside was dark compared to the lit interior of the shop. But it wasn't her face that Wynona was watching. Her dark eyes widened as she stared at her hand, consciousness slowly coming back into focus at the unusual sight.

Purple fissures began to creep along the glass, dancing in a zigzag pattern from her fingertips. The thick feeling of magic in the air intensified until Wynona felt her body begin to shake at the strength of it. She began to panic at the odd sensations, unsure what was going on, and tried to pull her hand back, but it was glued to the glass.

Wynona struggled to breathe. The strength of the magic and the panic coursing through her body sent her heart rate skyrocketing and she was positive she would have a heart attack at any moment. The sparks and lights shooting out from her hand began to grow in number and intensity.

The large window pane began to shake, rattling as strongly as the storm outside.

"Let go!" Wynona cried, yanking on her arm, but it wouldn't budge. Her arm began to burn and the purple lights began to move down her wrist, burning into her skin. "AHHH!" Wynona screamed, just as a massive bolt of lightning flashed in time with a clap of thunder strong enough to shake her entire building. Her palms slapped the hardwood floors, just keeping her chin from cracking against it.

"Wynona!"

Gasping, she turned to see a dark figure in the room entrance. The person was wearing a heavy cloak that covered their head, water dripping into puddles at their feet. Despite not being able to see their face, Wynona would know that voice anywhere. "Rascal," she croaked.

He threw off his raincoat and dashed to her side. "What happened?" he asked, helping her carefully to her feet. "Did you hit your head?" His hands ran over her head and shoulders as he checked for injuries.

Wynona wished she could have enjoyed the feel of his warm hands on her skin, but her entire body felt as if it had been struck by lightning, and she couldn't concentrate at all. "The window," she panted, pointing a shaky finger at the pane. She was shocked to see it still intact, having been certain it would be in pieces.

Rascal looked over, then back. His dark brows were furrowed together. "What about the window? Is there a leak?"

Wynona shook her head. "No. I don't think so." She looked down at her hands, but the red marks from whatever had burned her were gone. Her white skin was completely unmarred. She flipped her palm around, studying the front and back, but there was nothing to see.

"Then what is it?" Rascal asked, breaking into her thoughts.

Wynona's mouth opened and closed a few times. She had no idea what to tell him. Anything she said would sound crazy, even in the paranormal world. Since when did someone get attacked by purple lighting or have their hand suctioned to a window? "Nothing," she managed, her teeth chattering a little. "Sorry." She tried to smile, but she wasn't sure she pulled it off. "I guess that last bit of thunder scared me."

Rascal studied her face for a moment. He didn't seem convinced at all, but he didn't push her, for which she was grateful. Wynona had no idea what was going on, and she didn't want to risk alienating one of her few friends, especially when their relationship was so new.

He chuckled, though the sound was slightly strained. "I was worried about you in this storm. If a little bit of thunder is making you run for cover, then I suppose it's a good thing I stopped by."

Wynona laughed softly, her muscles finally easing slightly as the tingling in her body slowly dissipated. "Well, Violet hid under the bookcase before the rain even started, so I suppose she and I are a little more alike than I'd like to admit."

Rascal's laughter was more genuine this time as he put his arm around her and led her to the closest table to sit down. "Hang on a sec," he said, starting to walk away. "I better hang up my coat before Old Lu comes in here and chases me out with the broom."

Wynona eyed the floor. "Or the mop," she said wryly.

Rascal winced. "Sorry."

She smiled. "It cleans easily enough."

A mop flew past her head and Wynona jerked back.

"Ow!" Rascal rubbed the side of his head where the wooden handle of the broom whacked him. "Dang it, Lu! Is that any way to treat a friend?"

Wynona jerked her head around to see Lusgu standing with his hand out in the doorway of the kitchen.

"Ow! Lu!"

Lusgu's hand went back and forth and Wynona turned, realizing that the mop handle was following every movement, conveniently hitting Rascal with every turn. "Lusgu!" she scolded. "Enough!"

The brownie's dry brown lips pinched before his fist clenched and a clattering sound let her know that the mop had fallen to the floor.

Wynona closed her eyes and she slumped in her seat. "Thank you," she said softly. "We'll clean up the floor, okay?"

Lusgu huffed and disappeared back into the kitchen.

Wynona started to stand up, but Rascal cleared his throat. She looked at him to see his hand in the air.

"Don't bother," he said. "I got it." He winked one golden eye. "I made the mess anyway."

"Only because you were coming to save me from the storm," Wynona argued, but she sat back down. She still felt shaky from the odd experience at the window. "You're not in uniform," Wynona suddenly blurted. Heat infused her cheeks when he grinned at her.

"I'm off duty tonight."

Wynona bit her lip. They'd never gotten that walk he invited her on the other day, and while tonight was certainly not a good night for a walk, perhaps they could have dinner together or something. Problem was, Wynona wasn't sure if she should be the one to ask, or wait for Rascal to make another move.

Wynona jumped in her seat when another crack of thunder hit.

"We haven't had a storm like this in years," Rascal mused, his eyes glancing at her front window. "I'll bet the nature paras are having a grand time."

Wynona nodded. "I'm sure. Prim was excited when the forecast warning came through. She said her flowers were going to triple tonight if she played her cards right."

"Do you think Gnuq and Kyoz will have some new baked goods for you to try?" Rascal's voice was slightly muffled as he moved around, mopping the water from the floor.

"Maybe," Wynona mused. She pushed against the table, coming to a stand. Her knees held, for which she was grateful. "How about I make us some tea. You're probably freezing."

Rascal made a point of looking at his wet shoulders. "Yeah...nobody likes the smell of wet wolf."

Wynona laughed. "I don't see how tea will fix that, but at least it'll warm us up." She went into the kitchen and quickly put together a tray, grateful that she had water still hot on the stove. Holding the tray in her hands, she used her back to open the door and walk back into the dining area. "I happened to have a few rosemary rolls left," she announced, smiling at Rascal as she set up the table. "Thought you might enjoy some fresh bread."

"Ahh..." Rascal sighed in contentment as he sank into a seat. "You've found my weakness." He reached across the table, accepting the cup and saucer she offered. "Thank you."

"Rosemary is your weakness?" Wynona asked, tilting her head playfully. "That's a pretty easy kryptonite for a police officer."

Rascal splayed his hands to the side. "What can I say? I'm an easy guy."

Wynona laughed softly behind her tea cup. "Somehow I doubt that."

Rascal put his elbows on the table and leaned forward with his cup in his hands. "You think I'm complicated?"

"I think everyone is complicated," Wynona said easily. "I learned that all too well during your last murder investigation."

"*My* last investigation?" Rascal took a drink, then set the cup down before reaching for a roll. "I do believe you were just as involved in that investigation as I was."

Wynona snorted. "Not by choice."

He nodded sagely. "True. But still..." Rascal gave her that slow, delicious grin of his. The one that sent sprites racing through her core. "Have you given any more thought to joining my team?"

Laughter bubbled from Wynona's lips. "Not a chance," she said. "Just like I learned that people are far more complicated than we give them credit for, I also learned that I have no desire to ever get involved in a murder investigation again."

Rascal narrowed his eyes. "You keep saying that, but I'm not buying it. You were too good at it. You like solving problems. I have a feeling that given the chance, you'd jump back in without a second thought."

Wynona shook her head, more laughter slipping out. "Not only do I never want to see another dead body," she said firmly, "but I also value my neck." Wynona set her cup down. "I don't think that angering grumpy vampires is going to keep my jugular safe."

Rascal chuckled. "I'll give you that one. You know, I never have figured out what he's got against you."

Wynona smiled, but didn't speak. She had a couple of ideas about why Chief Ligurio hated her...and her family. Rascal was slightly correct that there was a part of her that liked to figure things out. The chief's grudge was just such a mystery. There was some kind of connection between Chief Ligurio and Wynona's sister, Celia, though Wynona didn't know all the details yet.

As the ruling family of Hex Haven, Wynona knew her family had a lot of enemies, but Chief Ligurio's derision was stronger than most. Even after she had helped solve the murder of Chef Droxon,

Chief Ligurio had barely been civil to her. In fact, he'd spent most of the investigation trying to pin the murder on her.

Rascal had been a key component in not only keeping the chief off her back, but allowing Wynona enough space to actually be able to put the pieces together.

Rascal held his last bite of roll in the air. "Those two imps are a major pain in the neck, but man...can they bake."

Wynona grinned. "It's why I keep them around. Despite how much Prim hates them."

Rascal barked out a laugh. "Yeah...I don't usually get asked to arrest people because they're well loved." Rascal's grin turned to a frown as his phone buzzed. He pulled it out of his back pocket and silenced it. "Sorry. They should know I'm off duty tonight."

Wynona watched as he set the phone down and it immediately went off again.

Sighing, Rascal picked it up. "Excuse me." He pressed a button. "Deputy Chief Strongclaw." His face immediately went serious and he sat up straighter. "Where? When? Is the unit there?" Rascal nodded. "Okay. I'm on my way."

Wynona slowly set down her cup. "Everything alright?"

Rascal shook his head, drained his cup and then stood. "Considering what you just told me, I don't think you want to know."

That dang curiosity. Wynona found herself leaning forward. She paused before she asked, catching herself before giving into the intrigue.

Rascal's golden eyes flashed with humor. "It's eating at ya, isn't it?"

Wynona shrugged, trying to act casual. "Not at all."

He laughed and held out his hand. "Well, come on. There's been a murder. You might as well come along."

Wynona shook her head. "No way. I don't want anything to do with another investigation." This time it was Wynona's phone that buzzed. She glanced at it and answered with her heart in her throat. "Celia?"

"WYNONA!" Celia screeched.

Wynona winced and pulled it away from her ear.

"She's dead!" Celia continued. "You have to come. You've done this before! You have to come!"

"Celia, I—" Wynona cut off when the line went dead. She looked at the phone, then Rascal. "I don't understand."

Rascal sighed. "Come on, Wy. I'm guessing we're headed to the same place."

Wynona rose and took his hand. It was strong and warm and instantly put her at ease. She had no idea what they were headed into, but between Rascal's description and her sister's cryptic words, Wynona began to worry that her wonderful life had suddenly come to a screeching halt.

CHAPTER 4

"Should have brought an umbrella," Rascal grumbled, pulling the hood of his raincoat farther over his head. The ground squished under his boots as he and Wynona tromped through a very wet and soggy field.

"I'm still not sure I understand what's going on," Wynona whispered. She clung to his arm for balance with one hand and held the hood of her coat with the other. The worst of the storm had passed, but the wind was still quite wet and cold as it whipped through the meadow and surrounding treeline. "Celia was hysterical, but didn't really say what had happened. And you only said there'd been another murder."

Rascal took a deep breath. "I'm actually not sure murder is the right word," he explained. Before Wynona could ask him to clarify, he stopped walking, forcing Wynona to stop as well. "Look. There they are."

Wynona followed the line of his arm to see a massive spotlight and dozens of smaller lights moving through the grass. "Is that the police?"

"Yep," Rascal responded. "I don't have all the details. Why don't we go get caught up?"

Wynona grumbled but followed. She really didn't want to be here. She'd already been involved in helping solve two murders, and a third was just asking for trouble. If Celia hadn't been so upset, Wynona wouldn't have come at all. She would have simply sent Rascal on his merry way. But despite the fact that Wynona and her sister didn't get along, Wynona couldn't quite bring herself to ignore Celia's pleas. She wasn't sure what Celia wanted her to do, but hopefully it would only involve driving Celia back home, and then they'd be done with all this mess.

"Deputy Chief Strongclaw!"

Wynona looked up, recognizing the female's voice. "Hello, Officer Nightshade."

The female vampire paused and an instant smile spread across her face. Her bright white teeth were still easily visible beneath her rain hood. "Why, Ms. Le Doux. What in the world are you doing here?"

Wynona smiled sheepishly. "My sister called. I think this is where she is."

"Ah." Officer Nightshade nodded thoughtfully. "I didn't think of that. But yes, Ms. *Celia* Le Doux is here." The vampire leaned in. "I won't even tell you where. All you have to do is listen to the screeching."

Wynona groaned. "I'm so sorry."

Officer Nightshade chuckled. "Don't be. I'm just grateful I only have to deal with the difficult side of your family once in a blue moon."

"Where's the chief?" Rascal interrupted.

Officer Nightshade jerked to attention as if realizing she was overstepping her boundaries. "He's still overseeing the other officers as they comb the area for evidence, sir."

Rascal nodded and Wynona noted that he looked far more serious than he had earlier. Apparently he had put on his professional face now that he was on duty. "Come on," he said to Wynona. Instead of offering his arm like before, Rascal guided her with a hand on her back.

She had to admit she missed the more informal touch, but understood his position. "Is Celia over here?" she asked.

Rascal shook his head. "I'm not sure, but if Nightshade is correct, I'm guessing the high-pitched squawking is her."

Wynona pinched her lips between her teeth to keep from laughing. She could barely hear what the sharp-eared shifter could, but considering how Celia had screeched on the phone, Wynona was sure Rascal was right.

"You can be sure I'll be telling my father about this!"

"Aaand there she is," Wynona murmured.

Rascal started to chuckle, but cut it off by coughing as they got closer. "Chief?"

A dark hood turned and then was flipped back, revealing the face of Chief Deverell Ligurio. His slicked back dark hair blended into the night, but his deathly pale complexion stood out clearly. "Strongclaw," he snapped, then paused. "And Ms. Le Doux." The sarcasm dripped heavier than the rain from the night's storm. "Why am I not surprised to see you here?"

Wynona held back an eye roll. She had thought they'd left the last investigation a little better than this, but apparently any progress had been erased during their absence from each other. "Hello, Chief Ligurio. I received a call from my sister. She asked me to come."

"I thought you weren't on good terms with your family?" he pressed, his red eyes narrowing in consideration.

"I'm not," Wynona said firmly. "But even if I'm not exactly close, when a family member calls in hysterics, I try to be the type of person who'll respond."

The chief snorted, then waved a hand to the side, toward the continual shouting. "Be my guest."

Taking a deep breath to fortify herself, Wynona gave the chief a nod and murmured her thanks to Rascal. Her pants were practically soaked to the knee by now after their romp through the wet grass. She pulled her coat tighter around her throat. "Celia," Wynona said as she got close enough to get her sister's attention.

Celia spun. She must have been using magic to keep herself dry and put together. Her hair was down and silky, floating through the air in an attractive manner. Her clothes were flowy and dry, accenting all the right curves while still looking like she could blend into Mother Nature without even trying. "Wynona," she said with a sharp smile. "You came."

Wynona folded her arms over her chest. She felt completely frumpy in her heavy raincoat next to her perfect sister, but right now there was little Wynona could do. Besides, Celia had called her here. "I did."

Celia huffed. "Figures you would. You always were a bleeding heart."

"You asked for my help, Celia," Wynona snapped. "I guess if you don't need me, I can just go home." Wynona started to turn, but Celia sighed loud and dramatically enough to wake the dead.

"As long as you're here, you might as well help these...idiots," Celia sneered, waving her arm at the police walking around.

Wynona shook her head. "No. You know what? I don't need this. The police aren't idiots and I'm sure between them and our parents, it'll all be taken care of soon." She turned to walk away again, but ran into a wall. An invisible wall.

"I don't think you understand...*sister*..." Celia said, her voice low as she came up behind Wynona. "Dear Mommy and Daddy don't ever need to know that I was out here."

Wynona spun, facing her sister nose to nose. "Whyever not? I just heard you threatening to call them. Why keep it a secret? There's no way the ghost reporters won't splash this over every page of the newspaper."

Celia's eyes narrowed, but she didn't answer.

Wynona's jaw went slack. "You weren't supposed to be out here, were you?" She barked a sarcastic laugh. "What do you think will happen? Mom and Dad will cut off your allowance?"

Celia rolled her eyes. "You're so naive, Wynona."

"No. I'm free. And it sounds like it's the exact opposite of you at the moment."

"Wynona!"

Both women turned toward the shout. Rascal was walking purposefully toward them, his face etched in stone. "Ms. Le Doux," he said, nodding at Celia before turning to Wynona. "Wy, if you'll come with me, please?"

"Wy?" Celia snorted.

Wynona ignored her sister. She shouldn't have come. No matter what panicked emotions had caused Celia to ask for help, it was clear offering anything to her sister was only going to come back to bite her. "Of course, Officer Strongclaw." She walked away, knowing the wall her sister had put up would be gone. If the police caught Celia using magic at a crime scene, she'd have been in far more trouble than what she already was. "Thank you," Wynona whispered, knowing Rascal's ears would pick it up amongst the noise.

Rascal grinned and winked at her. "You looked like you could use rescuing." He shook his head. "But I'll apologize ahead of time because bringing you with me means that you'll get stuck listening to everything that's going on."

"That's fine," Wynona replied. "Anything is better than dealing with Celia."

Rascal chuckled as they approached a group of women. One woman was sobbing into a handkerchief while another wrapped her arms around the first. None of the women looked very happy to be there. Wynona was positive they were all witches, just like her sister, since not one of them appeared to have been touched by the storm and were wearing similar long, flowing dresses.

Rascal took his hand from Wynona's back and pulled a notebook from his pocket. "Ms. Umbra?"

The crying woman looked up. "Yes?"

Rascal consulted his notes. "It's Callista Umbra, correct?"

She sniffed and nodded.

"And it was your sister...a, Indigo Stocker, who disappeared?"

Again, the woman nodded.

Wynona tilted her head, watching the sister. She was a pretty woman. Light blonde hair and small features. Nothing about her would stand out in a crowd, except that right now she looked particularly frail as she leaned into her friend.

"Do you mind telling me why you were out here tonight?"

One of the women scoffed. "We already went over this with your chief."

Rascal nodded. "I understand, but I'm asking again."

"It's alright," Callista said softly. She took a deep breath as she looked at Rascal. "We were out here for the storm," she explained. "Our coven was working together to draw the power of the lightning into some...um..." She bit her lip and looked at the other women.

"Oh, just say it," the loud one snapped. "It's not like they don't already know."

"Leave her alone, Adel," the one holding up Callista argued. "It's not like this is her fault."

Adel huffed and turned away.

"We were capturing the lightning in stones," Callista explained.

There it was. Now Wynona understood exactly why Celia didn't want their parents involved. Capturing lightning took a great deal of power, which was probably why there was a whole coven of witches out here. Petra Luminis, or stones with lightning trapped inside, could be used for large bursts of power, whether for destruction or for extra potent spells. But the most important thing was...they were illegal.

Rascal growled low in his throat, but nodded for her to continue.

"We were on our third stone when there was a particularly large burst of light." Callista's voice grew softer and her tears renewed. "I was blinded in the moment, and by the time I opened my eyes, my..." She sniffed and dabbed at her face. "My..."

The woman holding her sighed and squeezed Callista tighter. "Her sister, Indigo Stocker, was gone."

"Gone?" Rascal asked.

"Gone," Adel snapped, ignoring Callista's wail of distress. "Nothing but a black streak in the grass."

Wynona put her hand over her mouth. "How awful," she whispered.

Rascal huffed softly beside her. "Were you all blinded by the light?"

Every head in the group nodded.

"So no one actually *saw* what happened to Mrs. Stocker?"

"No," Adel said, her voice finally softening. She pushed a hand through her hair. "I just don't understand how this could actually happen. We had everything under control."

"There's a reason why this kind of magic is banned," Rascal stated firmly. "Is there anything else you can tell me? What time were you out here?"

"We met at eight," Callista said, having gotten a hold of herself again. "But we didn't open the circle for receiving until ten."

Rascal made a note.

"Indigo disappeared at ten thirty-two," Adel offered. "I know because my phone went off right as we realized she was missing."

Wynona nodded, though she wanted to ask a couple of questions. It seemed a little strange that anyone would be distracted by their phone when a person had gone missing. Still...

"Stop pushing me!"

Wynona closed her eyes and wished she were anywhere but in that field as Celia came over to join the group.

Celia huffed and stormed her way to the middle of the group. "Are we done here, yet? Don't you think you've asked enough questions?"

"We'll be done when I say I'm done," Rascal said with a cool but polite nod.

"Oooh," Celia drawled. Her eyes went to Wynona. "Looks like you got yourself a strong one."

Wynona had had it. She opened her mouth to put her sister in her place, but someone else beat her to it.

"I suggest you close that mouth of yours, Ms. Le Doux," Chief Ligurio said in an icy tone as he walked up to Rascal's other side. "Unless, of course, you have something to add to the case?"

"And if I don't?" Celia demanded, putting her nose in the air.

"Then perhaps I'll have to send you downtown for illegal magic. And when your family comes to pick you up, I'm sure they'll be thrilled to hear what you were up to this evening." The words were said as smoothly as if he were talking about the weather, but the threat was clear as a crystal ball.

Celia's nostrils flared and her dark blue eyes flashed with irritation, but she kept her bright red lips closed.

"I need to figure out how he does that," Wynona murmured under her breath. She bit her cheek to keep a smile in check when she felt Rascal start to shake beside her.

"Ladies," Chief Ligurio said, as if he hadn't just threatened one of them with jail time. "For now we are releasing you, but please stay in town. I'm sure we'll eventually have additional questions." His red eyes fixed on Celia and one dark eyebrow slowly rose up. "And when we do, we want to know where to find you."

Wynona stood still as the women began to slowly move away. She held her breath when Celia walked in her direction.

"If you breathe a word of this to Mom or Dad, I'll make your life miserable," Celia whispered as she walked past.

"Careful, Celia," Wynona said. "Remember that you called me here." She turned, frowning. "Speaking of which, you never have exactly said why."

Celia scoffed, but it was Chief Ligurio who answered. His vampire stealth made him hard to detect when he wanted to be under the radar, but the aura of his power was unmistakable.

"My guess would be she wanted you to use your newly developed sleuthing skills to help keep her from spending time behind bars," the chief said wryly.

Wynona looked over, but Chief Ligurio was still glaring at Celia, who was currently seething. Sparks of silver magic dripped from her clenched fists. "My...skills? What in the world do you mean?"

"Your sister was standing right next to Mrs. Stocker," the chief answered. "Which makes her a prime suspect in the disappearance."

"Callista was on Indigo's other side," Celia snapped. "I don't see you threatening her with arrest."

Chief Ligurio nodded in acknowledgement. "True. But you're the only one who seems to be...unconcerned about Mrs. Stocker's possible death. At least her sister is mourning. You, on the other hand, don't seem to care at all." He tilted his head to the side. "Why is that, Celia? Was there bad blood between you and Mrs. Stocker? And that doesn't even take into account that your accounting of the evening is a bit...shaky."

Celia huffed. "No. I just don't like to waste time crying when we don't even know if a person is dead." She sneered. "Now if you'll excuse me, I need to get home."

"We'll be in touch," Chief Ligurio drawled.

Wynona tugged on Rascal's sleeve. "I think it's best if I went home too," she whispered. "Can you spare one of the officers?"

Rascal looked torn. "I'm sure we can figure it out," he said. "I'm sorry I can't take you myself, but..." He made a face.

Wynona patted his arm. "Don't worry about it. I understand." She started to walk away, but Chief Ligurio stopped her once more.

"You might as well take her," the chief said with a sigh, then he turned to face Wynona head on. "Once home, be sure and stay there, Ms. Le Doux," he said, his voice as smooth and cold as ever. "Too many Le Douxs might just ruin this pot."

"I have no intention of getting involved," Wynona assured the vampire. "I've had enough of investigating to last me a lifetime."

CHAPTER 5

Before Wynona and Rascal could get back to his car, Celia stood in their way.

Wynona wanted to groan. Why couldn't her sister just leave things alone? "Excuse us," Wynona tried to say, starting to walk around, but Celia just sidestepped, once again blocking the path.

"I need to talk to you," Celia hissed.

Wynona pinched her lips together. "I think you've said enough tonight, don't you?" Wynona wanted to scream. Her nerves were completely frayed tonight. Between the experience with the lightning at her window, followed by the heavy moment with Rascal, and now her sister's horrid behavior? Wynona felt as if she had whiplash. Her body was begging for mercy and her brain wanted nothing more than to shut off and go to sleep. It was well past midnight at this point and she had patrons on the schedule for tomorrow.

"Sister," Celia said through clenched teeth. "If I didn't know any better, I would say you don't want to spend time with family."

Rascal stepped forward, but Wynona put out her hand. The last thing she needed was him stirring the cauldron.

"I can handle this," Wynona whispered in a barely audible voice, knowing his wolf hearing would pick it up.

Rascal's tiny nod let her know he understood. He straightened and folded his arms over his chest in an intimidating stance instead, letting both of them know he wasn't leaving, but he wasn't interfering.

Celia rolled her eyes dramatically. "Looks like wolfy boy is a bit territorial."

"Don't talk about him," Wynona said before she thought better of it. She wanted to close her eyes and disappear when Celia smirked. Nothing said "terrorize me" like declaring something off bounds. "You wanted to talk," Wynona hurried to say. "You've got two minutes."

Celia huffed, but turned away from Rascal. "You can't tell Mom and Dad about this."

Wynona threw her arms out to the side. "Is that all that's worrying you? Well, worry no longer, because I haven't spoken to either one of them since I left home. Now if you'll excuse us..."

Celia shook her head and sidestepped to stop Wynona again. "I mean it, Wynona. If they knew I was out here, I'd be confined to the grounds for a year."

"I get it," Wynona said. "That's fine. I won't tell anyone. Now let us go."

Celia opened her mouth, then shut it again. It was clear she wanted to say more, but she was hesitating.

Wynona's interest was piqued. Maybe Rascal was right that she was drawn to mysteries. "Was there something else?"

"H-how are you?" Celia asked, the words sounding foreign as they came out of her mouth.

Wynona froze. "What?"

Celia folded her arms over her chest in a defensive manner. "Can't I ask after my sister?"

"Are you talking about the sister you've treated like refuse ever since you could talk?" Wynona demanded. "That sister?" She couldn't believe she was being so bold. Wynona had sworn when she'd escaped her family that she would never be like them, and that included how she treated her tormentors. Apparently being tired made her snippy.

She didn't like it.

Closing her eyes and pinching the bridge of her nose, Wynona spoke before Celia could. "I'm sorry. That was unkind." She dropped her hand and tried to force her body to relax. "I'm doing well. Thank you for asking. But I'm also very tired and would like to go home. I'm sure you have other things to do as well, so if you're done?"

Celia's nostrils flared, but she didn't answer right away. She looked as if she wanted to shout and yell in her usual tantruming fashion, but she was holding herself back. Wynona had no idea why. This entire exchange was bizarre to say the least. "How well do you know Chief Ligurio?"

Ah. There it was. The real reason for this conversation. "We're not exactly friends, if that's what you're asking," Wynona said carefully. Her eyes flickered to Rascal, but he looked like a statue. Completely unmoved by the entire exchange. His golden eyes, however, were glowing ever so slightly, meaning his shifter was very close to the surface.

"You worked with him when you solved that murder a couple months back, didn't you?" Celia demanded.

Wynona nodded. "Of course we crossed paths. But it wasn't because we enjoyed each other's company. It was out of necessity."

"But he listens to you?"

Wynona shook her head. "No. He doesn't. Look, Celia. I have no power with him at all. I only came tonight because you called me, screaming like you'd been hurt, and I was..." Wynona hesitated to admit it, but it was the truth. "Worried for you. Since you're fine, I'll be going home and forgetting this whole thing ever happened."

Celia ground her jaw, but she didn't stop them when once again Wynona began to walk past her.

"What the heck was that all about?" Wynona whispered as she and Rascal gained a little distance from the crime scene. She tucked a soggy piece of hair behind her ear. Wynona could practically feel the frizz in her locks and knew she probably had short curls all around her forehead from the dampness in the air. What she wouldn't give for just a touch of the magic that kept Celia and the other witches looking so perfect even in this weather.

"I don't know," Rascal said just as softly. He glanced over his shoulder. "But I don't like it."

"The situation with the coven or my sister?"

Rascal opened the passenger side door of his truck and helped her in. "Both," he said before closing it and walking around to the driver's side.

"You know," Wynona said as they began to drive back to town, "Roderick mentioned something about Chief Ligurio and Celia before you came in and pounded him into the floor." She grinned when Rascal chuckled.

"My wolf got away from me that night," he admitted with a shrug.

"You know..." Wynona tapped her bottom lip. "You never did explain to me how you knew where I was." The humor she'd been feeling faded when Rascal stiffened.

"Maybe I can smell trouble," he said finally, glancing at her in the darkness, his gold eyes bright. "And you, Ms. Le Doux...are definitely trouble."

Wynona relaxed at his teasing. She put her hands in the air. "I promise I don't go looking for it. It has a habit of finding me."

"That's what they all say," Rascal said wryly. There was a moment of quiet in the cab. "But seriously, what did Roderick say?"

Wynona shook her head. "Not much. Just that the chief was using me to get back at her." She scrunched her nose. "My guess is they dated. But it wouldn't have lasted very long. Celia goes through men like Lusgu goes through brooms."

Rascal's laughter grew. "That's pretty impressive."

Wynona pursed her lips and nodded. "I know. She always had a new man she was bragging about every time I saw her." Wynona felt a deep sense of gloom settle over her at the reminder of her upbring-ing. Celia might be younger than her, but that hadn't stopped Celia from lording over Wynona whenever she got the chance. There was no love lost between them...at least on Celia's side.

There were times when Wynona still mourned for what might have been, but mostly she was extremely content with her life. She'd done well for herself after Granny helped her escape, and, of course, after a week of difficulties with Chef Droxon's murder. But now things were good and there was a hope of something even better if Rascal felt the way Wynona hoped he did.

Which was the exact opposite of the situation with her family. Wynona held no foolish hope at all, that they would ever be recon-ciled. Mostly because she knew her family didn't care. Celia's rude-ness tonight was just a taste of what Wynona had escaped.

They didn't want her, they didn't want her to succeed and if giv-en half a chance, they'd rather see her back in her closet than have her be traipsing around Hex Haven using their name. But as long as Wynona kept her head down and didn't upset the status quo, she knew her parents would leave her be. Dragging her back to the cas-tle would cause a media uproar which wouldn't be good for their im-age. As long as she wasn't doing anything to hurt their reputation, Wynona knew she was safe.

Celia, on the other hand, had reason to worry.

She really shouldn't have been out in the middle of the night making those Petra Luminis. "What could they possibly want them for?" Wynona murmured out loud.

"What was that?" Rascal asked.

"Oh. Sorry," Wynona responded. "I was just wondering what Celia and her coven wanted the light bombs for. Not that I have any experience with something like that, but I've read that they pack a real punch. Just what kind of magic are they utilizing that would re-quire that kind of power?"

"That's a very good question," Rascal muttered as he pulled into a parking spot near Wynona's shop. Instead of getting out, Rascal turned off the engine and then shifted in her direction. One arm lay across the top of the steering wheel as he looked her way. "It seems to me they had to be planning something. But what?"

"Is the head of the coven going to be arrested? I didn't see a coven mother," Wynona said.

Rascal shook his head. "I doubt it," he said tightly. "Do you know which coven your sister belongs to?"

Wynona shook her head, suddenly feeling foolish. Not knowing the name of her sister's coven was just another bit of evidence of how isolated Wynona had been.

"Tonight you met a good portion of The Sisters of Eternity," Rascal explained.

Wynona's eyes widened. "Are you serious? Celia is part of that group?" She might not know her sister's comings and goings, but everyone...*everyone*...knew the name of that coven. It had been around as long as paranormals had kept records, hence the name "Eternity". It was filled with the best and brightest, and the group's ability to perform complicated spells was unparalleled.

That darn jealousy churned in Wynona's stomach again.

Rascal nodded. "Yep. Unfortunately, they hold too much power for us to do much against them for collecting the lightning."

Wynona understood that all too well. Her family, after all, was the epitome of politics being greater than the law.

"But you're right. The coven mother wasn't there, so I'm guessing the younger sisters were working without permission." He huffed a laugh. "They might get in trouble within the coven for that." He tilted his head, looking out the windshield. "Or perhaps, they were on an errand for the mother and she simply didn't want to be involved. It could go either way, actually."

"But you can still investigate the disappearance of Indigo, right?"

Rascal turned back to her with a smile. "Yeah. We can't do anything about the illegal magic, but as long as one of the witches is missing, we can use that as an excuse to do some digging." Rascal waggled a finger at her. "It's eating at you, isn't it? You want to figure this out."

Wynona put both hands in the air and shook her head. "Nope. Absolutely not. I was dead serious when I told Chief Ligurio that I wasn't going to get involved." She dropped her hands to her lap. "I came because Celia called for help. But as you saw for yourself," Wynona was grateful for the dark as her cheeks burned with humiliation, "Celia wasn't really interested in my help. I'm still not sure why she called me in the first place. So I'm out. I won't interfere at all." She knew full well, however, that that wouldn't keep her from wondering what was going on. Perhaps Rascal wouldn't mind giving her updates once in a while.

As if he could read her thoughts, Rascal chuckled. He reached over to tweak her nose. "I'll believe it when I see it."

"Well, you can see it right now," Wynona said, thrusting her chin in the air playfully. She grabbed the door handle. "Thank you for the ride. Both directions," she clarified. "But I'm going to go inside, ride home and *not* think about this case again." Her smile was wide as she climbed down from the truck, listening to Rascal's laughter.

The truck didn't move as Wynona walked up to her shop, unlocked the door and went inside. In fact, the truck didn't move until she was on her mint green Vespa and riding on the empty streets home.

Wynona's cheeks hurt from smiling so much by the time she parked in her tiny garage and waved the large pickup off. Rascal was the ultimate protector, and on this dark, stormy night, Wynona was grateful she was the recipient of that.

Something weird had happened tonight, first at the shop and then in that field, and although Wynona wasn't ready to share the odd experiences she'd been having, it was nice to know someone like Rascal was on her side.

After getting inside, she immediately headed to the kitchen to make herself a cup of tea. She was going to need help getting to sleep tonight. Her mind kept going over the story the women were telling in the meadow.

She disappeared at ten thirty-two.

Wynona tapped her fingers on the countertop as she waited for the tea to steep. It was odd that they could be so precise. It was also odd that someone would bother to look at their phone when a person had just gone missing.

"Stop it," Wynona scolded herself as she dunked her infuser in the water a few times. "You're not getting involved in this. At all." With a firm nod, she carried her tea to her bedroom. If she was lucky, she would be able to get a few hours of sleep before needing to fulfill her duties tomorrow at the tea shop.

The police would take care of the missing witch and Celia would go back to the palace, their parents none the wiser for the coven's illegal activities.

None of it affected Wynona in the least, and she wasn't the least bit interested in getting involved.

She wasn't.

Not at all.

CHAPTER 6

Wynona fingered the petals of a white and pink calla lily. She loved visiting Prim's greenhouses. Not only did it always smell wonderful, but the colors and greenery were a feast for the eyes as well as the senses.

"I can't believe she treated you that way, after *she* called you to come," Prim grumbled. Her hands were splayed over the top of a tiny plant. Slowly, but surely, the leaves began to tremble and start to reach for Prim, growing bigger with each passing moment. After a couple of inches, however, the plant's growth petered out and collapsed. Prim huffed and put her hands on her hips. "See? I'm so ticked off I can't even grow properly."

Wynona sighed. "I'm sorry. I shouldn't have brought it up." She had come by Prim's this morning to talk about next week's arrangements, but had taken the opportunity to complain to her best friend about Celia's behavior last night.

"Oh, you definitely should have," Prim argued. "That's what friends are for. But geez, that witch makes me mad. Next time she calls, tell her to stuff it."

Wynona laughed softly. "Somehow, I'm guessing that would lead me to something worse than having my powers bound."

Prim pursed her bright pink lips. "Let her try it." She wiggled her fingers and the vines of a nearby plant began to dance in the air. "I think you and I can take her."

Wynona smiled broadly. She adored Prim's feistiness. "I'm pretty sure that with a snap of her fingers, Celia could kill everything in here."

Prim's shoulders deflated. "I know. But that doesn't have to stop me from dreaming." She scrunched her nose. "Dang witches." Prim's pink eyes widened and she turned to look fully at Wynona. "Present company excluded, of course."

"Don't worry," Wynona said. "I knew you didn't mean me. It's not like I'm a real witch anyway." The words might have been true, but that didn't make them any less painful. Thirty years and she was still struggling to come to grips with her curse. A person would think that should be enough time to not care, but Wynona wasn't sure if she would ever reach that point.

Living in the paranormal world only made her crave her magic more, rather than less. In fact, if she didn't have such good friends and love her shop so much, she would probably look into moving into the human world. At least there, she wouldn't be reminded of her disadvantage at every turn.

Prim squeaked in disdain and rushed over to Wynona, grabbing her by the shoulders. "Wynona, there is not a creature living that wouldn't call you a real witch." She made a face. "That sounded better in my head."

Wynona laughed. "I know what you meant. And thank you."

Prim shook her friend's shoulders slightly. "No. I mean it! Your kindness and moral ethics are what we all wish other witches would be. Our world would be a lot less corrupt if all witches and warlocks were willing to help others, rather than looking for ways to rule over them."

Wynona sighed. "I know. And my family are the worst offenders of all. If I had any sway over them, I'd do my best to help, but they'd just as soon lock me up as look at me."

Prim grunted. "Their loss, my gain." She winked before going back to her plants. She picked up a spray bottle and began squirting it into the air, letting the droplets gently land on the nearby foliage.

"Besides, not all witches are horrible. Your grandmother is a good example of that."

Wynona nodded as she sauntered through the greenery. "True. She was a good woman."

"She was," Prim agreed. "We need more like her." Prim grinned. "And you."

This was exactly what Wynona needed this morning. She had woken up feeling a little down and Prim was the ultimate shot in the arm. "Thanks, Prim. I'm fond of you too."

Prim fluffed her pink hair. "Of course you are. Isn't everyone?"

"Well if they're not, they should be!"

Prim bounced on her toes and began to work her way down her line of pots. Only the sounds of water and the slight rustling of leaves could be heard for a few precious moments. "But seriously," Prim inserted. "Why do you think she called?"

"I honestly don't know," Wynona said. She leaned in to sniff a flower that reminded her of a rose but had more petals. "Oooh. That is wonderful. What's this?"

"A Floribunda Rose," Prim replied. "It's cultivated for its scent."

"Can we use some of these in the shop?"

Prim tilted her head back and forth. "We can, but I'm a little concerned about the smell mixing with your teas. The herbs are pretty strong. Do you think it would be too much? Some of your patrons have overeager olfactory senses."

Wynona pointed a finger at Prim. "This is why you're paid the big bucks."

"Nice to know I have you fooled," Prim teased. "But if you're looking for something similar in looks, try the peonies. They're a favorite of mine." She raised up on tiptoe and pointed. "Over there. The far corner."

"On it." Wynona worked her way around the table and workbenches. She found the section Prim was talking about and was almost stunned into silence. "You're right!" she hollered over her shoulder. "They're amazing!"

"Some of them have a strong smell," Prim called back. "But some don't. We can go over what will blend and what won't."

Wynona nodded. "Sounds good!" When their conversation quieted down again, her mind went back to Prim's question. Just why had Celia called last night? What exactly had she wanted Wynona to do? Celia had sounded panicked, but once they were at the field, she had been nothing but nasty.

It didn't make sense. Even for Celia. There had to have been a reason that Celia had called for Wynona in the first place.

"Whatcha thinking?" Prim asked right behind Wynona, making her jump.

"Prim!" Wynona gasped, putting her hand over her racing heart. "Don't do that to me."

Prim cackled. "Sorry. Couldn't resist."

Wynona shook her head. "Next time I'm slipping licorice into your tea."

Prim stuck out her tongue. "Gross."

"Exactly."

Waving a dismissive hand in the air, Prim began watering the peonies. "Have you figured it out yet?"

"Figured what out?"

Prim gave Wynona a wry look. "Where the witch disappeared to?"

Wynona rolled her eyes. "I wasn't even thinking about that."

"Maybe not, but it'll hit you sooner or later. Eventually, you'll realize Celia is just a jerk who makes no sense and you'll move onto something else." Prim waggled her pink eyebrows. "Like what happened to that woman."

Wynona pinched her lips. She didn't want to admit that the question had been niggling at her. Instead, she forced herself to shrug. "I don't know what any of that has to do with me."

Despite being willing to share family squabbles, Wynona had yet to tell Prim about any of her encounters with the wild magic. Her fairy friend had no idea what had happened at the shop window the night of the storm and it was going to stay that way.

Even if Granny Saffron was trying to connect to Wynona, which was the only explanation Wynona could think of, the whole set of incidents was crazy. Only once had Wynona ever brought the topic up and it was when she'd been working with the police on the murder she'd helped solve a few months back. But even in the paranormal world, a ghost helping the living was odd. Ghosts always had their own agenda. If they wanted to stick around, it was usually as part of the ghost reporter squad or to haunt someone who had wronged them in life,which took a great deal of power. Not just anyone could be a ghost.

So why would Granny decide to stick around and help Wynona? Or was she really helping? The magic seemed to crop up at odd times and wasn't always helpful. The only part of the experiences that was consistent, was the color purple. Wynona hadn't missed how each spark and sizzle had been the color of the lavender growing on the far side of Prim's greenhouse. But what exactly did that mean?

"There it is," Prim said ominously.

Wynona blinked rapidly to bring herself out of her insane thoughts. "There what is?"

Prim pointed a manicured finger at Wynona's face. "The look that says you're interested in figuring it all out."

Wynona did want to figure it all out, but it wasn't just about the missing witch. "I have no interest in getting involved," Wynona said, putting her hands in the air. "None whatsoever." She had enough on her plate and she definitely didn't want to rock the boat more than it already was.

Prim snorted. "I'll believe it when I see it."

Wynona put her hands on her hips. "Have you been talking to Rascal? Just what is it about you two that has you both so sure that I want to get involved?"

Prim's eyes flashed with excitement. "Oooh. Have you been spending time with the hotty wolf shifter?"

Wynona spun on her heel. "That's none of your business."

"Of course it is!" Prim hurried after her. "I'm your best friend. I'm supposed to live vicariously through you."

Wynona laughed. "It'll be a very boring life then."

"Says you," Prim argued. She paused to brush her fingers over a wilted plant. It reacted instantly, reaching for Prim and looking far healthier than it had a moment before. "I haven't had anyone flirt with me in months. Not since Roderick said a few token things when all he really wanted was you."

"Roderick didn't want me," Wynona grumbled. "He wanted my family's power."

Prim shrugged. "Tomato, tomahto. In the witch world, it's all the same."

Wynona rested a finger on the tip of a sharp thorn. "Maybe so," she said softly. "But I don't want that world."

Prim pulled Wynona's hand away. "And I don't want that Venus Fly Trap to take off your fingers." She smiled softly. "That particular one is a little more powerful than most."

Wynona stuffed her hands in her pockets. The dangerous plant was a reminder that not everything was as it seemed. Just like Roderick. He'd been suave and flirty and sweet. And a murderer.

"Focus on the shifter," Prim called out as she walked past Wynona. "He's better looking anyway."

Wynona laughed softly and tucked a piece of dark hair behind her ear. "You know, I think he was going to ask me out the other day."

Prim's mouth dropped. "Really?"

Wynona nodded. "Yeah. But then we got interrupted."

Bright pink lips pursed into a deep pout. "Crud. Hopefully he doesn't get cold feet and wait another two months." She paused. "Wait. You *do* want to go out with him, right?"

Wynona shrugged. "I wouldn't say no."

Prim rolled her eyes. "How very proper of you."

Wynona shook her head, a grin tugging at her lips. "I better be getting back. My first appointment is in about an hour."

"I'll make up some designs with the peonies and send them over soon," Prim said.

"I'd love that, thank you!" Wynona waved and started to walk out of the greenhouse.

"Oh, and Nona?"

Wynona paused in the doorway. "Hmm?"

Prim's grin could only be described as mischievous. "When you decide you want to work on that case, just let me know."

This time it was Wynona's eyes that rolled toward the ceiling. "I've already retired from investigating!" she said dryly.

Prim's laughter followed Wynona out into the bright sunshine. Despite her response, Wynona's brain wasn't as onboard with her answer as the rest of her. There were several mysteries churning in her brain at the moment and none of them had easy answers.

Wynona slipped onto the seat of her Vespa and headed toward home. She loved the feel of the breeze over her face. There was something so freeing about it. And it was that free feeling that she was so desperate to hold onto.

Yes, she wanted to know why Celia had called her in a panic. Yes, she wanted to figure out why Granny Saffron's ghost seemed to be sticking around. Yes, she was curious about the missing witch and the odd answers from the coven members.

But no...she wasn't willing to risk everything she had gained in order to find those answers.

Wynona had only allowed herself to get involved in the first investigation because it was the only way for her to open her shop on time and save her reputation. This time, however, the situation was different. Sticking her nose in an investigation that involved her sister, and therefore her family, would only put Wynona on their radar. A place she wanted to be as far away from as possible.

It didn't matter how many questions and curiosities plagued her. She was going to resist her personal nosiness and stay out of it all.

She had a shop to run, customers to please, several custom tea meetings this week and a friend group to enjoy.

There was absolutely no time or need to add anything else to her plate. No...Wynona had plenty to do. And if she was lucky and Rascal was brave, she might have something in her future to look forward to that had nothing to do with investigations at all.

CHAPTER 7

Wynona stood on the street, the noise of children playing in the apartment building yard almost deafening. With a poof of fur, one of the children turned into a small lion cub and the squealing of the other participants tripled as they ran to escape.

"No fair! No shifting in tag!" one of the younger girls shouted as she climbed to the top of the jungle gym.

Wynona grinned. Her isolated growing up was so different from this. Even now, her life was mostly quiet, with only occasional interruptions. These children, however, were never quiet. Ever.

"Are you going to stand there staring or go inside?"

Wynona spun to see a smaller, elderly woman glaring up at her. If Wynona wasn't mistaken, it was the woman who lived just down from Rascal. "Mrs. Reyna, isn't it?" Wynona stuck out her hand. "I'm Wynona Le Doux. Nice to officially meet you." Normally, people looked impressed at her last name. Especially when they were speaking to Wynona about business matters, but apparently her family wasn't as adored on this side of town.

If anything, Mrs. Reyna's eyebrows furrowed even further. Instead of shaking Wynona's hand, she huffed. "Why are you standing out here in the blazing heat?" She shook her white head. "No sense. No sense at all." Turning, Mrs. Reyna began marching up the stairs.

"Can I help you?" Wynona asked, trying to take the woman's elbow.

"I can walk," Mrs. Reyna grumbled, shaking herself loose.

"Sorry," Wynona said softly. She stopped walking, figuring the woman would prefer some distance between them. Once Mrs. Reyna was inside, Wynona would work up the courage to go in and see if

Rascal was home. She really should have called ahead, but her head was still buzzing with questions after her chat with Prim yesterday, and Wynona had hoped Rascal would help alleviate her curiosity without Wynona actually having to get involved in anything.

"Are you coming or what?" Mrs. Reyna snapped, her hand on the door of the building and her body language screaming impatience.

Wynona couldn't help but point to herself. "Me?"

Apparently, it wasn't only teenagers who were good at rolling their eyes, since Mrs. Reyna could perform the act with the best of them. "What he sees in you, I'll never know," the woman mumbled. "Yes. You. I thought you wanted to come in?"

Wynona nodded stiffly. "Yes. Thank you, I was going to visit—" She snapped her mouth shut. It really wasn't anyone else's business who Wynona wanted to visit, though Mrs. Reyna more than likely knew that Wynona was here for Rascal.

"As if we don't already know," Mrs. Reyna said sarcastically. "He's home in twenty minutes. Might as well come make a cup of tea while you wait."

"Um..." Wynona waffled a little. Maybe it was best to wait outside. She wasn't comfortable entering Rascal's home without him.

"Was the gossip wrong?" Mrs. Reyna demanded, still holding the door. "They say you have a bit of Saffron in you, girl."

Wynona jerked. "You...knew my grandmother?"

One white eyebrow shot up and a smirk appeared on thin, wrinkled lips. "The answer to that will depend on how well you make a cup of tea." She disappeared through the doorway and Wynona raced after her without stopping to think about the consequences.

"H-how did you know her?" Wynona asked as they waited for the elevator. She rocked back and forth on her heels, her energy suddenly restless. Her grandmother had been one of the most powerful witches in the entire paranormal world. It seemed odd that she would know a wolf shifter from the opposite side of town. Especially one that, as far as Wynona knew, didn't have any kind of elevated powers or run in the upper circles of society.

"That, my girl, is a story." Mrs. Reyna laughed, the sound dry and raspy. "Old Saffron and I had lots of those."

"Stories?" Wynona clarified. The elevator doors shut and the machine began to move up, soft music playing in the background.

Mrs. Reyna made a face at Wynona. "You don't keep up very well, do you?"

Wynona stiffened. "I'm sorry, Mrs. Reyna, but I wasn't expecting to run into someone who knew my grandmother, and I'm afraid I'm a little caught off guard."

Mrs. Reyna shook her head as she exited the elevator and shuffled her way to her door, just a little bit down the hall from Rascal's. "Being ready for the unexpected is the only way to survive in this world."

Wynona didn't answer, but she did follow Mrs. Reyna into her apartment. There was truth in the elderly woman's words, but right now Wynona was still trying to get her footing under her before she worried about preparing for other ventures. She had just started to feel like her life was on track when suddenly it had been interrupted again.

"Herbs are in the cupboard," Mrs. Reyna said, pointing a gnarled finger at her kitchen. "Pot's on the stove. Water's in the faucet."

Wynona held back a grin. She had definitely not given Mrs. Reyna a good first impression if she felt the need to break it down so much. "Cups and saucers?" she asked as she set about getting the necessary ingredients.

"Next cupboard."

Wynona nodded. After setting the kettle on, she turned and eyed Mrs. Reyna. Narrowing her eyes, Wynona let her intuition take over. Sometimes the voice was quieter than others, but if she listened, she could almost hear the voice of her grandmother help her figure out the exact tea for each person. It was one of the skills Granny Saffron had been so insistent on, and was the lifeblood of Wynona's business.

People loved coming for tea parties, but it was the custom tea blends that were her strongest success. Granny had been an amazing teacher and Wynona's record was flawless.

"Ginger, thyme and tumeric," Wynona muttered to herself. Without a second thought, she went about making the tea, then presented it to Mrs. Reyna who was waiting, as impatient as ever, on her couch.

The older wolf shifter picked up the cup and took a sniff. She grinned and her brown eyes sparkled. "Well done. I didn't know if you had it in you." She eyed Wynona as she took a sip. "Saffy used to make me the same tincture before she passed."

Wynona sat down across from Mrs. Reyna a little harder than she'd intended. "You really did know her."

Mrs. Reyna nodded. "Yes."

Just as Wynona leaned forward to ask some questions, the door banged open.

"Mama Lina! What in the world is so—" Rascal cut off and his brown skin darkened, along with the tip of his ears when he spotted Wynona. "Wy. What are you doing here?" His golden eyes flashed back and forth between Wynona and Mrs. Reyna.

"She made me some tea for my arthritis," Mrs. Reyna said with a sniff. "No thanks to you."

"No thanks to..." Rascal folded his arms over his chest. "What in the world is that supposed to mean?"

Mrs. Reyna sniffed and shrugged.

Wynona's head felt like a ping pong ball as it whipped from one of them to the other. "Uh..." She tried to smile, but it felt like more of a grimace. "Hey, Rascal. I was coming to ask you a few questions." She started to rise, but Mrs. Reyna pointed a finger at her.

"Sit."

Wynona promptly sat down again. She pinched her lips together and made a face at Rascal.

He chuckled and sauntered the rest of the way into the room, closing the door behind him. "Welcome to Mama Lina's apartment. She's a tough one to resist."

Mrs. Reyna snorted and took another long sip of her tea before setting the cup on the saucer, then transferring both to the coffee table. "Now...Wynona. Ask your questions."

Wynona felt her eyes widen. Which questions was Mrs. Reyna referring to? The ones about Granny Saffron or the ones she was going to ask Rascal? Neither seemed appropriate in this now crowded situation.

Rascal sat down on the couch a little down from Wynona, his arm going across the back of it, just barely missing her shoulder. "It's alright," he said. "Mama Lina knows it all anyways."

"I..." Wynona's eyes darted between the two wolf shifters before settling on Rascal. "I was going to ask you a few questions about the case," she said in a whisper.

Rascal grinned. "Just couldn't stay out of it, could you?"

She gave him a mock glare. "I just had a few questions. I don't want to get involved."

Grabbing an apple off the bowl on the coffee table, Rascal rubbed it against his shirt, then took a large bite. "Ask away."

Wynona glanced at Mrs. Reyna, who was watching the two of them with a very peculiar look on her face that Wynona couldn't decipher. "Is it alright to ask...here?"

Rascal nodded. "Mama Lina already knows everything before it reaches the public anyway. There's nothing to hide."

Mrs. Reyna wheezed slightly as she snickered. "You young folks think you're so secretive." She winked at Wynona and tapped the side of her nose. "Nothing is secret if you know where to look."

"Oh." Wynona had no idea what to say to that. In fact, this entire situation was a bit bizarre. Just who was this woman? And how did she know Granny Saffron? It seemed like the more Wynona learned, the more questions she had. She reminded herself to take things one question at a time and turned back to Rascal. "I was curious if you've found that missing witch."

Rascal shook his head, taking the time to swallow before answering. "No. She's still missing."

"And no body has shown up?" Wynona frowned. "Is Chief Ligurio assuming she's dead at this point?"

Rascal made a face. "Nope. It hasn't even been forty-eight hours and without a body, he refuses to declare a murder. It's driving the family crazy, especially Callista, the sister. Keeps saying something about letting her brother-in-law, Indigo's husband, grieve properly."

Wynona tapped her fingers against her knee. "Hmm..."

Rascal chuckled. "Go ahead. Ask."

"Well...I just..." Wynona huffed. "I wonder what the sister's deal is. Wouldn't she *want* her sister to be alive? Want to believe there's a chance she's out there somewhere?"

"You'd think," Rascal said, settling deeper into the couch cushions. He jumped slightly and grimaced. "Hang on a sec." Fishing his phone from his pocket, he punched a button. "Deputy Chief Strongclaw. Oh, hey, Chief." Rascal's face grew serious as he spoke with his boss. "Uh-huh...no..." Rascal's eyes darted to Wynona. "Actually, Ms. Wynona Le Doux is with me right now."

Wynona winced as the voice on the other side of the phone grew louder. She could only imagine the words Chief Ligurio was using to talk about her.

Mrs. Reyna laughed softly and picked her tea back up. "What in the world did you do to that man?" she asked quietly. "He doesn't like you at all." She cackled under her breath before finishing her cup of tea.

Wynona shrugged. "Nothing. I barely know the man."

"But your sister does."

Wynona tilted her head. "How do you know all these things?"

A slow smile grew on Mrs. Reyna's wrinkled face. "Age brings all sorts of knowledge."

Wynona didn't say anything. She knew full well that Mrs. Reyna was being purposefully cryptic and Wynona didn't want to fall for it. Granny Saffron was often like that as well. As a small child, it had driven Wynona crazy. As an adult, she had learned to wait. When Granny was ready to talk, she would talk. Pressing beforehand only brought frustration.

"Good girl," Mrs. Reyna murmured.

Wynona raised an eyebrow. It was one thing to be patient, it was another to feel like she was being mocked. "Thank you for your time, Mrs. Reyna, but I believe it's time I headed home."

So much for getting time to ask Rascal a few questions. He had stood up and was currently arguing with Chief Ligurio about who knew what, and Wynona had had enough of Mrs. Reyna's smug attitude.

Mrs. Reyna tsked her tongue. "Don't get all bent out of shape. Some things have to happen in their own time."

Wynona nodded as if she understood, though she didn't. "Right. I'll see you around." She stood and walked to the door. Just as she was pulling it open, Rascal called her name.

"Hang on!" he said, stuffing his phone in his pocket and hurrying to her side. "Let me walk you out."

Wynona's smile softened into something much more genuine. "That would be nice. Thank you."

Rascal winked, his signature greeting. "It's the least I can do since you came to see me and got hijacked along the way."

Wynona laughed softly and they headed out into the hallway. "I'm sorry for whatever Chief Ligurio said to you when he was complaining about me."

Rascal laughed. "It wasn't really about you," he explained. "Just the Le Doux family in general." Rascal stuffed his hands in the pockets of his uniform pants and shook his head. "I, uh, couldn't help but notice the difference between you and your sister the other night." He glanced sideways at Wynona. "It's no wonder you said you don't have much of a relationship with them."

Wynona nodded sadly. "Well, when a person's personal goal is to be the exact opposite of their family, odds are they don't get along very well."

"That'll do it," Rascal said, holding his hand against the elevator door until Wynona was inside. They stood side by side as the machine started to take them down to the ground level. "Any other questions for me before I head back to work?"

Wynona pursed her lips and squished them to the side. "I don't know. I just..." She sighed. How could she explain that something about the whole situation just seemed...off...to her? There was no evidence of it, but Wynona had a gut feeling that the coven hadn't told the whole story the other night.

"Just what? Just want to get involved? Just wish Mama Lina would mind her own business?"

Wynona laughed softly. "No. I don't want to get involved. I was just curious. And yes, I kind of wish Mrs. Reyna would mind her own business." They stepped into the sunshine and Wynona paused and put her hands on her hips. "She said she knew my grandmother."

Rascal paused. "Wow. Really? The one you named your shop after?"

Wynona nodded and squinted up at the apartment building. "I'm not sure what to think of that."

"Sounds to me like you have a good excuse to come back."

She turned back to Rascal and smiled. "I guess so."

Rascal jangled his keys. "If you make sure I'm going to be here, I'll act as buffer when Mama Lina gets too weird."

"Deal." Wynona headed over to her parked Vespa. "Hey, Rascal?" she asked as she settled onto the seat.

"Yeah?"

"When you find Indigo, will you let me know?"

Rascal gave her a half smile. "Yes. But don't tell Chief. He already threatened to drain me if you began poking around."

Wynona held her hands up. "I promise. I'm just worried for her…" Wynona tilted her head back and forth. "And a little curious. Her sister, Callista, seemed nice, so I'd hate for her to be grieving if she doesn't have to be."

Rascal nodded. "So noted." He gave her a mock salute. "See ya later."

Wynona smiled in return. "Come by for tea sometime."

"And pastries?"

"Of course!"

"Done." With one last wink, Rascal headed to his truck and Wynona pulled onto the street.

That niggling feeling that something was wrong wouldn't leave her alone, but she ruthlessly pushed it aside. This wasn't her case. Rascal and even grumpy Chief Ligurio were perfectly capable of handling it. She would leave them to the mysteries and Wynona could go home and handle her teas. That was where she belonged and that was where she planned to stay…for the time being.

CHAPTER 8

"Everything looks delicious!" Wynona gushed as Kyoz and Gnuq scampered toward the back door. "I'm excited to try those strawberries with the fruit dip." She kept her smile up as the two imps giggled and looked at each other. They had been up to more mischief than usual today while they dropped off the fresh baked goods. "Thank you!" Wynona called out as soon as they crossed the threshold, followed by a quick slamming of the door. She leaned her forehead against the metal, taking in a deep breath. "I think they get worse every day."

A huff from behind her had Wynona spinning to see Lusgu cleaning up the spilled eggs.

"Oh, Lusgu, I can take care of that," Wynona said, rushing over. "It's my fault they were in the fridge to begin with." Kyoz had mentioned she needed some cream to finish her eclairs and Wynona had told her where to find it instead of getting it herself.

True to form, the imp had taken full advantage, and now Wynona had a large mess on her hands only thirty minutes before her doors opened for the day. She was getting started later than usual, since it was Saturday and Wynona only opened for afternoon teas that day.

She always spent the morning with Prim, going over flowers, and then came to the shop to receive her fresh pastries, but that trip to Rascal's had put Wynona a bit behind. Though it had also opened up a few curious doors that Wynona planned to examine later, when she had the time.

"They'll take you for all you're worth," Lusgu grumbled as he waved his hand over the broken eggs.

Wynona stilled and allowed herself to enjoy the magic show as the floor soon sparkled with the rest of the kitchen. No matter how much she tried to help, Lusgu beat her to every mess and did a wonderful job of keeping everything in order.

He definitely deserved a raise...if he wasn't so grouchy with the patrons.

Wynona had to make sure Lusgu stayed in the back of the shop while she had customers, or else he would mutter complaints and insults to every person who dared enter their doors. For a creature whose feet looked like they had never been cleaned his entire life, Lusgu was oddly obsessed with cleanliness from everyone else.

A knock came from the kitchen door and Wynona looked back with a frown. She had no idea who would be coming by since all her packages had already arrived. She turned to Lusgu. "Thank you, Lusgu. You always do such a wonderful job."

The only sign that he heard her compliment was the slight reddening of the very tip of his pointed ears. Otherwise, the brownie kept his head down and moved on to cleaning the next spot he deemed unworthy.

Wynona hurried to the door. "Yes?" She pulled it open and immediately covered her eyes from the sunshine.

"It's about time," Celia snapped as she pushed her way past her sister.

Wynona stood gaping like a confused spectre as she watched her sister storm inside as if she owned the place. "Celia! What are you doing here?"

Celia sniffed and began to take off her jacket. "I needed to speak to you." Her eyes moved around the kitchen as she huffed. "And I assumed this was the best place to do it." Celia's lip curled as her eyes landed on Lusgu. "I didn't expect you to have company."

Lusgu, to his credit, ignored the rude witch.

Celia, however, didn't seem to appreciate his discretion. "Can't he go back to his hole or wherever he's from?" she demanded, waving a dismissive hand toward him.

Wynona hurried over. "Celia, stop," she hissed. "Lusgu is my employee and...my friend." It was an odd word for their relationship, but Wynona figured the brownie had very few friends and she was willing to be at least one.

Celia sniffed again. "I should have suspected you would befriend the lower class."

Wynona pinched her lips together and closed her eyes. "Celia, if you have a purpose for coming, I suggest you get to it. Otherwise, I'm going to have to ask you to leave. You coming into my shop and insulting my workers is not on my agenda for the day." Wynona glanced at the clock. She only had a few more minutes before she needed to open the front door. Saturday afternoons were always busy and Wynona knew that if she didn't get Celia out the door quickly, Wynona would pay the price when her attention was on her patrons rather than keeping track of her sister.

Celia folded her arms over her chest. "I told you. I need to speak to you."

"I only have a few minutes until I open."

Celia rolled her eyes. "I won't stop you from running your ridiculous little shop," she snapped.

A retort sat on the edge of Wynona's tongue, but was held back, just like it had been so many times during their growing up years. If Celia grew angry, Wynona had no way to protect herself or her shop, and she just couldn't risk that. Reminding herself that Celia was a product of her upbringing, Wynona waved toward the door that led to the rest of the shop. "Why don't we go to my office?"

Celia's heels clipped on the hardwood floor as they walked through the shop and down the hall.

Wynona closed the door behind them before walking to sit at her desk. "Have a seat," she said to her sister, waving at a plush chair off to one side.

Celia eyed the seat, but didn't sit down.

Wynona ignored the insult and leaned back in her own chair. "What did you want?"

Celia put her hands on her hips. "I need to know what kind of influence you have with the police department."

Wynona's nonchalant attitude disappeared and she leaned forward. "Excuse me?"

"You heard me," Celia snapped. "That...shifter guy. Are you dating?"

Anger began to bubble in Wynona's stomach, but she kept it from rising. Celia's entitled, demanding attitude was something Wynona should be used to by now, even if she didn't like it. "We're friends," Wynona stated carefully.

Celia growled in frustration. "I should have realized no one would make a move on a magicless witch," she grumbled under her breath.

Wynona put her hands on her desk and pushed herself upright. "If you're done, Celia, I think you should leave." For the first time that Wynona had ever seen, fear flashed across Celia's face and it made Wynona's conviction falter.

"You need to speak to him," Celia demanded, though her voice shook slightly.

"Speak to who? Rascal?"

Celia cackled. "Rascal? That's his name?"

Wynona waved away the rude words. "You need to explain yourself." She glanced at the wall clock. "I've got five minutes until I open my doors, and if you haven't finished by then, I'll have you kicked out."

Celia's plush lips became white as she pinched them together. Her dark eyes went to the wall as her jaw ground back and forth in indecision. "I need help," she finally said tightly.

"With what?" For the life of her, Wynona couldn't figure out what exactly was going on. This was starting to remind her of the panicked Celia that had called her just the night before. "Did they ever find your friend? The one who disappeared?"

Celia shook her head. "No. And that's exactly why I'm here."

"Celia," Wynona moaned. "I'm confused and I'm out of time." She began to walk around her desk. "You're going to have to leave," she said, waving toward the door. If her sister wasn't going to be more forthcoming with her information, then Wynona wasn't going to waste any time and energy on figuring it out.

"They think I did it," Celia whispered.

That froze Wynona in her tracks. "What?"

Celia's eyes were filled with that fear again when she looked up at her sister. "The police think I killed her."

Wynona's jaw dropped. "Indigo is dead? I thought they hadn't found her."

"They haven't," Celia spat. "But Deverell is convinced I'm behind the whole thing."

Wynona folded her arms over her chest. "Just what happened between the two of you?"

Celia's perfectly manicured nails suddenly became very interesting as she ignored her sister's question.

Wynona shook her head and let her arms drop. "You can't have it both ways, Celia. You said you want my help, but you won't tell me anything. It's not going to work. If you want help, you have to be willing to share. Otherwise...out."

Celia hissed. "I'm not sharing the details of my personal life."

"Then I don't see how you really need my help," Wynona said plainly. She walked to the door and held it open. "I have a shop to run."

Celia started to stomp to the door, then paused. She took a deep breath and seemed to swallow some kind of emotion before her facial features softened. "I really do need your help."

"And I need answers." Wynona wasn't about to fall for her sister's emotional tricks. She'd done it too many times when they were growing up. Wynona had been so desperate for acceptance that she'd fallen for Celia's manipulation again and again, only to end up being the one hurt. And while Wynona didn't want to be like her family, she also didn't want to leave her boundaries open.

Celia rolled her eyes. "I don't think my dating life is any of your business, but I'll tell you everything else."

Someone rang the bell at the front of the shop. "Be that as it may, I can't listen right now," Wynona said. "If you'd like to come back at closing, we can talk then. But if I don't open, I'm going to have several upset patrons, and I'm not willing to do that."

Celia stepped up and grabbed Wynona's arm. "Please," she begged. "I'm innocent."

Wynona stared at her sister. This wasn't like her at all.

"Please."

The word tugged at Wynona's heart. She hated to see Celia begging, even if the spoiled princess deserved to be brought down a peg or two.

The doorbell rang again and Wynona jumped. She looked back and forth between the front and Celia. "Sit down," Wynona said, pointing to the side chair. "I'll be back when I can, but I can't promise when it will be. If you come out here and bother any of my customers, so help me, I'll call Chief Ligurio and tell him you're here waiting to confess. Is that clear?"

Celia's lips curled into a smug smile. She flounced to the chair and sat, crossing her legs. "Like a crystal ball," Celia said sweetly. Too sweetly.

Wynona already knew she was going to regret this, but she didn't have time to worry about it. Rushing down the hall, she unlocked and opened her doors, forcing a plastic smile on her face as all her regulars began to swarm the front room. It would take quite a while to get back to Celia, but Wynona had to admit her curiosity and her empathy were piqued.

Obviously, Celia had gotten exactly what she wanted when Wynona had agreed to listen, but Wynona still wasn't sure exactly what her sister's endgame was. She wanted help. But what kind of help?

Help convincing Chief Ligurio that Celia was innocent?

Wynona wasn't convinced of that herself, though she erred toward it. Celia was many things; mean spirited, rude, entitled and spoiled, but she wasn't a killer. What would have been the purpose in killing Indigo? What would have been *anyone's* purpose in the killing? Rascal hadn't mentioned any kind of motive they had found in regards to enemies for Indigo.

The coven had all been working together to gather lightning. It seemed an odd thing for one of them to kill a fellow sister during such a ritual.

Two hours passed before Wynona had a break. The few customers still in the shop were a pair of older druids who always sat and chatted for hours. Wynona knew they would be fine if she went and checked on Celia.

Just as she headed down the hall, a scampering sound caught her attention and Wynona paused to let Violet reach her. Since she was wearing a skirt, she bent down and put her hand down on the ground for the mouse to get on. "Feel like I haven't seen you in a while," Wynona said with a smile. She put her hand up to her shoulder, which was Violet's favorite place to settle. Once the creature was on her shoulder and nuzzling her neck, Wynona felt her emotions begin to calm down. She reached up and scratched Violet behind her ear. "Thanks," she whispered.

Violet chattered her own response.

Wynona paused, her hand on the office door. "Wish me luck," she whispered, smiling when Violet nuzzled her again. Wynona had no idea what she was going to find when she opened the door. She hoped that nothing had been destroyed or hexed while she was away. The door opened to find Celia sitting in the same seat, a book in her hands.

She turned her deep blue eyes to Wynona and raised her eyebrows. "You're busier than I expected for a..." The words trailed off when Wynona raised her own challenging eyebrow.

If Celia was going to continue to be derogatory, she was gone. Celia must have recognized her sister's thoughts because she smiled placatingly.

"Thank you for coming back to see me." The insincerity was so thick it fairly dripped from the words.

Wynona reached up for Violet again, the soft fur helping calm her nerves. "I don't have long," she said as she walked to her desk. "Now...I need to know what is going on and what exactly you're expecting me to do about it."

Celia set the book aside and sighed. "I already told you. Deverel thinks I killed Indigo."

"No one is even sure that Indigo is dead," Wynona said. "How can they charge you with a murder?"

"He hasn't charged me," Celia sniffed. "At least, not formally. But he made it very clear that as soon as they find the evidence, he'll put me behind bars himself."

The words were all too familiar to Wynona, since Chief Ligurio had threatened herself with that many times. "And will they? Find evidence?"

Celia's spine stiffened so tightly Wynona was worried her sister would snap. "You think I killed my friend?" Celia's voice was low and dark and silver sparks began to drip off her fingers.

Wynona put up a hand. The magic worried her, since she herself was defenseless, but she tried not to show it. "It's a question I have to ask, Celia. You promised answers."

Plush red lips pinched into a tight line. "No," Celia snapped. "I didn't kill anyone."

Wynona leaned back in her seat. "Then I don't think you have anything to worry about with the police. If you're innocent, they won't be able to find any evidence to the contrary."

Celia looked away quickly, as if hiding something.

Wynona's eyebrows pulled together. "Celia?" Her sister didn't turn back. "They won't find any evidence, right?"

Celia once again became completely absorbed with her fingernails.

Wynona groaned and Violet scampered down to the desk. "You promised answers," Wynona warned.

Celia looked back, then did a double take. "What in all of Hex Haven is that?" she pointed to Violet.

"Another friend," Wynona said, not wanting to bring up Celia's botched hex that had turned the mouse purple in the first place.

"You're going to get turned in for a health code violation if you keep that thing around," Celia said with a smirk.

"She doesn't get anywhere near the food," Wynona defended. "And I'll remind you one more time that you promised me answers."

Celia fluttered her eyes while rolling them. "I didn't do anything to hurt Indigo, but I need your help to keep the police off my back because..." She turned away for a moment, her jaw set tight. When she turned back her eyes were nearly black with anger. "Because I lied to them."

CHAPTER 9

Wynona followed Celia into the mansion. Almost every part of Wynona was screaming for her to run and not come back. This wasn't her problem. Her sister was an adult and should be able to handle it on her own. No one actually knew if Indigo was dead.

The excuses went on and on, but a very small voice in the back of her head had spoken up while Wynona had been speaking to Ceila, and that voice seemed to be running the show.

She's your sister.

Those three words had seemingly trumped every other argument that her frantic brain could think of, though Wynona wasn't quite sure why. It wasn't like Celia treated her well, or had ever treated her well. In fact, most of the time, Celia went out of her way to make sure Wynona was miserable or at least knew she was worthless. A fact Wynona not only knew well, but struggled to contradict even on her best days.

The only reason Wynona could truly justify what she was doing was her vow to never be like her family. If Wynona had come crawling to Celia, begging for help because she had lied to the police, Celia would have shut the door in her face, laughing all the way.

Wynona didn't want to be that way. Terrible or not, Celia deserved justice to be served, and she said she hadn't hurt Indigo. So Wynona believed her...mostly. She didn't think Celia would hurt a fellow coven sister, but she did think Celia would hurt others if the situation called for it. Her favorite choice of weapons, however, were words. Celia was sharper tongued than the oldest hag or ugliest harpy. Lashing out physically just wasn't in her M.O.

Which was why Wynona now found herself walking into Adel's family home where the Sisters of Eternity were waiting for her. It felt like she was walking into the troll's den and once again, Wynona was completely helpless.

Her fingers trembled as she clutched her purse across her chest. Her Banshee Scream was in her purse, but it gave her little comfort. An entire coven of witches was more than enough of a match for an ear splitting scream that only lasted a few seconds. All it would take was a quick non-hearing spell and not one of the powerful women would be affected by the weapon.

"Ms. Le Doux," the butler intoned, bowing his head to Celia. He paused slightly, when his yellow eyes met Wynona's. They quickly darted back and forth between Wynona and her sister as if comparing how similar they looked. "Ms..."

"Le Doux," she supplied, pleased that her voice wasn't shaking as badly as her hands.

The butler was very well preserved for a zombie, Wynona noted, but not even a good spell could quite hide the surprise that lit his face, causing his dead eyes to sparkle and his patched jaw to drop. "Excuse me," he stammered, collecting himself quickly. With another head bow, he addressed her in a similar manner to her sister. "Ms. Le Doux. If you'll follow me."

The butler's back was so stiff, Wynona worried he'd break his decaying bones, but they made it in one piece to a large and lavish sitting room. Wynona had never met a zombie in person, though she'd read about them. They were a show of power and wealth, and apparently the Thornhearts had both in abundance. Anyone who had the magic to keep a wild being sane, while also keeping their body intact, had to be at the top of the magic food chain.

The Thornheart mansion was also one of the more impressive homes in Hex Haven. Between the power and the money, it explained why Adel was part of the Sisters of Eternity coven. Despite its grandeur, however, Wynona was able to keep her gawking to herself, since the castle she was raised in outdid every other wealthy family in the area. She wasn't particularly proud of that fact, but it did help keep her from looking like an idiot when she visited with the elite.

"Welcome, sister," Adel purred as she sashayed across the room to kiss Celia on each cheek. After the greeting, both women turned to look at Wynona, who stood back, knowing she wasn't going to receive the same reception.

"Hello, Adel," Wynona said, putting her chin in the air just a little. Just like with her family, Wynona knew showing any bit of weakness would bring dire consequences. Between Adel and the other sisters in the room, Wynona was the weakest one here and that would be used against her if she wasn't careful. "Callista." Wynona inclined her head. Her eyes moved to the other women in the room. Not all of them had been in the meadow the night of the storm. "Ladies," she said politely. "My sister has asked me to help, as I can, with this case and I was hoping you wouldn't mind answering a few questions for me."

Callista crossed her legs under her flowing dress. Her bottom lip poked out like a pouting child. "I don't understand why we need to do this. We spoke to the police and you the other night."

"Daughter," an older woman scolded. "Ms. Le Doux has offered her services." Her emerald green eyes were sharp, even if her face was lined with wrinkles. "One of our own is missing. We should welcome such help."

"I don't see what a magicless witch can do for us," Adel muttered, walking away from Celia and sitting down in a chair.

If Wynona hadn't heard those very words a thousand times, they would have stung worse than they did. But as it was, she brushed them away and enjoyed the angry chittering of Violet, who had emerged from Wynona's hair.

Adel jerked upright. "What is that?"

Wynona raised an eyebrow. "A friend. Now...do you want my help or not?"

Adel's eyes narrowed, but it was Celia who responded.

"We all know that if we don't get this figured out, Deverell is going to find a way to pin this on me, and I haven't done anything wrong," Celia sniffed. She sat down in a seat across from Adel and pinned her friend with a glare. "Wynona helped solve the murder of Chef Droxon, so she already has an 'in' with the police. Why not let her give it a try?"

Adel huffed and sat back in her seat. "I just don't see how she can accomplish something we can't. Our magical abilities outweigh anything she can do."

"Have you found Indigo?" Wynona interrupted.

The room went deathly silent.

"That's what I thought," Wynona said firmly. "If your magic hasn't found her at this point, what does it hurt for me to give it a try?"

The older woman walked over and stood toe to toe with Wynona. Those green eyes saw too much, but Wynona felt helpless to pull away. It wasn't until they darted to Violet that Wynona felt as if she could take a breath. The woman spun around and walked to the couch. "Let her help."

The words were said with finality and Wynona had to assume the witch was the coven mother, since no one objected to her statement.

Violet nuzzled Wynona's neck. "Thank you, Madam...?"

The woman's eyes sparkled with humor. "Augustus Murik. Mother Murik if you wish."

Wynona filed away the name but she wasn't about to call Madam Murik *mother*. Wynona was *not* part of this coven, nor would she ever be. "Madam Murik, again, thank you."

The older woman's lips twitched as if amused at Wynona's small rebellion.

"Callista," Wynona said. "I'd like to start with you."

Callista jerked and looked around before facing Wynona. "I already told you everything I know."

Wynona nodded. "I know, but I'd like to hear it again please. The night of the storm, I was only an observer. If I'm to help, I need to rehash the evening."

Callista pinched her lips together, looking anything but pleased. "Like I said before, we went to the meadow to capture the lightning for the Petra Luminis."

Wynona nodded and tilted her head. "About what time was that?"

Callista shrugged. "We arrived at eight and set up everything we needed for the ritual."

"Which was?"

Adel rolled her eyes. "If you were a proper witch, you would know this."

"Adel," Madam Murik said calmly.

The fact that Adel snapped her mouth shut was a clue to Wynona that Madam Murik was a very powerful witch. As head of the coven, she would have to be, but for the women to follow her orders without question...that was a whole new level of power.

A shiver ran up Wynona's spine and she saw a few purple sparkles in her peripheral vision. Ignoring them, she went back to Callista. "Please tell me about this ritual."

"We form a circle, with our backs to the middle," Callista explained in a bored tone. "As the lightning is breaking across the sky, we join hands and reach for the sky, chanting the spell necessary to bring the lightning to the chosen rock in the middle of the circle."

Wynona nodded. "So you were holding your sister's hand when she disappeared?"

Callista hesitated before shaking her head. "Uh, no. We actually weren't touching at that point."

Wynona frowned. "I thought you were next to each other."

"We were, but our connection had broken." Callista began to fiddle with a thread on her skirt.

"Was anyone in contact with Indigo when she disappeared?" Wynona asked the group. "Who was on her other side?"

Celia growled as she lifted her hand. "I was in contact with her...until I wasn't."

Why did it always come back to Celia? Wynona had agreed to help prove her sister's innocence, but with each thing she learned, Celia seemed deeper and deeper involved. "Please explain."

Celia twirled a piece of hair. "Our hands were connected after the second stone, but when the light flashed, blinding us, she was simply...gone."

"Gone," Wynona clarified. "Just gone. No residual magic or anything?"

Celia shook her head. "Who could tell if there was residual magic with all that power from the storm running around?"

Wynona nodded. That was true. It would have been difficult to tell one from the other. "I understand." She chewed her lip for a second. "Can you remind me again of when Indigo disappeared?"

Callista looked at Adel, who gave a very subtle nod, before she turned back to Wynona. "I believe it was ten thirty-two."

"Ten thirty-two," Wynona repeated.

Callista nodded. "Yes. Exactly."

"And you knew this how?"

Adel sighed long and loud. "I already told you that I got a text right after she had disappeared. My phone said the time."

"Right," Wynona responded. "I forgot."

Adel rolled her eyes and relaxed deeper into her seat.

"What else do you need to know?" Madam Murik asked, carefully watching Wynona.

Wynona shifted her weight from one foot to the other. She actually wasn't sure what to ask next. Just like last night, she got the feeling that she was being lied to. Something about Adel's excuse just didn't sit well with Wynona. Not to mention, she wasn't quite sure what her sister had lied about.

After Celia's admission, Wynona had been forced to go back out to handle a new batch of patrons. After closing, she and Celia had come straight to the Thornheart mansion. She should have taken the time to find out what Celia was holding back, and then it would have helped Wynona be more prepared to dig a little deeper. "You're absolutely sure about the time?" Wynona gave them the opportunity one more time to tell her the truth.

Callista once again looked to Adel, who groaned. "Yes. I am *absolutely* sure."

Wynona nodded. She wasn't sure how, but in her gut she could feel the words were a lie. Perhaps it was best to solve that first before asking for more information. If they weren't going to tell the truth, Wynona wasn't going to get very far anyway.

"Thank you for your time, ladies," Wynona said. "I think I've got enough to get started." She could hear Adel grumbling under her breath, but Wynona ignored her.

"You'll tell the police, won't you?"

Wynona spun and frowned at Callista. "Tell them what?"

Callista sunk in her seat, looking just as weak and vulnerable as she had the night of the storm. It was interesting that such a woman was part of such a powerful coven. "That Indigo is dead?" Her smile looked pained. "It's been forty-eight hours, but Chief Ligurio still refuses to declare my sister dead." She sniffed and pulled a handkerchief out of her sleeve to dab her eyes. "My brother-in-law...and the rest of my family, deserve the opportunity to put her to rest." She looked hopefully up at Wynona. "Perhaps as you do your research, you can make sure the chief allows Niam...and the rest of us, a chance to grieve properly."

Wynona could only assume that Niam was the widower. "I'll, uh, do my best," Wynona said carefully. There was no way Chief Ligurio was going to listen to her about something like this. But Wynona had to agree...if Indigo hadn't shown up after this amount of time, it was more than likely she was dead.

Ignoring the green eyes still boring into her, Wynona nodded and left the room. She didn't even bother to see if Celia was coming with her. One of these days, Wynona would pin down her sister, but as long as the other witches were around and keeping their own secrets, this wouldn't be a good time to do it.

"Ms. Le Doux," the zombie butler said in a monotone voice as he held the door open for her.

"Thank you," she said before stepping out into the fading light. The evening was quickly coming on and Wynona needed to get home. The air smelled wet, letting her know another summer storm was on the horizon, and Wynona wanted to be tucked away at her home, drinking tea and eating her leftover alfredo before it hit.

"Maybe while we're there, we can figure out what those witches are lying about," she whispered to Violet.

Violet grumbled and paced on Wynona's shoulder.

"Yeah...I can't quite figure it out either," Wynona responded. She reached up to pull her friend off her shoulder and set Violet in a small cargo basket attached to the back of her Vespa. "Hang on. Let's get home and then we'll chat."

The ride home was longer than Wynona would have liked, but she purposefully lived on the opposite side of town from the wealthy elite, making tonight's commute longer than normal.

She had just pulled into her garage when the first raindrops began hitting her roof. "Whew," she breathed, picking Violet up out of the basket. "That was close." By the time they were inside the house, the spatters had turned into a downpour.

Wynona set Violet on the dining table and headed straight for her teapot. "First...tea." She glanced over her shoulder. "Then we need to figure out why those witches were lying...and what they're trying to cover up."

CHAPTER 10

"You're not going to be in trouble with the chief, are you?" Wynona asked as she jumped out of Rascal's large pickup truck. He had been kind enough to drive her out to the meadow the witches had been in. Wynona was hoping to find evidence of what really happened that night, though she wasn't positive it would be anything the police hadn't already figured out.

But she was still positive that the members of the coven were lying. She just needed a single piece of evidence to prove it.

"Nah," Rascal drawled. "I'm off today anyway, and he's too busy fighting off the Umbra family to do much else."

Wynona raised her black eyebrows. "Fighting them off? Why?"

Rascal shook his head and reached out to take her elbow as they walked over a patch of uneven ground. "Most of them are convinced that Indigo is dead and they want the chief to declare it officially."

"Yeah...Callista mentioned that last night when I spoke to the coven." She bit her lip when Rascal gave her an amused look.

"So, am I to believe this is you *not* getting involved?"

Wynona sighed. "Celia came begging again."

His face hardened.

"I know, I know," Wynona hurried to say. "I don't owe her anything, but..."

"But what?" Rascal asked. "I don't get it. The woman treats you like yesterday's garbage," he spat.

Wynona had never seen him quite so worked up. Rascal was the epitome of smooth and cool, approaching every situation with a level head on his shoulders. Seeing him so angry that hair was starting to sprout on the back of his clenched fists was a little disconcerting. "Uh...Rascal?"

His golden eyes were glowing brightly when he looked at her, letting Wynona know the wolf was taking over.

She silently pointed to his hands and Rascal looked down, then groaned. They paused their walk while he took a couple of deep breaths and pulled himself back together.

"Sorry," he said sheepishly. He rubbed the back of his head. "I just don't like seeing you treated with less than you deserve."

Wynona gave him a smile. "That's really sweet," she said. "But I'm okay. I'm used to it."

Rascal gave her a look. "That doesn't make it any better."

She shrugged, then turned to keep moving. They were almost at the meadow now. "Maybe not, but when I was trying to decide whether or not to help my sister out, I had a thought." She began to study the ground, her attention diverted by the possibility of finding a clue.

"Wy?"

"Hmm?" She glanced up.

"What thought did you have?"

"Oh!" Wynona's face heated. "Sorry. I got distracted." She tucked a chunk of hair behind her ear. "I just remembered that my goal in life was to be the exact opposite of my family." She smiled. "And since I *know* that my sister wouldn't do anything at all to help me if I was in a similar situation, it made sense that I should."

Rascal stared at her, then closed his eyes and gave his head a hard shake. "I'm not sure I follow that logic."

"It doesn't matter," Wynona said. "What does is that I told them I would look into it. If I can help, I will." She glanced sideways. "But mostly I'm here to keep Chief Ligurio from charging my sister with murder just because they have a history together."

Rascal snorted and he studied the flattened grass at his feet. "He really does have it out for your family."

"You don't say," Wynona grumbled sarcastically. She slowly moved around the area, her eyes trying to pay attention to every nuance within the dirt and plants. She had no idea what she was looking for, but surely there was something there.

With her lack of magical powers, Wynona wasn't particularly good at feeling residual magic or recognizing if a spell or hex was used, but she did have a good eye for detail and she was hoping that would help her in this situation.

"Hey, Wy?"

She looked up from her study. "Yeah?"

Rascal pointed to the ground. "Here's where Indigo went missing."

Wynona hurried over, seeing the burnt streak in the grass well before she arrived. "Callista mentioned that," Wynona murmured.

Rascal nodded, his hands resting on his hips. "Yeah...I'm not quite sure what to make of it. It almost looks like she got hit by the lightning, but even if she had, there'd still be some burnt remains."

Wynona swallowed hard. She wasn't particularly squeamish, but that didn't mean she enjoyed talking about dead bodies. "You'd think there would be something," she agreed. She tilted her head and walked in a circle around the mark. Other than the fact that it appeared burnt, there was little else to see. "If lightning had hit, wouldn't the fire have spread some?" she asked.

"Maybe not," Rascal responded. "It was raining so hard that any fire was probably out before it began."

"True, but it still seems like the burn is very...precise."

Her companion nodded. "Yeah. That is strange."

Violet must have decided it was safe to emerge, because she finally poked her nose out of Wynona's pocket.

Wynona put out her hand and brought the mouse into the open. "I thought you were napping in there," she teased.

Violet made a disgusted sound and squeaked in indignation.

"Sorry, sorry," Wynona said with a smile. "We probably should have left you home though. There's not much to see out here."

Violet peered over the edge of Wynona's hand, then pointed at the ground.

Wynona frowned, then glanced up at Rascal. "Did she just..."

Rascal chuckled. "That's quite a mouse, Wy."

Shaking her head in disbelief, Wynona squatted low enough to let Violet get off her hand. "Okay. Have a look."

Violet scurried back and forth over the black streak. Multiple times, she stopped and sniffed, only to run around again.

"Find anything?" Wynona asked.

Violet raced over and climbed up Wynona's leg and body until she was resting in her favorite place on Wynona's shoulder. After getting comfortable, she chittered for a long time.

Wynona listened carefully. Well, as carefully as she could to a mouse. WIthout magic she didn't have the ability to speak to animals, but there were times when she and Violet just seemed to...click. Plus, Violet had proven very helpful in the past when it came to unraveling mysteries. Wynona couldn't have solved her first one without the rodent's help.

Violet's little paws swirled through the air as she continued in an animated fashion.

"Huh," Wynona said, her eyes moving back to the ground.

"Are you telling me you understood all that?" Rascal asked. He reached out and let Violet climb onto his hand. After cradling the mouse against his chest, he began to pet her, much to Violet's delight, who melted into a gooey puddle of satisfaction. "I'm part animal and it was still beyond me."

Wynona made a face. "Sort of? I mean, I don't really *understand* her, but sometimes I can get the gist of what she's saying." Wynona bent forward and studied the black mark closer. Cautiously, she reached out and let her fingers trail along the mark. Purple sparks shot into the air, startling the group. Wynona gasped and jerked away so fast she fell on her backside. She held her burning hand against her body, afraid to look at what damage she'd caused. Her breathing was shallow and rapid and she had to blink rapidly to get the lavender stars to clear from her peripheral vision.

"Wy!" Rascal quickly tucked Violet in his pocket and rushed over to help Wynona to her feet. He tugged her into his chest and turned them around so his body was between her and the mark.

"I'm alright," she panted, leaning into his side as he wrapped his arms around her. A small part of her lamented that this was how her first time in his arms had come about. Secretly, she had been hoping that it would be a far more romantic scenario, but still...beggars couldn't be choosers.

"Let me see," he insisted, pulling on her hand.

The burning had lessened and Wynona allowed Rascal to tug her hand out into the open, spreading her fingers wide. Her eyes widened as the last drop of purple glitter swept away with the wind, leaving her fingers perfectly whole. There wasn't the smallest mark on them.

"I thought you'd gotten hurt," Rascal said, turning her hand over and back.

"Me too," Wynona responded. "It was burning after I touched the mark."

"Well...whatever it was," he grumbled, "it looks like it didn't do any permanent damage."

"I suppose so," Wynona said softly. Rascal's touch had gone from medical inspection to something a little more gentle. His large, warm hands engulfed her smaller, more delicate one, sending pleasurable tingles up her arm. When he started to caress her knuckles, she suddenly had a very vivid understanding of how Violet must have felt only moments before.

"Wy," he said in a low tone, "there's something I've been wanting to ask you."

Violet poked her head out of his pocket and began to whimper.

Sighing, Rascal dropped her hand and pulled out the mouse. "Sorry," he said. "I was checking on our lady."

Violet sniffed and turned to Wynona, who put out her hand. She loved her little mouse friend, but right now Wynona wished Rascal was still holding her instead of her having to deal with a scared mouse. "I'm okay," Wynona said, putting Violet on her shoulder.

The mouse shifted into the crook of Wynona's neck and nestled in. It was her favorite place to be.

The moment between them was definitely lost, but Wynona wasn't willing to let it stay that way. "You had something you wanted to ask me?"

Rascal scratched the back of his head. "Yeah..." He cleared his throat. "Would you like to have dinner with me?"

A slow smile crept across Wynona's face. She had been waiting for this moment for a couple of months now and having it come to fruition was one of the best feelings in the world. "I'd love to," she gushed. She knew her response was a little too enthusiastic, but Wynona couldn't conjure up the self control necessary to act cool and composed.

"Really?" Rascal asked, his eyebrows shooting up his forehead.

Wynona laughed softly. "Did you think I'd turn you down?"

He scrunched up one side of his face. "I think every guy worries about that." Her response must have bolstered his confidence, however, since he boldly reached out and entwined their fingers. "But I had hoped you'd say yes."

Wynona was sure she was glowing. If she had any magic at all, she knew it would be shooting into the sky like fireworks. As it was, she was sure she was floating a couple of inches off the ground. She even glanced down to be sure, but her sneakers were firmly planted on the soil.

"Is there anything else you want to see here?" he asked with a frown. "I'm a little disinclined to let you touch anything though."

Wynona shook her head. "No. I don't think there's much to see." She turned to the burn. "Other than the mark." She brought her hand up and examined them once more. "I'm not exactly sure what happened though," she murmured. "It's almost like there was some kind of spell there."

"They were casting a spell," Rascal reminded her.

"True, but it's not the type that should have affected me," Wynona countered.

"But what they were doing required an insane amount of power," Rascal said. "Maybe what you felt was the leftover power when that last gathering went wrong."

"Could be," Wynona agreed. She sighed and rubbed her forehead. "I wish I understood magic better. I always feel like I'm running blind in these types of situations. One of the other witches would probably know exactly what was going on."

"And yet you said the other witches are lying," Rascal said, tugging her away and toward the truck. "Who's to say they know anything at all?"

"Why are they lying though?" Wynona argued. "What are they covering up? Did Indigo accidentally die in the lightning flash and they're trying to cover for it? We already know they were doing illegal magic, so it seems ridiculous to perpetuate a lie that would keep us from finding their sister."

Rascal shook his head. "I have no idea."

Violet emerged from her spot and tapped Wynona on the cheek.

"Hmm?" Wynona asked, leaning her head back so she could look at her shoulder.

Violet began to push on Wynona's chin, as if to force her to face upward.

"What's going on?" Wynona asked, pulling Rascal to a stop.

Violet chattered and pushed the underside of Wynona's chin again.

Sighing, Wynona looked up. "Happy now?" she asked.

Violet patted her cheek and seemed to say "yes".

Rascal turned and looked up as well. "What am I supposed to be seeing?"

"I don't know..." Wynona began, then trailed off. The last of the clouds from last night's storm were still in the sky, but as Wynona stood still, a strange phenomenon occurred. She could see the clouds moving. They slid quickly and seamlessly across the sky, making Wynona's head spin. "Do you see that?" she whispered.

"The clouds?" Rascal asked. "Yeah. What about it?"

"The way they're moving?" Wynona said, her excitement growing.

Rascal was frowning when he looked over at her. "They do that a lot. Is it supposed to mean something?"

Wynona reached her free hand over and grasped Rascal's arm. "I think I know what the witches were lying about," she said.

His dark eyebrows shot up. "You do?"

"Yes." Her eyes darted around as she came up with a plan. "Can we run to my office? I need to look something up."

"My place is closer," Rascal said, walking once again toward the truck.

"That works," Wynona replied. "I only need a few minutes, and if my hunch is correct, then I think we have a coven to confront."

CHAPTER 11

"So what exactly are we looking for?" Rascal asked as they drove back to his apartment.

Wynona's knee was bouncing like crazy and she couldn't quite contain the excitement at having a small breakthrough. True, it didn't get them any closer to finding Indigo, but forcing the coven to tell the truth might at least get them on the right path. "It's the storm," she said.

"The storm?" Rascal clarified, glancing her way before turning back to the road. "What about it?"

Wynona shifted in her seat to face him, then froze when she felt Violet having to adjust. "Sorry," she said softly after making sure the mouse was alright. "Anyway, the whole coven was insistent that Indigo disappeared at ten thirty-two," Wynona continued.

"Yeah..so? Adel said she received a text at that time."

"Don't you find that a little weird?" Wynona pressed. "A woman had just disappeared and Adel was willing to look at her phone? If one of my sisters disappeared, I sure wouldn't be worrying about whether or not my pocket was buzzing."

Rascal scratched his chin. "It does seem a little odd, but Adel doesn't strike me as the warm and fuzzy type. Maybe she honestly just doesn't care."

"True..." Wynona agreed. "But I think there's more to it than that."

"Such as?"

"I think they're all covering for someone."

His head jerked toward her. "Covering? So you think someone hurt Indigo on purpose?"

Wynona shrugged. "I don't know. We don't have a body, so I have no way of knowing whether she's hurt or not, but we do know that Indigo isn't here. She's gone and I think someone helped her be gone."

"And what does this have to do with the storm?" He cranked the wheel of his truck as he turned them into the apartment building parking lot.

"Hold that thought," Wynona said. "I'm hoping I can answer it when we get on your computer."

"Well come on up, m'lady," Rascal teased. "My laptop awaits."

Wynona grinned when he winked at her. She didn't want to admit how excited she was to go on a date with him. Ever since her crash and burn with Roderick, Wynona had found herself crushing more and more on Rascal. No matter how much she told herself to slow down, she just couldn't seem to get the flirty wolf shifter out of her head.

They went inside and rode up the elevator quite quickly. The walk to Rascal's door, however, wasn't quite so fast.

"Shoot." Rascal grabbed Wynona around the waist and ducked them both around a corner.

Her back was to the wall, with Rascal pressed up against her. "What's going on?" she whispered.

Rascal put a finger to his lips.

From this close, Wynona could see flecks of green in his golden eyes and she found herself almost hypnotized by them. If he had been looking straight at her, she knew for sure she would be a goner. As it was, despite the fact that they were pressed up against each other in a very intimate way, his attention was somewhere else. His eyes were fixated on the hallway they had just come from and Wynona could almost see his ears twitching as he listened for whatever had spooked him.

Wynona did her best to breathe in a shallow manner as she waited for him to decide they were safe. This close, she could smell his unique woodsy scent and it was a little more enticing than she was comfortable with.

"I think she's gone," he whispered, his attention still caught in the other direction.

"Who are we hiding from?" Wynona finally managed to ask, now that his hand had fallen to his side.

Rascal turned to look at her and immediately froze. His wide, surprised eyes slowly began to glow as if he was just now realizing how close the two of them were. His nostrils flared as he took in a long breath and his eyes fluttered for just a second as if he was savoring it.

Wynona had been right. Having him look straight at her made her knees feel weak and she was warm all over. The longer the silence went on, the faster her heart raced. At the rate she was going, Wynona was sure she was about to have a heart attack. "Rascal?" she whispered again.

The glow of his eyes quickly disappeared when Rascal blinked several times and seemed to come out of his trance. He stepped back so quickly that his arms flailed for a split second. "Sorry," he rasped, then cleared his throat. He scratched behind his ear in an irritated manner. "I could see Mama Lina coming out of her apartment."

"Ah." Wynona nodded knowingly. She hoped he couldn't see how bereft she felt at his retreat. Her insides were trembling worse than when she'd been shocked by the magic in the meadow. It took more work than it should have for her to control her breathing and calm her pulse. "Yeah...now's not a great time to get caught up in conversation with her."

Rascal snorted and waved his arm toward the main hallway. "It's never a good time, but that doesn't ever stop her. Today, however, we have an agenda, and I didn't want to break it."

Wynona peeked around the corner, then grinned over her shoulder. "All clear."

"Make a run for it," Rascal said. "The door's open."

They raced to the door and Wynona found herself giggling as they closed it behind them. "Why in the world do you leave your door open?" she asked through her laughter. "It seems to me you would be one of the first ones to know how dangerous that is."

Rascal shrugged as he headed toward the kitchen. "I'm not too worried about it."

Wynona stood around, feeling slightly out of place. "Oh? Why is that?"

Rascal came back with a couple bottles of water. "Because anyone who actually wanted anything from my place would be an idiot and I could track them down just by smelling them, so odds are they wouldn't get very far."

"Not to mention Mrs. Reyna would more than likely see them before they could do anything," Wynona teased as she accepted the bottle. "Thanks." She unscrewed the cap and took a long drink. "Wow. I didn't realize how thirsty I was."

Unfortunately, she was far thirstier for something else, but she wasn't about to be that bold. Rascal had barely asked her on a date. There was no way she could press for a kiss just yet.

He drained his bottle and set it on a side table. "Let me grab my computer."

With him gone again, Wynona took the liberty of grabbing the empty water bottle and taking it into the kitchen in order to find a garbage can. Once done, she glanced around and noticed that Rascal might just be as messy as Lusgu said. Or at least, he didn't do the dishes everyday. Maybe it was a bachelor thing.

"Wy?"

"Coming," Wynona answered, walking back into the sitting room.

Rascal's ears had gone red again. "Well, now that you're done cleaning up after me and realizing what a slob I am, why don't you show me what you think you figured out?"

Wynona laughed. "I promise I wasn't judging. But apparently, Lusgu is wearing off on me because I never leave things sitting around anymore."

Rascal set them up at the table and pulled out the seat next to him. "Even for a brownie, the guy is ridiculously neat."

"True." She accepted the computer from him and immediately pulled up a search engine and got to work.

"Pictures of the storm?" Rascal read from the screen. "What do you need those for?"

Wynona didn't answer right away as she picked through the relevant answers until she found what she wanted. "Bingo."

"I'm still lost," Rascal said, leaning in closer.

"Hang on," Wynona mumbled. She clicked through several pictures, keeping an eye on the statistics until she found exactly what she wanted. "Got it!"

Rascal shook his head and then scratched the back. "I always thought I was pretty intelligent, but I'm feeling like an idiot at the moment."

Wynona scrunched her nose. "Sorry. That wasn't my intention." She pointed to the screen. "Do you see that?"

"Yeah."

"That's the main part of the storm."

Rascal's eyebrows went up. "Uh-huh."

"Well, that's where most of the thunder and lightning originated from," Wynona explained.

"Okay," Rascal said slowly, as if asking her to keep going.

"If you narrow in and look at the map," Wynona said, using her fingers to shift the picture around, "you can see that at ten thirty-two, the main part of the storm was..." She trailed off, leaving him room to solve the situation himself.

Rascal's eyes widened. "Clear on the other side of town," he said in awe.

Wynona nodded. "Yes! Just like the women described, I remember that extra large flash of lightning. It was right before you showed up at the shop."

Rascal nodded quickly. "Yeah. The dang thing nearly blinded me while I was driving."

"Right. It definitely wasn't in a position to have struck that meadow. Which means the witches aren't telling us the truth about what happened to Indigo." Wynona sat back in her seat while Violet, who had climbed down from her shoulder, ran circles on the table.

"But how did you figure that out?" Rascal inquired. "What happened in the meadow that made you realize what they were lying about?"

Wynona pointed to Violet, who stopped her racing long enough to preen a little. "It was Violet's suggestion that I look at the sky. Seeing the clouds move so fast across the horizon reminded me that the storm would have been moving as well. And when I remembered the flash at the shop, I realized it couldn't have been in the meadow. The odds of two strikes of lightning that severe are pretty minimal. Not to mention the storm should have already gone past the meadow by the time the women claim they were collecting the lightning."

Rascal whistled low under his breath. "First off..." He jumped from his seat and retrieved a package of cookies from his cupboard, giving one to Violet. "Well done, little one."

Violet chittered happily as she ate the treat.

"And second..." Rascal turned to look at Wynona and gave her a teasing salute. "I bow to your intelligence and ingenuity. I'm thinking at this point that you need to lead the homicide team, not just join it."

Wynona felt her usual blush creep up her cheeks. She waved a dismissive hand at him, trying to play off her enjoyment of his praise. "I have no doubt you would have figured it out soon," she said. "Besides...I had help." She sent a silent thank you to Granny, since Wynona was still convinced her grandmother was the source of the strange magic that had been happening around her lately.

If Granny Saffron hadn't created that weird scene at the window, pulling Wynona's attention to the storm, she wouldn't have realized that the lightning strike couldn't have been in both places at the same time.

Rascal leaned back and folded his arms over his formidable chest. "The question is...now what do we do?"

Wynona groaned. "I think I need to meet with the coven again."

Dark eyebrows shot up. "Not a fan?"

"If you were a prey type shifter, instead of a wolf, would you enjoy being in a den of lions?"

Rascal snickered, then coughed to hide it, but Wynona didn't blame him. It was kind of funny. "But you're also a witch," he pointed out.

"A magicless one," Wynona reminded him. "I'm not on equal ground with those women."

"You're right," Rascal agreed, much to Wynona's chagrin.

She hoped she hid the pain his words sent through her. It was the truth after all.

"You're way above those entitled princesses."

Wynona jerked her head back to stare. "What?"

Rascal grinned and winked, as usual. "It doesn't matter how much magic they have," he said softly. "They'll never manage to catch up to the saint you are."

Wynona just knew her cheeks were hot enough to roast marshmallows on. "You're a flirt," she said with a grin.

"Maybe so, but I'm a truthful one." He pushed his chair back and stood up. "Should we go confront some witches?"

"You want to go with me?" Wynona asked, closing down the computer.

"I think this is something the department should be a part of, don't you?" He paused. "In fact, I hate to say it, but I should probably let the chief know what we're doing."

Wynona scrunched her nose. "And I probably need to message Celia. She should be able to get the whole coven together."

Rascal headed down the hall to make his phone call and Wynona reluctantly pressed her sister's number. "Wish me luck," she whispered to Violet while the line rang.

"This is Ms. Le Doux's private line," Airian, Celia's personal assistant, intoned. "How may I help you?"

"Hi, Airian," Wynona choked out. "It's Wynona. Is my sister available?"

There was a shuffling on the other end and Celia's voice came through quickly. "Have you solved it?"

Wynona rolled her eyes. "No, Celia. I haven't, but I do need to speak to the coven again."

Celia huffed. "Again? We've already told you all we know."

"No, actually, you haven't," Wynona snapped before she could stop herself. She squeezed her eyes shut and took a deep breath in through her nose. "In fact, you mentioned yesterday that you lied to the police, Celia, but you never have told me what about."

Wynona had a sneaking suspicion that it was *not* what she had just discovered.

Celia sniffed. "What I told Deverell has little to do with the case."

"But it still has to do with it," Wynona pressed. "I need to know what it is, Celia." Wynona could practically hear her sister roll her eyes.

"I might have told him that I was in the circle the whole time."

Wynona's eyes widened. "Excuse me? You weren't there the whole time?"

Celia huffed. "I was running late, alright? Sometimes it takes a little longer to prepare for these kinds of occasions."

Wynona pinched the bridge of her nose. She knew her sister well enough to know that she was either coming in late from a date or she was primping because she had a date later. Either way, it still meant that Celia could have snuck in and done something to Indigo without out anyone knowing about it. "We'll talk about this later," Wynona said firmly. "Right now I need you to get your sisters together. It's important."

"Fine," Celia said with a groan. "But they won't be happy about it."

"That's fine," Wynona said with forced sweetness. She was about to lose it. This conversation needed to end now. "I appreciate your help. Thank you."

The line went dead before Celia responded and Wynona shook her head before stuffing her phone in her back pocket. "I have no idea how that woman and I are related," she said to Violet.

Reaching out, Wynona picked Violet up and set her on her shoulder, where the mouse attached herself in the usual way.

"Now we just need..." Wynona spun as she heard footsteps from down the hall. Her smile fell when she saw Rascal's face. "That bad?"

Rascal snorted. "I made the mistake of telling Chief that you figured it out and were coming with me."

Wynona sighed. "One of these days he's going to have to realize I'm not his enemy."

Rascal shot her a sarcastic smile as he opened his front door for her. "I'm guessing it'll happen at the same time Lu and I become bosom buddies."

CHAPTER 12

"You ready for this?" Rascal asked as he put his truck into park.

Wynona blew out a breath as they stared up at the Thornheart mansion. "Nope. But we better do it anyway." She turned to look at him. "Are we waiting for Chief Ligurio?"

Rascal's attention was caught in the rearview mirror. "Speak of the devil."

Wynona spun in her seat and watched the patrol car pull up behind them, essentially blocking them in. "I don't think he wants to let you leave anytime soon."

Rascal snorted. "At least not until he can ream me in person."

She frowned. "Is it really going to be that bad? I promised Celia I'd help, but I don't want you in trouble."

Rascal winked. "I'm not too worried about it. I'm the best nose he's got on the force. I'm not going anywhere."

Anxiety still fluttered in her stomach, but Wynona nodded and climbed out of the vehicle. She waited beside Rascal for his boss to reach them. "Chief Ligurio," she said politely. "Thank you for being willing to meet us here."

The chief's red eyes narrowed. "This better be worth my time, Le Doux."

Wynona nodded. "I think it will be. I believe that after this chat we'll have a much better chance of going in the right direction on this case."

"*We* won't be going anywhere," Chief Ligurio growled. He pointed a finger at Wynona. "After this, you'll be backing away while my precinct takes care of the rest."

Wynona sighed. "I'm not trying to step on toes, Chief Ligurio," she explained calmly. "I'm simply trying to help my sister."

The chief snorted, then glanced at the house. "You witches, you're all the same."

Wynona glanced up at Rascal, who gave her a small shrug.

"Why don't we go in?" he suggested.

The chief nodded and Wynona stayed near Rascal's side as they traipsed into the same sitting room as before. The zombie butler had once again let them in and Wynona still found herself awestruck at how well put together he was.

"Ms. Le Doux," Madam Murik said with a respectful tilt of her head. She glanced at the men. "Chief Ligurio, Deputy Chief Strongclaw. Welcome."

Wynona didn't miss the fact that Madam Murik had greeted her first. Neither did Chief Ligurio if his clenched jaw was anything to go by. "Thank you, Mrs. Murik. We promise not to take up too much of your time."

The older woman nodded again, then walked to a couch, sitting down elegantly and crossing one leg over the other. "What can we do for you?"

Wynona looked around the room. The women were all in similar spots to where they had been before, as if it were their habit to be in a certain order. "I wanted to ask one more time about when Indigo disappeared."

There were several small groans, but no one gave a vocal objection.

Not knowing quite where to start, Wynona turned to Callista. "I'd like you to tell me what really happened that night."

Callista jerked back, upsetting the perfect flow of her long dress. "What do you mean? We told you what happened." Her pale hand fluttered to her throat.

"I'm sorry, Callista, but it's not true." Wynona tilted her head to the side, feeling sorry for the nervous witch. "I checked the storm's progress and the worst of it was well past the meadow during the timeframe you all testified about. The strike of lightning you described did happen, but it didn't happen the way you're saying."

The room had gone eerily quiet and Wynona turned around to meet the gazes of the other witches, including her sister.

"You've been lying to us and we want to know why. Not to mention the true story of what happened."

Adel's eyes moved and Wynona was sure she was glaring at Callista. "Don't do it," Adel warned.

Wynona spun and saw Callista struggling to breathe. Her pulse was visible in her neck and her face was paler than normal. "I can't do it anymore," she rasped.

Wynona frowned and leaned down a little, worried the woman was going to hyperventilate. "What happened, Callista?" she asked softly, rubbing the woman's back for comfort.

Callista's eyes were darting around over Wynona's shoulder, so Wynona stepped directly in front and squatted down on the witch's level.

"Right here," Wynona whispered, drawing Callista's eyes to her. "Just tell me what happened."

Callista was breathing rapidly and she swallowed a couple of times before answering. "It all happened so fast," she whispered.

Wynona nodded. "It's okay. Go on."

"I-it was me," Callista blurted out. "I killed my sister."

Wynona's eyes widened. She hadn't expected such a confession, and she quickly looked over to see Rascal and Chief Ligurio looking as shocked as she felt. Turning back to Callista, Wynona tried to control her reaction. "Can you tell me about it? How did you kill her?"

Callista nodded jerkily. "I...I lost hold of her hand during the chanting." She swallowed audibly. "I knew that if we weren't connected, the strength of the spell would go down, leaving me enough magic to do what I needed to do."

"You killed her on purpose?" Wynona's eyes nearly bugged out of her head. If she felt like she was shocked before, it was nothing compared to now. She had assumed something had simply gone wrong, that the situation had been an accident. Apparently she had been wrong.

Callista shrugged. "Yes. You don't know her like I do." Her eyebrows drew together. "In public she was sweet, but Indigo always thought she was better than me. She treated me like a second class citizen!"

Wynona stood and stepped back. This was getting a little too intense.

"She deserved it!" Callista shouted as she began to cry. Tears poured down her cheeks and she folded into herself. "All those years...even her husband knows how horrible she is..."

Adel rushed over and sat on the arm of the chair, her arms going around her coven sister. "Can't you see she's been through too much?" Adel snapped at Wynona. "We were only trying to protect her."

Callista let out a wail and her sobbing grew worse.

Wynona shook her head and continued to back up. She had come today to find the truth, but she had gotten much more than she bargained for.

"I killed her," Callista cried, turning her head into Adel's lap. "It's all my fault."

Warm hands gently took Wynona by her shoulders and began to pull her backward. "Let's get out of the way," Rascal whispered, leading Wynona off to the side.

Chief Ligurio, looking more somber than usual, walked up to Callista with another officer at his shoulder. "Ms. Umbra, I think it would be best if you came with us...now."

Wynona tuned out the noise as Callista's crying grew worse with every word the chief said, though she didn't fight when the officer pulled her from her chair and cuffed her with a hag thread. The light of the enchanted string glowed eerily against Callista's porcelain skin.

"You have no idea what that woman has been through!" Adel was shouting as the officer walked Callista out of the room. "She can't be held responsible for her actions!"

Wynona stepped a little closer to Rascal when Chief Ligurio stood in front of Adel, his hand in the air. "Hold on, Ms. Thornheart. That's for the law to decide."

Adel's hands were clenched into fists at her side and red sparkles began to shimmer and drip to the floor.

Wynona felt Rascal tense before he stepped slightly in front of her.

"Indigo was a jerk," Adel argued. She jammed a pointed finger toward the door. "Callista has been through enough at her sister's hand. Anyone would have broken."

"Her mental health will be examined along with any extenuating circumstances," the chief assured the irate witch. When Adel's anger didn't abate, Chief Ligurio put his hand on the magic stun gun at his side. Lots of inventions had been created to help those who didn't hold magic of their own, but needed to be able to control those who did. Every officer held one of those stun guns, which rendered magic useless within a certain range, depending on the make and model.

Wynona held her breath as she waited for Adel to back down.

"Right now, I could arrest each and every one of you for obstruction of justice," Chief Ligurio hissed, his normal grumpiness coming back to the forefront. "But I'm more concerned about helping your friend."

The chief backed up a few steps and eyed the rest of the room. "What will it be, ladies? Should I take you all down? Or will you allow me to do my job?"

Celia, who up until now had been surprisingly quiet, walked up to Adel and put a hand on her coven sister's arm. "Let them go," she said softly. "I'm sure Callista will be treated fairly."

Wynona almost choked. She had never heard her sister be so calm and compassionate. A small spark of jealousy hit Wynona in the chest, but she shook it off. Now was not the time to psychoanalyze her situation with her family.

Apparently, Wynona wasn't the only one who was surprised by Celia's words because Chief Ligurio stilled for a split second before he was back under control. "Stay in town, ladies," he said as he began to walk toward the door. "There could easily be more questions in the future."

Rascal gripped Wynona's wrist and they walked quickly after the chief. He didn't need to worry since Wynona had no desire to be left behind with the angry coven, but she was grateful for his concern all the same.

The afternoon sun was blazing as they came out of the mansion and Wynona covered her eyes so she could see.

"Are you okay?" Rascal asked, dropping his grip on her arm.

Wynona nodded and shrugged. "I suppose. When I accused them of lying, I certainly wasn't expecting for Callista to give a full confession."

Rascal nodded and sighed. "Me neither." He glanced back at the mansion. "They were all in on it. They were all harboring a murderer."

Wynona squished her lips to the side but didn't speak.

"What're you thinking?" Rascal asked.

She didn't answer him right away. Something was niggling at Wynona, but she wasn't sure what. Shaking her head, she looked him in the eye. "Nothing. Can I go with you to the station?"

Rascal scratched behind his ear. "I don't see why not. I'm guessing Chief won't give you a hard time at the moment. Not after what you managed to accomplish." He gave her a wink, but it lacked its usual playfulness.

Wynona smiled, but she too struggled to feel flirty at the moment. Callista's confession was sitting heavily on her. A sister killing a sister. It was so hard for Wynona to wrap her head around it.

She had been verbally abused her whole life, but not once had Wynona ever considered killing any of her family. Of course, it's possible that Granny Saffron was part of the reason for that.

The older woman's kindness certainly gave Wynona hope during a very dark period of her life. Maybe Callista didn't have the same anchor in the storm. Perhaps her family offered no support and the problems had simply been too much for her to handle.

"Ms. Le Doux."

Wynona came out of her maudlin thoughts to see Madam Murik in front of her. "Hello." Wynona hadn't noticed that the coven mother had followed Callista and the officer outside. Perhaps she had been offering some comforting words before Callista was taken away.

Madam Murik was studying her again, just like she had the day before. "You will take care of her?"

Wynona jerked a little and looked at Rascal, who was none too happy with the question. "I'm afraid I don't understand."

Madam Murik folded her hands in front of her and lifted her chin. "Sisters take care of each other."

"Is that what you call this?" Rascal muttered. He folded his arms over his chest. The move showed off his physique, making him quite intimidating as he stood over the two smaller women.

Madam Murik ignored his sarcasm and continued to look at Wynona expectantly.

"Callista is not my sister," Wynona said carefully. She didn't want to anger the witch, who had to be very powerful if she was in charge of this coven, but Wynona also refused to be pulled into something she wanted no part of.

The witch community at large shunned Wynona for her lack of powers, declaring her beneath their notice. Just because she had managed to become independent and ran a successful business, didn't mean she would welcome their embrace now.

One white eyebrow rose high. "You are a Le Doux."

"That means nothing in this case," Wynona answered.

"Every Le Doux witch has been a member of this coven since its inception."

Wynona had to give the older woman credit. She didn't like to hear no, and she was obviously skilled at getting her way, but Wynona had learned how to stand up for herself as well. "Apparently not every Le Doux witch, since I have never been involved and never plan to be involved," Wynona said firmly. "Now...if you'll excuse us." She and Rascal walked around the coven mother to head toward his truck.

"Wynona."

Wynona stiffened but slowly turned around. Right now she was very grateful they had left Violet at Rascal's apartment. She just knew the tiny creature would be screaming right about now. Violet was very protective of Wynona and seemed particularly harsh toward species with strong magic.

"Your grandmother would want this."

Okay...now she had gone too far. Wynona stepped forward. "My grandmother was the whole reason I managed to build a life for myself *outside* of my family's home and influence. She would have no desire for me to tie myself to a group who only recognizes me because of my last name." Wynona tilted her head to the side. She worked very hard to be kind and polite, but sometimes being firm was a necessity. "Up until a few months ago, you didn't even know I existed," Wynona said. "And my last name isn't enough to make up for my lack of magic, which I'm sure you're aware of, so I see no reason for me to build ties with a group who values power above all else."

Her voice grew a little, but Rascal's hand on her lower back helped Wynona keep herself under control.

"You already have my sister. I'm sure she's enough of a representative of our family to help continue the legendary name of your coven, and her magical contribution is far more than mine would be." Wynona tilted her head. "Now, if you'll excuse us, we have work to do."

Spinning on her heel, Wynona marched to the truck in record time. She didn't want to give Madam Murik any more chances to stop and argue a point. By the time Wynona sat down and buckled in, her face was flushed and she was breathing heavily.

"You okay?" Rascal asked as he backed out of the driveway.

Wynona nodded. "I will be."

"For the record...you were awesome." He grinned, his sharp canines showing in his enthusiasm.

Wynona slumped in her seat as the anger and adrenaline began to ease from her body. "I hate confrontations," she whispered.

Rascal reached over to pat her knee. "Well, you handled it beautifully. You were firm, truthful and still respectful." His wink this time was much closer to normal. "Just another reason you should join the squad."

Wynona laughed in a breathy tone. "You're ridiculous."

Rascal shrugged. "Can't blame a guy for trying."

Wynona's smile lasted most of the ride to the precinct. It wasn't until they parked that she felt her humor disappear as she remembered why they were there. Callista Umbra had killed her sister.

Wynona had so many questions, and she was grateful Rascal had let her tag along. She had no jurisdiction here, but Wynona was learning she had an insatiable curiosity, much to her dismay. She knew she wouldn't be able to walk away from this case until everything was tied up in a neat little bow.

They walked inside the busy station.

"Here we go," Rascal said under his breath.

Wynona nodded her agreement. "Here we go."

CHAPTER 13

Wynona held her breath as she and Rascal walked up to the interrogation room. She felt like she deserved the chance to hear what Callista had to say, but there was a part of Wynona that was certain Chief Ligurio was going to throw a fit.

"Should we go to the listening room instead?" Wynona whispered.

Rascal shook his head. "No. I want to be able to ask questions, and I want you to be able to as well." He gave her a sad grin. "You see things from a different angle and it always seems to come out in our favor."

Wynona rolled her eyes. "Now if only your chief thought so."

"He knows," Rascal assured her. "He just doesn't want to admit it." Without further ado, Rascal turned the knob and pushed his way into the room. "Sorry for the delay, Chief," Rascal said, holding the door open long enough for Wynona to slip inside.

Wynona nodded at the police chief politely, more grateful than she could say when he only sneered at her appearance. Maybe Rascal was right and Chief Ligurio was getting used to having her around.

Wynona sat carefully in a metal chair toward the back of the room and behind Chief Ligurio, where she could see all the proceedings. Despite Rascal's compliment, she wasn't sure she really wanted to participate in the questions, but Wynona did want to hear and see Callista's reactions. Something about the dramatic confession was eating at Wynona, but she wasn't sure why.

The witch in question was slumped in a seat similar to Wynona's, her hands now free, and holding a steaming styrofoam cup. Callista looked more pathetic than normal with her hunched shoulders and tear streaked face.

Rascal came to stand by Wynona's side, giving her shoulder a quick squeeze.

She glanced up and gave him a small smile before he dropped the softness and the big, bad wolf took over. His stance widened, his folded arms accentuated his muscles and all humor dropped from his face, making it look carved from granite.

It was as appealing as it was terrifying, and Wynona forced herself to look at Callista and Chief Ligurio instead of admiring those sharp cheekbones and two-day-old stubble.

Chief Ligurio, for his part, was seated across a desk from Callista, a laptop in front of him and several other officers scattered throughout the room. "Ms. Umbra," the chief said in a low tone, "why don't we start from the beginning and you can tell us exactly what happened with your sister."

Callista took a shuddering breath and set the cup down on the desk. "My sister treated me like a servant her whole life," Callista whispered. She looked up at the chief. "I lived with her, you know. Helped take care of the house and chores." Callista slumped again. "I'm actually not quite sure what I'll do now that she's gone."

Her voice broke on a sob and Chief Ligurio pushed a box of tissues toward the emotional witch. The remorse was understandable. It seemed as if the murder had been a crime of passion and now Callista was feeling confused by her actions.

"Thank you," Callista said thickly, taking a tissue and wiping her face. She took a deep breath and tried to straighten in her seat again. "Despite me doing everything I could to please her, Indigo was never happy." Callista's eyes fell again. "Her marriage was falling apart." Long blonde hair fell in Callista's face as she shook her head. "And who could blame her? Niam was always gone. She treated everyone so terribly, it was no wonder."

Callista suddenly straightened, her voice growing angry. "Her selfish behavior sent him to spend more time than he should have on *business trips*." From the way she said "business trips", no one in the room had any question to what Callista was really referring to.

"And what does her failed marriage have to do with her death?" Chief Ligurio pressed.

Callista shook her head. "Nothing. I'm just trying to help you understand." She was tearing the tissue to pieces.

"So you had a bad relationship with your sister," Chief Ligurio said matter of factly. "How long have you been planning to kill her?"

"I haven't," Callista said softly. "It just...came to me while we were in the circle the other night."

"Tell us about it."

Callista sighed and closed her eyes, as if picturing the event. "The worst of the storm was already gone," she said, confirming the lie Wynona had uncovered earlier. "The power had been dangerous during the heart of it, so we waited until the second half." A small smile played on her lips. "Everyone was euphoric. The natural magic in the air was enough to have the entire sisterhood giddy with power."

Wynona scrunched her nose. Callista made it sound like a drug, and Wynona didn't like that description at all. She'd never heard that magic was addictive in any way, but if it was, she was, for the first time ever, grateful she couldn't access it. She enjoyed being in control of herself and her future. Being under the control of an outside influence was not the least bit appealing.

A small bump to her shoulder had Wynona glancing up at Rascal, who gave her a questioning look. Apparently, he was wondering the same thing she was.

Wynona gave a tiny shrug and shake of her head. Maybe that was something she would have to do more research into.

Rascal frowned, then turned back to look at the interrogation.

"As we combined our powers to make the stones, a heavy buzzing filled the air." Callista took a deep breath as if she could still smell the magic. "Indigo was to my right and before we could fill a third stone, she pulled away from me."

The small smile on Callista's face disappeared and anger took over. "Indigo said my hand was clammy and she wiped her own on her dress." Callista shook her head. "It was raining and everything was wet. I wasn't clammy in the least, but Indigo said it anyway." Callista sneered, her eyes still closed as she relived the scene. "She was always trying to make me feel like I was less than her. Her hair was always better and she always reminded me that her clothes were more expensive." Callista's lips began to tremble. "She even bragged about how she had a husband and I never would." The tremble was gone and Callista sneered again. "As if Indigo could hold onto him."

"The field, Ms. Umbra," Chief Ligurio reminded her.

Callista stilled, then nodded. "When Indigo made fun of my hand, she also took note of the dress I wore, declaring that it looked like a potato sack and was unworthy to be a part of our circle."

The witch's breathing was growing faster and Wynona automatically leaned back. The old hag thread was gone. If Callista got upset and tried to use magic, there was no one here to stop her.

Rascal's hand was large and warm as it landed on her shoulder and Wynona felt herself relax ever so slightly. Her eyes darted up to his and he nodded toward the door.

Frowning, Wynona looked over to see an officer standing at ease. She looked back up at Rascal.

"Black hole," he mouthed.

Wynona's eyes widened. A black hole was rare. They were essentially human, except that their magic was that they didn't have magic. In other words...they neutralized any magic around them. No matter how upset Callista grew, she wouldn't be able to use any powers with the officer around.

"Right after she said those words, another flash of lightning hit the sky," Callista snapped. Her cheeks were a bright red and her fists clenched as she continued with her story. "I was so *tired* of Indigo's cruelty. So tired of being made fun of, so tired of watching her always be one step ahead, so tired of seeing her walk away with the prize..."

Wynona narrowed her eyes. There was something Callista had left out of that sentence. But what?

"As the power built in the air, I suddenly had the thought..." That weird smile came back to Callista's face. "That *I* had the power to stop it. I had the power to make her regret the way she treated me and everyone else who found themselves in her path."

Wynona found herself growing more tense with each word that came from Callista's mouth. Wynona knew the end result, Indigo had been killed. But even so, she was invested in the story. No matter how horrible her family had been to her, Wynona had never once considered harming any of them. Even now that she was emancipated and on her own, she never thought of revenge.

Okay...she had to admit to herself that revenge had crossed her mind, but it was never a thought she allowed to be entertained. The idea of hurting Celia made Wynona sick to her stomach. Literally.

Her hand fluttered to her abdomen in response to her thoughts and Wynona had to concentrate on breathing. This was exactly why she had no desire to be a part of investigations such as this. She absolutely loathed the emotional toll situations like this took on her. Wynona allowed herself to care and feel too deeply to be so involved in criminal cases.

"I waited," Callista said softly, her voice dropping in tone and volume. "I waited until we could feel the vibration in the air, letting us know the next strike was on its way." Her eyes fluttered closed again and Callista's head slowly leaned back, her face to the ceiling. "The spell built in my palm and I drew from the magic in the air.

When Indigo finally reached over to complete the circle, the spell ignited. Killing her instantly."

No one seemed to breathe as Callista's words sunk in.

It felt as if the room were stifling and the air thicker than normal. It took a great deal of concentration for Wynona to keep her heart rate under control and not jump up from her seat and run out the door. Her eyes remained glued to Callista, which was lucky, as Wynona would have missed it otherwise. When Callista's eyes opened, a flash of emotion went across the witch's face and it took Wynona a moment to figure out what it was.

Fear.

But why? Why would Callista be afraid now? Was she afraid of the consequences? Was she afraid of what others would think of her, knowing that she had committed murder?

"Where is your sister's body?" Chief Ligurio asked.

Callista cleared her throat. "I, uh...I'm not quite sure."

Wynona frowned.

"You said you killed her instantly," the chief argued. "Did you bury her? Did the coven help you? Did her body simply dissipate with the spell?"

Callista shook her head adamantly. "No, no, nothing like that." She licked her dry lips. "It was the spell. I collected the equivalent of a bolt of lightning in my hand," Callista said hoarsely. "When Indigo touched me, it would have more or less electrocuted her."

"Then her body should have still been there," Chief Ligurio argued.

Callista rubbed her forehead before she snapped up to look straight at Wynona. "You're a witch," she said with a tight smile. "You understand, don't you?"

Chief Ligurio spun to glare at Wynona, then faced Callista again. "She has nothing to do with this. What I want to know is where your sister's body is."

"I had no control over that!" Callista cried. "It was a lux spell. Those are notorious for being difficult to handle."

Chief Ligurio's hands slapped down on the desk. "That still doesn't answer my question!" he all but roared.

Wynona winced and scooted back in her seat. Angry vampires were not someone you wanted to mess with.

"I can't answer it!" Callista wailed. Her shouts broke into sobs and soon she was bent at the waist, crying uncontrollably. The woman's mood swings were enough to make a person dizzy.

Chief Ligurio slumped in his seat. After several moments, when Callista failed to get a hold of herself, he motioned to the officer at the door to come take her away.

While the emotional witch was led out, Wynona considered all that had been said. They were still lacking answers on several ends. It was obviously not premeditated, but would that make much of a difference in the long run? The right lawyer could spin this whole story as an accident, or that Callista wasn't in her right mind, too drunk on nature magic to make good decisions.

"Le Doux!" Chief Ligurio snapped, not bothering to look her way.

Wynona straightened in her seat. "Yes, Chief Ligurio?"

"Here."

Wynona made a face at Rascal, who hid his chuckle behind a fist. It was probably the first time the police chief had ever actually wanted her close rather than telling her to get lost, but his execution could use a little work. Manners mattered. "Yes, Chief?" she asked, stepping up to the desk.

"This spell she mentioned. The lux one." He finally looked up from his computer. "Explain it to me."

Wynona sighed. "I'm not sure I'm the right person for this." She pointed to herself. "No magic. Remember?"

His dark eyebrows pulled together. "Are you really telling me that that inquisitive mind of yours has never studied anything to do with your kind?"

He had her there. Wynona probably knew the history of witches far better than most other women her age. Since she couldn't practice spells or potions, she had spent her time in other pursuits. Most of which involved her granny or books.

Chief Ligurio smirked. "That's what I thought. Now tell me about it."

Wynona put her hands on her hips. "There's not much to tell. Callista was right when she described it as basically having a piece of lightning in her hand. Indigo wouldn't have stood a chance against that kind of power."

"But what about the body?" the chief growled. "Wouldn't there have been some charred remains or at least some ash left behind?"

A delicate shudder ran up Wynona's spine. It seemed so callous to speak of someone this way, though she understood the need for it. "Not necessarily, though there's no way to know." Wynona scrunched up her nose. "That amount of power could have thrown Indigo a half mile into the forest. Or it could have burned her into oblivion." Wynona shook her head slowly. "I'm sorry, but I honestly don't have a good answer for you."

The chief grumbled and rubbed the bridge of his nose. "That's all. You may go."

"Chief, I—"

"You may *go*, Ms. Le Doux," Chief Ligurio said tightly. He opened his eyes to stare her down, obviously having made up his mind.

Wynona bit her tongue and swallowed her observations. Nodding, she began to walk toward the door. Maybe it was better that she not speak to the chief right now anyway. She tended to think better if she had time to stew on the information she gathered. A nice cup of tea, a chat with Violet and a few hours of thought would help Wynona figure out what had bothered her about this whole situation.

Rascal stepped into the hall with her. "Officer Nightshade is going to run you to my apartment to pick up Violet, then take you home," he said. Frowning, his shoulders sagged. "I need to stick around for a while."

Wynona nodded. "It's alright. I get it." She smiled at him. "Thanks for taking me to the field and the coven and..." She waved her hands in the air. "Everything else today."

"It wasn't quite how I expected our time to turn out," Rascal admitted.

"Me neither, but hopefully this means we're that much closer to putting Indigo's murder behind us."

Rascal gave her an odd look at her choice of words, but didn't press. "I'll text you. See you soon."

Forcing a pleasant smile, Wynona nodded, then turned to go find her friend Officer Nightshade, the vampire who worked the front desk. The sooner Wynona got home, the better. She needed to set her head straight on a few things, and a busy police station was definitely not the place to do it.

CHAPTER 14

By the next morning, Wynona still couldn't find herself settled about Callista's confession and subsequent arrest. The whole situation seemed a little too...contrived. The witch had seemed almost deranged during her confession and in the earlier talks with her, Wynona hadn't gotten that impression at all.

Callista had appeared a little shy and nervous, but definitely not insane. Not to mention there was something about the way Callista told her story that sounded practiced. It struck Wynona as similar to the cover up by the coven. They all knew exactly what to say, making the story a little too detailed.

"Still," Wynona said to Violet, who was munching on a cracker near her bookcase, "if I killed my sister, it's possible every detail would have been burned into my memory as well."

Violet chittered, but didn't look up from her food. After being picked up from Rascal's apartment, Wynona had shared everything that had happened and the tiny, purple furbaby had been miffed ever since.

Wynona huffed and put her hand on her hip. "For the last time, I wasn't trying to leave you out!" she said in exasperation. "I caught you up, didn't I? You know as much as I do."

Violet glanced up and her tiny eyebrows seemed to furrow. With her own puff of air, she mimicked Wynona's posture with her paws on her haunches. Violet was obviously ready to talk it all out, since she scolded and chattered for a full ninety seconds before taking a break.

Wynona sighed and her shoulders deflated. "I'm sorry," she said, squatting down so they were on a more level playing field. "I had no idea that things would become so crazy." Holding out her hand, Wynona smiled when Violet reluctantly climbed on. "I left you at Rascal's because I was afraid I might make the coven upset, and who knew what magic they would throw around." Wynona gave Violet a significant look. "Need I remind you of the first time you and Celia met?"

Violet scrunched up her adorable nose and hissed.

"Exactly," Wynona agreed. "We all assumed you were safe away from a large group of magic users. But the point is, it's over and done. I've told you everything I know. Can you please forgive me and let's move on?"

Violet stared Wynona down for a moment before finally nodding.

"Thank you," Wynona said, breathing a sigh of relief. She scratched the little creature behind her ear. "Now...I need to finish setting these tables."

Violet scrambled up Wynona's arm and nestled into her hair.

Humming a happy tune, Wynona made her way through the dining room, placing tea settings at every seat.

"You pinch me again and I'll sic Lusgu on you!"

Wynona paused. "Oh, dear." She immediately recognized her best friend's voice, and had an inkling as to who Prim could be shouting at. Wynona glanced at the clock and groaned. Kyoz and Gnuq were due to drop off their fresh goodies for the day and if Prim had decided to drop by...well, that could only spell trouble.

A crash came from the kitchen and Wynona ran over as quickly as she could without dislodging Violet from her shoulder. She threw open the swinging door and gasped.

Prim had cornered the two imps and was threatening them with a steak knife. "Go ahead," Prim growled. "Move. I dare you."

"Prim!" Wynona scolded. "What on earth are you doing?"

Prim didn't even bother to look over her shoulder. "I'm escorting these two hooligans out of your kitchen before they destroy everything you've worked for," she said matter-of-factly. Prim jerked her head toward the back door. "Come on. March."

Gnuq stepped away from the corner and smoothed down her dress. Sticking her nose in the air, she sniffed disdainfully at Prim and moved toward the door as if it had been her idea the whole time.

Kyoz, however, was still in the corner, and didn't look like he wanted to move any time soon.

Wynona watched as the look on his face went from one of fear to one of...was that admiration? Wynona's jaw grew slack as Kyoz puffed out his chest and *sauntered* toward Prim, who was still aiming a knife at him.

Prim scowled harder and Kyoz changed his trajectory just enough to miss the point of the knife, though not by much. As he walked past, he turned his head and winked at Prim, giving her an air kiss.

"Get. Lost," Prim snapped, jabbing the knife in his direction.

A high-pitched squeal came out of Kyoz as he scampered the rest of the way to the door, throwing it open with a small burst of magic.

Wynona had to admit she was impressed he was capable of that. Imps were very small creatures, only about shin high to a normal sized human, and their magic was the same way. It was just enough for them to pull tiny pranks like pulling on a person's hair or pinching them in impossible to reach places, which just happened to be one of their favorite pastimes with Prim.

Being able to open a full sized door meant he was a little stronger than the average imp. Wynona tucked the information away for future use. She looked at Prim once the door had closed. "If I didn't know any better, I'd say you have a new admirer."

As a fairy, Prim wasn't a lot larger than the imps, reaching mid-thigh on Wynona. Her normally plush, pink lips were pinched so tightly, they were a thin, white line. "If he ever tries to actually kiss me, I'm gonna bind him in ivy so tight he can't breathe."

Wynona held back a laugh. Violence wasn't supposed to be funny, but with Prim still in her fairy form, she looked quite humorous, since the kitchen knife was almost as big as she was. Deciding a change of subject was in order, Wynona glanced around. "Where's Lusgu? I heard you threaten the imps with him."

Prim straightened and reached up to put the knife on the counter. "He disappeared into the pantry when they showed up." Her pink eyes rolled. "I think he simply hides until they're gone, then comes out to clean up whatever mess they leave."

"If only we all could do the same," Wynona mumbled. She stepped in and noticed several pots on the floor. That must have been the crash she'd heard. She walked over to pick them up and started stacking them in the sink. "What brings you by today? I don't remember having a flower order."

"You didn't," Prim said in a snippy tone.

Wynona paused and turned around to see why Prim was upset.

The fairy poofed herself into her human form, making her a little taller than Wynona. "Did you forget to share something with me?" Prim asked, the hurt easily audible in her tone.

Wynona hung her head. Prim usually kept her fairy form around her because she felt safe from ridicule for her wingless state. The one exception was when they were having tea together. Being the size of a regular human made sitting at the same table much easier.

Now, however, they weren't having tea and Prim had resized herself before confronting Wynona. It told the tea shop owner everything she needed to know about her friend's frame of mind.

"I'm sorry, Prim," Wynona said softly. She looked up from under her lashes. "I promise I haven't been trying to hold out on you."

Prim's face flushed pinker than her hair. "I had to hear from Triwyn, who heard it from Lula, who had gotten it from Woodwink when she was getting her hair done at the Curl and Die, that you forced a confession from Callista Umbra for her sister's murder!"

Wynona shook her head. "That's not exactly how it happened."

"It doesn't matter!" Prim cried. "You're my best friend! You should have told me what happened."

Violet began scolding from Wynona's shoulder and suddenly she felt surrounded. With a sigh, Wynona grabbed a tea kettle and began filling it with water before setting it on the stove. As she rummaged through the cupboard for the herbs she wanted, she heard the pot begin to whistle. She glanced over in surprise, then relaxed when she saw Lusgu shuffling his way through the kitchen, cleaning up the invisible mess left by the imps as he grumbled under his breath.

"Thank you," she said sweetly, taking the kettle and leading Prim out to the front room. Instead of using the teacups already set on the table, Wynona set down the kettle on a trivet and went to grab a couple of cups and saucers from her antique collection. The collection had been inspired by Granny Saffron and was reserved for her closest friends. "Please sit down," Wynona said to Prim, who huffed but obeyed.

Violet scurried down Wynona's arm and waited patiently until Wynona handed her a cracker to nibble on.

Wynona took the filled diffusers and poured everyone's cup before passing them around. "What would you like to know?" she asked Prim.

Prim pouted. "Everything."

Wynona nodded and proceeded to relay everything she knew. The longer she went on, the bigger Prim's pink eyes grew.

"Holy orchids," Prim breathed. She shook her head. "I can't believe you caught another murderer!"

Wynona winced. "I'm not sure I'd go that far."

"Well, what else would you call it?" Prim took a sip of her tea and immediately relaxed. "Oh my goodness. You always know exactly what to make."

"Rosehip and lavender," Wynona said. She winked. "Good for relaxing and a boost for the immune system."

Prim looked sheepish. "Sorry. I probably went a little overboard with the imps, since I was already upset when I came."

Wynona raised a single eyebrow.

"Okay," Prim threw her hands in the air. "I went a lot overboard." She pointed at Wynona. "But seriously, those two are horrible. They pinch me every time I come over here."

"Threatening dismemberment might be a harsh punishment for a little pinch," Wynona said wryly, although truthfully she didn't exactly disagree with Prim's actions. Those pinches hurt.

Threatening to break their contract had given Wynona a free pass as far as future pranks went, but that didn't mean the imp twins left her staff, friends or property alone. They were mostly harmless, but they were enough to drive a person crazy if given half a chance.

"I wouldn't have stopped at dismemberment," Prim grumbled into her tea.

"Prim," Wynona said on a sigh.

Prim gave her a too-wide grin. "So...now that we've gotten the whole story out of the way..." She glanced at her cell phone. "Shoot. We gotta make this fast. The roses will be hungry soon." She turned her pink eyes back to Wynona. "I want to know why you're not happier about this. Celia should be out of your hair again, so why not celebrate?"

Wynona pinched her lips and crumbled a cracker with her fingers. "Sorry," she mumbled to Violet, when the mouse glared and began to pick up all the usable chunks. Wynona brushed her fingers together and leaned back with a sigh. "Because something about it doesn't sit right with me."

"Oh?"

Wynona nodded. "Her confession was a little too...too."

Prim's pink eyebrow rose high. "Too, too?"

Wynona nodded. "Yeah. It was too dramatic. Too detailed. Too...practiced."

Prim's teacup slowly lowered to her saucer. "So what? You think she's lying?"

Wynona shrugged. "Maybe."

"But why would she lie about something like that?" Prim argued. "Having the title of 'sister killer' definitely isn't something that most people would want hanging over their heads."

"I agree," Wynona said with a nod. "But I still think there's something we don't know." She tapped her lips. "I just can't place my finger on it."

The room was quiet for a moment.

"Want to know something funny?" Wynona asked.

"What's that?"

Wynona tilted her head and tucked a piece of her black hair behind her ear. "Despite the fact that I've followed Rascal around like a lovesick puppy dog during all of this investigating, not once have I seen Indigo's husband."

"Pssht." Prim waved a hand through the air. "That's because he's out of town."

Wynona frowned. "How would you know that?"

Prim put down her cup and leaned in, obviously ready to share a bit of juicy gossip. "Word in the salon is that he's in the human world. No one can get a hold of him, so he doesn't even know his wife is dead yet."

"That's horrible," Wynona whispered, her hand fluttering to her throat. "Are you sure?"

Prim leaned back with a shrug. "As sure as I can be when I hear the information fourth hand."

Wynona chuckled. "That makes it a little hard to believe."

"I told the lilies and they agreed," Prim said with a little chin tilt. "They're great at dissecting truth from deception."

"You talk to your flowers?" Wynona asked slowly. "Like sentient beings?"

Prim gave her a look. "Of course! Where do you think the term 'heard it through the grapevine' came from?" She shook her head. "You wouldn't believe what the primroses outside the Sultry Spirits have to say," Prim said, referring to Hex Haven's oldest bar. It was run by women psychics, who were known for having your drink ready before you came in the door.

Having never been inside, Wynona could only imagine what kind of information a plant outside a bar would have to say. Probably not anything that she was interested in hearing. "And just what were *you* doing at The Sultry Spirits?"

Prim's cheeks soon matched her hair. She shifted in her seat. "Believe it not, sometimes even wingless fairies have dates."

"You had a date!" Wynona cried, then immediately brought her voice down. "Why didn't you say something?"

Prim pursed her lips like she'd tasted something sour. "Because the guy was a total loser. I left within the first ten minutes."

"Oh, I'm sorry."

Prim shrugged it off. "No biggie." She wiggled her eyebrows. "Nothing like what you're eventually going to tell me when you and Rascal actually manage to go out." She frowned. "I'm guessing this investigation is making it a wee bit difficult."

Wynona nodded sagely. "You could say that."

"What are you going to do about Callista's confession?"

It took Wynona's head a minute to catch up with the change in subject. "I don't know." She scrunched up her nose. "Do you think I should do anything?"

"What does your gut say?" Prim pressed.

"That we don't know the whole truth," Wynona answered without hesitation.

"Then you have to say something."

Wynona groaned. "Chief Ligurio isn't going to be happy with me."

Prim laughed and stood from her seat. "Like that's different from any other day? He already doesn't like you, so who cares if he doesn't like you even more?" Prim paused. "That last sentence came out weird."

"Maybe so, but I got your gist." Wynona stood as well and held out her arms, hugging Prim tight when she stepped over. "Thanks," Wynona whispered.

Prim pulled back. "Anytime." She grinned. "Someone has to keep your head on straight." She looked at the table. "Heaven knows Violet isn't doing it."

Violet immediately began to chatter, causing Prim to laugh.

She raised her hands. "I stand corrected," Prim said with a wide smile. She turned back to Wynona. "Gotta run. Say hello to Rascal for me."

"Will do," Wynona said, watching her friend slip through the kitchen door in order to leave through the back. Wynona glanced at the wall clock and gasped. "Vi. We gotta hurry or we won't be ready for our customers."

Making a mental note to send a text to Rascal when she had time, Wynona threw herself into the job she adored. There would be time for murders, confessions and missing husbands later. Much later.

CHAPTER 15

The police station was busier than normal when Wynona parked her Vespa out front and walked inside. There seemed to be an excited buzz in the air that was nearly contagious, until she remembered why she was there. Confronting Chief Ligurio with nothing more than a gut feeling wasn't going to be the smartest thing she had ever done.

"Ms. Le Doux!" Officer Nightshade called from the front desk. The vampire smiled with a toothy grin as Wynona approached the desk. "What brings you here today?" She gave a slow wink. "Looking for Deputy Chief Strongclaw?"

Heat immediately lit fire to Wynona's cheeks and Officer Nightshade chuckled. "Actually, no," Wynona said primly. "I need to speak to Chief Ligurio."

Officer Nightshade straightened. "Oh? Is something the matter?"

Wynona scrunched up her nose. "I'm not sure, but it has to do with the Indigo Stocker case."

Dark eyebrows pulled into a frown. "Are you sure you want to mess with that? Chief has already given you credit for helping solve it. I'm not sure I'd press my luck, if I were you."

Wynona sighed and nodded. "I know," she said softly. "But I really do need to speak to him." She hesitated before continuing. "And honestly, if Deputy Chief Strongclaw was available to help keep my jugular intact, I'd appreciate it as well."

Officer Nightshade snorted. "You might need more than a wolf to protect you if you mess this up." She picked up the phone and punched a button. "Hey, Clawman. I've got your favorite witch out here."

Wynona slapped her forehead. "Amaris," she scolded, dropping the formal title in view of the secretary's teasing.

Amaris laughed and hung up the phone. "That's funny. He just told me off as well...only his language was a bit more colorful."

Wynona closed her eyes and shook her head. "One of these days..." she threatened.

"One of these days I'll come by the shop and we can gossip over tea," Amaris promised as she straightened some papers. "I haven't had a date in ages," she admitted. "I need to live vicariously through someone else for a while."

Wynona shook her head. "There's nothing to live through," she said in exasperation. "We haven't even been on a date."

"Yet," Amaris offered, pointing a finger at Wynona. "I have a feeling it won't be long now."

"Wy!"

The women both turned to see Rascal standing in the entrance to the hallway.

The Deputy Chief glared at Amaris for a second before waving Wynona back. "Come on, or she'll never leave us alone."

Wynona walked away with Amaris laughing behind her. "Sorry," she said as she reached Rascal. "I actually need to speak to Chief Ligurio, but Amaris and I both thought having you around for protection might be a good idea."

Rascal blew out a breath. "That might be a tough call today. He's actually meeting with someone at the moment." His dark eyebrows furrowed. "Can you tell me what's going on?"

Wynona dropped his gaze and stared at her shoes. "I need to talk to him about Callista." She looked up from under her eyelashes.

"Why do I have the feeling he's not going to like what you have to say?"

Wynona made a face. "Maybe because I don't think she's telling the truth?"

Rascal folded his arms over his chest. "And why is that?"

Wynona shrugged. "It's not something I can actually put my finger on, more of an intuition."

Rascal's eyebrows went up. "Intuition?"

She nodded. "Yeah. The same one that told me the witch coven was lying to begin with."

Rascal pushed a hand through his wild hair, leaving it standing on end. "Okay, come on." He took her elbow and guided her down the hallway until they were outside the chief's office.

Shouting could be heard from the inside and Wynona cringed. "I was hoping he would be in a good mood when I spoke to him."

"Good luck with that," Rascal grumbled.

The door jerked open and Wynona and Rascal turned their attention to the noise.

"It's no wonder you and I are through, Deverell," Celia sneered. "You never could see any other opinion than your own."

"And you're a spoiled princess who never hears the word no," Chief Ligurio shot back. "Nothing you have to say is worth listening to."

Wynona's eyes widened as she watched the fight. She had heard those two used to be an item, but now she saw the evidence for herself.

Silver sparks shimmered all over Celia's body, outlining her body with a coating of magic.

"Ah, crap," Rascal whispered.

A bad feeling built in Wynona's stomach and she had the distinct impression that if she didn't do something, Celia was going to get herself into serious trouble. "Celia, no!" Wynona shouted, stepping in between the fighting couple.

A bolt of magic shot from Celia's hand and came straight for Wynona's chest before she could move. Wynona had just enough time to put up her hands and squeeze her eyes shut.

"What?" Celia screeched.

Wynona cracked open her eyes, to see a haze of purple smoke filtering through the air.

Celia looked at her hands, then back at Wynona. "How did you do that? You don't have any magic."

Wynona shook her head, her mouth gaping open and closed as she tried to come up with a plausible explanation. She had suspected for a long time that Granny Saffron was behind these random spurts of magic, but she didn't know for sure and there was no way that Wynona wanted Celia to know anything about it.

"He's a black hole," Chief Ligurio snapped, pointing down the hall.

Wynona breathed a sigh of relief as Officer Skymaw bore down on them with a fierce expression.

"I'm going to have to ask you to leave," the officer said to Celia in a firm tone.

Celia sniffed and threw her waist length hair behind her shoulder. "I was leaving anyway," she said snippily. Glaring first at Chief Ligurio, then Wynona, then the chief again, Celia sashayed down the hall in truly spectacular fashion.

No matter how Wynona felt about her sister, she had to admit that Celia knew how to make an entrance *and* an exit.

"Strongclaw," Chief Ligurio growled. "This better not be about the Stocker case."

Rascal rubbed the back of his neck and looked at Wynona with a sheepish expression.

"I asked him to join us," Wynona said to the chief hurriedly.

"Us?" Chief Ligurio snapped.

Wynona nodded. "Yes. I think we need to discuss Callista's confession."

The chief put up his hand. "It's done, Ms. Le Doux. Signed and formalized. There's nothing else to discuss." He turned to go back to his office and Wynona chased after him without stopping to think of the consequences.

She had just saved his life, after all. Surely the police chief wouldn't kill her without giving her a head start. "Didn't you find her confession a little too easy?" she asked, stopping at his desk to put her hands on it.

Chief Ligurio sat in his seat and leaned back. "No. I didn't."

"It was like a practiced theatrical performance," Wynona argued. "She obviously knew exactly what she was going to say beforehand."

"How lucky for us that she was prepared to tell all."

Wynona groaned. "You have to admit that something about the situation is off."

"I don't have to admit anything," the chief said, leaning forward. "But I am going to ask you to leave." One side of his lips curled up. "I've had enough of the Le Doux family for the day."

"Chief," Rascal said in warning.

The vampire turned to his deputy and raised a single eyebrow. "Got something to say?"

Rascal huffed. "She's shown us in the past that her hunches are right. The least you can do is hear her out."

"I've heard all I want to hear," Chief Ligurio snapped.

Wynona deflated. She had known this would be hard, but she hadn't thought it would be impossible. Curse Celia and her need to interfere. Celia and Chief Ligurio's past relationship was the whole reason the police chief hated Wynona on sight to begin with.

"Chief!"

All heads turned toward the still open door.

An officer Wynona didn't know stood there, looking worried. "They found the body."

Wynona gasped. "Indigo's?"

The officer nodded. "About two miles out of town, near the Grove of Secrets."

Rascal looked to Wynona, knowing that her house was on the forest's edge.

Wynona shrugged and shook her head. She knew nothing about it.

"Which side of the forest?" Chief Ligurio asked, eyeing Wynona skeptically.

"Half a mile from the foot of Spell Summit."

Wynona let out a quiet breath of relief. It was the opposite side of the city from her. Surely the chief couldn't use this against her.

"Grab the coroner," Chief Ligurio shouted, rising from his seat. "Strongclaw! With me!"

Rascal glanced at Wynona and waited for the chief to pass him before tilting his head in invitation.

Wynona pinched her lips together, but nodded in gratitude. Whether Callista was guilty or not, at this point Wynona was too deep in the mystery to stop before she saw it through. Besides, if her hunch was correct, the body might show them something that proved her theory about Callista not being guilty.

Ducking her head, Wynona followed the group of officers down the hall and when they got outside, she stayed close to Rascal so she could hop in his truck. Keeping up in her Vespa wouldn't be possible.

"Here we go," Rascal said, pulling out into the line of squad cars.

"How come you drive a truck instead of a regular car?" Wynona asked as she looked around the cab.

Rascal chuckled. "I negotiated it with my contract."

"Wow," Wynona said with a slow nod. "That's some pretty good power you have there."

Rascal winked at her. "I'm in high demand, didn't you know?"

"Well, I did, but I didn't realize everyone else knew it."

Rascal gave her a mock glare, then broke into a wide smile and chuckled. "Way to keep my ego from getting too big."

"Someone has to do it," Wynona said cheerily. They slowed with the traffic as they reached the outskirts of town. "I'm guessing she won't be a charred mess," Wynona whispered, her heart starting to pound. "Otherwise they wouldn't have known who it was."

"Good deduction, Detective Le Doux," Rascal said as he parked.

"Not a chance," Wynona sang with a saccharine sweet smile. Rascal was always teasing her about joining his team of detectives, but despite his insistence and her insatiable curiosity, Wynona had no intention of taking him up on his offer. She much preferred her tea shop, thank you very much.

Chief Ligurio scowled when he saw Wynona walking up with Rascal. "Why am I not surprised," he grumbled. "You just can't help yourself, can you?"

Wynona did her best to smile, though it was a bit shaky. "I promise I'm not here to step on your toes," she said. "I'm just here to see this case through." And if she could figure out why her sister was involved, then Wynona would like to figure that out as well. She had a feeling that Celia would be even more reluctant to share any information than she had been before the fiasco at the station.

Chief Ligurio rolled his eyes and turned away, but didn't argue with her anymore. "Might as well come see that Ms. Umbra's confession was true," he called over his shoulder.

Wynona glanced up at Rascal, who held an arm out toward the direction that the chief was walking.

"Thank you," she said softly, watching her step as she tromped through the uneven ground to the site of the crime. There was a crowd up ahead and Wynona assumed it was by Indigo's body. Wynona's heart reacted with each step she took closer and her breathing was soon a little too shallow and rapid for her liking. She didn't want to see another dead body. At least the last ones she had dealt with were nothing but ash, making them easier to handle. Wynona had a feeling, however, that this one wouldn't be the same.

"What is this?" Chief Ligurio shouted as he reached the group.

Wynona jerked back and nearly ran into Rascal. "What's wrong?" she whispered.

Rascal shook his head. "I don't know. I need to get over there." He gave her a questioning look. "Do you want to wait back here?"

She shook her head and swallowed hard. "No. I need to see."

Rascal nodded his understanding and settled his large hand on her lower back.

Wynona was more grateful for his support than she could utter at the moment. Taking a deep breath, she stepped forward again, ignoring the chief's shouts, and weasled her way into the group so she could see the body. "Oh my word," she breathed.

"Well, that changes things," Rascal grumbled. He pushed a hand through his hair, then looked down at Wynona. "Are you sure you don't have any magic?"

Wynona shook her head. "None."

He sighed. "Well, then your intuition ought to come with a warning label."

Wynona gave him a small, nervous smile, then turned back to study the body. Indigo was dressed in tight jeans and a T-shirt, and her feet were bare, which seemed odd for someone lying in the middle of nowhere. Bright blonde hair was thrown around her head, spread out in the crushed grasses underneath her body.

Wynona could almost imagine that Indigo was merely sleeping in peace, if it weren't for the most obvious part of the crime scene.

Indigo's lips were black, and the color bled in zig zagging lines across her lily white skin. It stretched across her face and down her neck, just peeking out from underneath the T-shirt sleeves.

"Do you know what it is?" Chief Ligurio asked, surprising Wynona, who was too focused to hear him step up to her side.

She looked up at him and nodded.

The police chief raised an eyebrow expectantly.

The scene was almost an exact replica of something Wynona had read about during her growing up years. Her parents' library had been vast and she had read almost everything since she hadn't been allowed to do anything else. She had seen this before, and it wasn't a good sign.

"Hex poisoning," Wynona said softly.

Chief Ligurio closed his eyes and his shoulders deflated. "There's no chance this had to do with Callista's lightning spell?"

Wynona shook her head. "No." She pointed to the body. "If she had been hit with light, there would be burns on the body at least a little bit. Not to mention, I'm sure you noticed that Indigo isn't dressed like the other women were in the field." Wynona shook her head. "If she had been killed the night of the storm, she'd still be wearing her ritual dress."

Chief Ligurio took a deep breath. "Don't go anywhere, Ms. Le Doux. You and I need to talk." At that, he walked away and began shouting orders to his men.

Wynona stepped back and stayed out of the way from the officers and medical officials who were handling the body. She put a hand to her stomach, feeling slightly nauseated as she thought of the horrible death Indigo would have experienced under the poison.

"What exactly is hex poisoning?" Rascal asked softly.

Wynona looked up at him sadly. "It means she drank a hex," Wynona explained.

"Drank it?"

Wynona nodded. "Yeah. Hexes can be made into all sorts of forms and some are liquid." Her eyes went back to the body and Wynona shivered a little. "It basically kills a body from the inside out."

Rascal rubbed her back. "Hang tight and I'll drive you back when we're done."

Wynona nodded and stepped farther out of the way. She was severely regretting getting involved in this case, but a flicker of determination was building inside of her as well...one that refused to be put out. With Callista in jail, she couldn't have been the one to do this, but someone had killed this woman, and no matter how badly the witch community treated Wynona, Indigo deserved justice.

And Wynona felt like she was just the witch to help find it.

CHAPTER 16

"Why are we waiting here?" Wynona whispered to Rascal. They were back at the station and Chief Ligurio had put them in an interrogation room, only to leave a few moments later.

Rascal scratched his three-day-old beard. "I think they're bringing Callista in here to talk with her again."

"Oh." Wynona tapped her fingers on her knee. "And the chief?"

Rascal shrugged. "I'm not sure."

The answer to her question came quickly, however, when Chief Ligurio burst back in with a mug in his hand.

Unconsciously, Wynona leaned back. She knew vampires needed blood to survive, and those who lived in the cities were quite civilized about it, but that didn't mean it didn't churn her stomach just a touch. Though the recognition of that made Wynona feel bad. In the paranormal world, different species all had different diets. Why should one disgust her more than the others?

Taking a deep breath, Wynona forced her uncharitable feelings aside and tried to act as if she had been waiting patiently, though inside she was squirming with eagerness to get this over with.

Chief Ligurio didn't seem to notice her at all as he sat down at the table in the middle of the room and opened a folder. He seemed to be studying its contents while they all waited for Callista to arrive.

When the door opened again, Wynona straightened in her seat. Callista was being led in with officers on either side of her. Her hands were still wrapped in a hag thread and Wynona wanted to scold them for keeping her locked up when they had full evidence she was innocent. She bit her tongue, however. There was a time and a place to pick a fight and right now wasn't it.

"Ms. Umbra," Chief Ligurio said in a more pleasant than usual voice. "Have a seat, please."

Callista frowned, but complied.

"Your hands."

Callista looked up at the officer at her side and held up her hands. Her eyes widened when he removed the thread. She slowly lowered her hands, rubbing the skin as if she was hurt, though the skin wasn't red at all.

"We found your sister," Chief Ligurio said carefully.

Wynona stiffened. There was something in the edge of his tone and she wanted to know where he was going with this.

Callista relaxed and smiled. "No wonder you brought me in here. You know about our plan."

Wynona frowned. Plan? What was Callista talking about?

Callista looked around. "So, am I free to go then?"

Chief Ligurio leaned forward on the desk. "What exactly do you think we found, Ms. Umbra?"

Callista blinked several times. "I thought you said you found Indigo. Didn't she tell you about our plan?"

"You told us point blank a couple of days ago that you killed your sister," Chief Ligurio pointed out. "Yet now you're speaking as if we should have found her alive."

Callista's face drained of color and she swayed slightly. "She wasn't alive?"

The chief slowly shook his head. "Her body was picked up about an hour ago at the foot of Spell Summit."

"Indigo's dead?" Callista rasped, as if she couldn't really grasp what the chief was saying. "Are you sure it was her?"

Chief Ligurio nodded slowly. "She's with the coroner at the moment, and we're still waiting for you or another family member to make a formal ID, but..."

There was no need for more. Even Wynona, who had only ever seen the Umbra family from a distance and between the sliver of an open doorway at her own family's balls and receptions, had known exactly who it was when she saw the body.

Callista's face crumpled and she buried herself in her hands, sobbing wildly. "She wasn't supposed to die! That wasn't part of the plan."

The chief tried to speak to Callista several times over her wailing, but it only caused the witch to cry harder.

Unable to sit and watch any longer, Wynona leapt to her feet and rushed over to Callista's side. She knelt at the chair and wrapped her arms around Callista's shaking shoulders, holding her tight. "We're going to get to the bottom of this," she whispered in Callista's ear. "It's going to be okay."

Callista, who wouldn't have given Wynona the time of day if they were in public, let her weight fall into Wynona and soaked up the comfort being offered.

Chief Ligurio scowled, but didn't stop Wynona from helping. He obviously wasn't completely comfortable with hysterical women, so Wynona put his grumpiness out of her head while she helped to calm Callista.

Slowly, the tears ebbed and Wynona pulled back, using her hands on either side of Callista's face to look her in the eye. "You need to tell us about this plan between you and Indigo."

Callista nodded and sniffed. "I know."

"It might help us find her killer," Wynona continued. "So please don't leave anything out."

Callista sighed and settled herself back in her seat.

Wynona stood up and grabbed a box of tissues from the desk, handing one to Callista. "Oh, thank you," she then said to Rascal, who had moved her chair to be right next to the grieving witch.

He gave her his signature wink, then stood back in the corner, once again surveying the situation.

Callista blew her nose and took another tissue to wipe her face before she spoke. "I already told you that Indigo's marriage wasn't...the best." Callista sighed and slumped against the back of the chair. "When I mentioned that Niam was spending more time away from home than he should, I meant it." She looked up. "Sometimes he's gone for weeks at a time. He always says he's in the human world, but we don't have a good way to make sure he's telling the truth."

"What does he say he's doing there?" Chief Ligurio asked, making a note on his computer.

Callista shrugged. "I don't know. Work?"

"He's a...politician, correct?" Chief Ligurio clarified after checking his notes.

Callista nodded. "Yes." She frowned. "Has he been told yet?"

The chief shook his head. "We can't get a hold of him."

Callista blew out a breath. "It's ridiculous that we can hide our entire community from the humans but we can't send a simple cell phone call through."

Wynona huffed a quiet laugh. She had to agree that of the two, a phone call sounded like it should have been the easier thing.

"Keep going, Ms. Umbra," Chief Ligurio demanded.

Wynona wanted to scold him, but she just took Callista's hand and warmed it between her own. Her energy was better spent helping Callista, rather than arguing with the chief about manners.

"Indigo was sure Niam was seeing another woman." Callista's eyes went to her lap. "So she wanted to give him a test."

"Test?" the chief snapped. "As in...what? Faking her own death?"

To Wynona's shock, Callista nodded. "Yes," she said softly.

"And you were willing to play along?" Chief Ligurio said incredulously.

Wynona almost dropped the hand she held. The horrible ramifications of such a prank were enough to have her completely disgusted with Callista and her sister. Had they no care for what others would think? How many people they would hurt with that kind of stunt?

"She's my sister," Callista argued, her back straightening as she defended herself.

"A sister whom you claim treated you badly."

Callista shrugged. "Everyone knew that Indigo was spoiled. It was part of who she was."

"And the rest of the plan?"

Callista sighed, her attitude changing so swiftly that Wynona once again had whiplash. Now the witch sounded irritated for being interrupted. "The news was supposed to get back to Niam about her death," Callista explained in a snippy tone. "Once he was back in Hex Haven, Indigo would follow him to see what kind of reaction he had to her death. You know, whether he was truly upset about it or not."

"And you couldn't do it because you would be in jail," Chief Ligurio stated.

"Exactly," Callista said with a smile. "We didn't want anyone else getting in trouble, so I had to confess in a way that was believable. When Indigo's situation with Niam was figured out, then she would present herself as alive and all the charges would be dropped."

Chief Ligurio leaned back in his seat, looking like he couldn't believe the story he was hearing. A quiet snort came from Rascal's corner, but Wynona didn't dare look his way. She completely agreed with both men. It was absolutely the most unbelievable scheme Wynona had ever heard. She couldn't understand why the women thought it was a good idea.

"Obviously, it didn't work out the way you planned," Chief Ligurio muttered, going back to his notes.

Callista began to sniff again. "No." She turned large, watery eyes on the police chief. "Why would someone kill her? I don't understand. Indigo was staying at the Hexmoon Inn. We signed her in under a false name. No one should have even known she was there."

Wynona relaxed a little. That answered one question. The Hexmoon Inn was near the Goddess's Table, which was on top of Spell Summit. It explained why Indigo was found in that area of town and why she might have been without shoes. She was more than likely killed at the hotel, then brought down to be hidden in the wilderness.

"Do you know anyone who was upset with your sister?" Chief Ligurio asked. "Anyone that would want to harm her?"

Callista rolled her eyes. "Indigo was one of the most powerful witches in Hex Haven. Of course she had enemies."

Wynona held back her own eye roll. Yes, the Umbra family was powerful, but they certainly weren't at the top like Callista was bragging about. Wynona was starting to think the witch was not fully there mentally.

"Have you ever heard of hex poisoning?" Chief Ligurio pressed.

Callista jerked back. "I'm a witch. Of course I know what hex poisoning is." Her eyes widened. "Is that how Indigo died?" she asked in a whisper. She brought her tissue to her mouth. "Who would do that?"

"That's what we're going to find out," the police chief assured her. He nodded to Officer Skymaw, who waited at the door as usual. "I think we're done for now, Ms. Umbra. As you were in prison when your sister was killed, you are no longer considered a suspect. You're free to go."

Callista looked to Wynona, who smiled and nodded. Rising slowly from her chair, Callista walked out, paused in the doorway as if she was going to speak, then hurried into the hallway.

The remaining officer closed the door behind her.

"What did you make of that?" Chief Ligurio asked the room.

Wynona looked at him to see who he was speaking to, and his red eyes were trained on her. She shook her head. "I think Callista worships her sister and is also a little delusional."

Chief Ligurio nodded. "There does seem to be a strange relationship between them."

Wynona found herself holding her breath. He had never spoken to her this way, and it was refreshing to have him actually treat her like an asset instead of a disease.

"So this hex poisoning," he said, leaning onto the table. "Tell me again what it is?"

"It's literally a hex in liquid form," Wynona explained.

"Can any witch make it?"

She squished her lips to the side and sighed. "Not exactly. Hexes come in all sorts of difficulty levels, so even young witches can create a hex. Turning it into liquid is a bit more difficult, but again, is dependent on the level of hex you were working with to begin."

"And one that would kill someone like Indigo?"

Wynona's shoulders fell. "I'm guessing it had to be fairly powerful. Witches with certain magic levels can sense other magic. Indigo wasn't quite as strong as Callista made her out to be, but if she's in the Sisterhood of Eternity, she should have noticed a hex before she drank whatever it was."

Chief Ligurio tapped a pen against the table. "Can you tell exactly what type of magic something is? Can a witch tell a hex from a blessing, for example?"

"Some can," Wynona continued. "At least according to my readings." She shrugged. "I'm afraid I don't have personal experience, nor am I positive of what exact level Indigo was. She was friends with Celia and I had seen her before, but I..." Wynona trailed off. She hated admitting how isolated she had been growing up. It made her feel inadequate and embarrassed.

"I think I understand," Chief Ligurio said tightly. His face had turned to stone as soon as Wynona had mentioned Celia's name. It was a mistake Wynona reminded herself not to repeat in the future. "I'll let you know if I need you again," he said by way of dismissal.

Wynona nodded and stood. Rascal followed her out into the hallway.

"I'll drive you home," he said quickly, but Wynona shook her head.

"My scooter is here," she said with a smile. She tilted her head toward the door. "Besides...I'm guessing Chief Ligurio doesn't really want you to leave for a while."

Rascal gave her a sad smile. "You're probably right."

Feeling a little bold, Wynona patted his chest. "I'm still holding you to that dinner you promised me."

Rascal's eyes began to glow as a slow, deliciously mischievous smile crept across his face. "And I'll be more than happy to provide it. But maybe when we don't have a dead body hanging over our conversation."

"I can get behind that," Wynona agreed. She gave him the wink this time. "See you soon."

Taking a lesson from her sister, Wynona may or may not have put just a little extra swing in her hips as she walked down the hall and away from Rascal. She wasn't quite sure when they'd get this case over and done with, but she wasn't completely opposed to letting him see what he was missing in the meantime.

Now if only she could put that confidence into her detective work. While Wynona was relieved to have seen an innocent Callista go free, they now had a true murder on their hands and a murderer who needed to be brought to justice.

Wynona gritted her teeth. It might be time to speak to Celia again.

CHAPTER 17

"You wanted to see me?" Celia said casually as she let herself into the tea shop the next morning.

Wynona held back a snappy retort. Each time she met with her sister, it was a little harder than before. This whole case was starting to wear on Wynona's nerves. Fake confessions, fake murders, real murders, questionable relationships...nothing was as it seemed and somehow, Celia knew more than she was sharing.

Wynona folded her arms over her chest. "Yes," she said carefully. "I have some questions for you."

Celia gave an unconcerned shrug and slipped into a seat at one of the tables. It was already set for the day and she began to play with one of the teacups and saucers.

Wynona walked over and took the cup, moving it to the other side of the table, before sitting down herself. "You heard about Indigo?"

Celia put a hand to her chest, her silver bracelets jingling with the shift. "That poor thing," she said with fake sympathy. "I can't imagine being killed with hex poisoning." She shuddered.

"Wow," Wynona couldn't help but say. "Your grief over a lost coven sister is overwhelming."

Celia rolled her eyes. "It's not as if we were close," she said. "The whole coven is one big vat of vipers." She grinned evilly. "Each and every one of them will stab you in the back if you dare turn around."

"I thought covens were supposed to be like a family?" Wynona asked, genuinely confused.

Celia leaned forward. "My dear *sister*," she said with enough derision to let Wynona know exactly how she meant that word. "When one must constantly compete in order to keep their spot, it makes it difficult to feel anything warm and fuzzy for the people around you."

"So...what? All that talk about protecting each other is just that? Talk? None of you actually care if someone is killed?"

"There are a dozen witches waiting to take Indigo's spot," Celia said, leaning back as if she hadn't a care in the world. "And with her gone, it means half the coven will move up a slot." She shrugged. "Other than her husband and sister, I doubt very many people will grieve over Indigo's death."

Wynona made a face. For the second time in her life, she was extremely grateful for her lack of powers. The idea of competing with those who were meant to be family and wishing for others to fail was in direct contrast to what Wynona wanted out of her life. But she was aware enough to recognize that if she had been raised with the same powers as Celia, Wynona knew she would more than likely be in the same position.

She simply wouldn't know any different.

"Don't judge me," Celia snapped, her voice turning angry. "You sit here in your tiny little shop with your ridiculous purple mouse and think you understand what my life is like?"

Wynona felt her heart begin to beat harder at her sister's anger. Silver was starting to spark on her fingertips and Wynona began to think her sister needed a lesson in emotional management. Celia's magic was a little too "at-the-ready" every time Celia got the least bit irked. A good witch was in control at all times, but Celia was far from it, despite being so talented.

A squeak caught their attention and a purple streak raced across the floor and up Wynona's leg until Violet perched on Wynona's shoulder, scolding Celia loudly.

Celia smirked. "I rest my case."

"First of all," Wynona said, feeling a little more confident now that she wasn't alone. A mouse really shouldn't have been that reassuring, but Violet was becoming a true friend and Wynona trusted the tiny creature. "I wasn't judging you." She held up a hand to stop Celia's argument. "I have no desire to live your life and despite your disdain, I love mine. I'm sorry things are so difficult for you."

Some of the silver fire in Celia's eyes dimmed, but she still looked on edge, as if the slightest wrong move would set her off again.

"But I'm trying to help bring a murderer to justice and I'm guessing that since Callista has been set free, Chief Ligurio is going to go back to his original list." Wynona gave Celia a significant look. "Which, unless my memory is faulty, included you."

Celia snorted. "It should include the entire coven," she muttered.

"From what you just said, it should include every witch in town."

"That too," Celia said with a smirk.

"I need to know what you were doing two nights ago," Wynona said bluntly.

Celia stilled, her red fingernails stopping mid-air from tapping on the table. "Excuse me?"

Wynona sighed. "I'm trying to help," she said softly. "You know that Chief Ligurio is going to eventually come calling now that we have a body and a time of death. I'm not asking anything he won't be asking as well."

"I just can't believe that my own sister would feel the need to ask—"

"Celia," Wynona groaned, throwing her head back. She smiled slightly when Violet went off again. Bringing her head back down to look her sister in the face, Wynona leaned into the table, giving her sister her best glare. "Believe it or not, I'm trying to help," she said through gritted teeth. "Although heaven only knows why. Ever since you asked for me to help clear your name, you've treated me with disgust, insulted my life, lied to me about your alibi, and tried to curse a police chief!" Wynona shook her head. "If I didn't know any better, I'd say you were *trying* to get thrown in jail! And if that's the case, then go for it! It's no skin off my nose!" Wynona pushed up from the table and began to walk away. "Close the door behind you," she tossed over her shoulder.

She was so sick of her sister's antics. Wynona honestly didn't think her sister had killed Indigo, but there was definitely information being held back. And if Celia refused to give it, then she could deal with the police herself. Wynona would go back to her tea making and friends and do her best to ignore the guilt she would feel about her sister.

"Wynona," Celia drawled.

Wynona ignored her.

"Wynona!"

She spun at the kitchen door. "What?"

Celia took a deep breath and deflated a little in her seat. Her fingers began to toy with several beaded pieces of jewelry that she wore on her wrist, the movement appearing like a nervous habit. "What do you want to know?"

Wynona slowly walked back, feeling a little like she was navigating a land mine. There was no way her sister was just going to conveniently cooperate after Wynona's little tirade. There were too many years of abuse between them for it to be that easy. "I want to know where you were two nights ago," Wynona said, standing at the table, but not sitting down.

"I was at home," Celia said, refusing to look at her sister.

"And who can corroborate your story?"

Celia glanced up, her look sharp, but she didn't argue. "Zysus," she stated.

"The butler is the only one who knew you were home?" Wynona put her hands on her hips. "How do I know you didn't pay him to give you an alibi?"

Celia studied her nails. "I guess you don't, but he's the only witness I have."

Wynona had an odd thought... "What exactly were you doing with the butler?"

Celia raised one eyebrow. "Are you sure you want to know?"

Wynona scrunched up her nose. "Really? The butler?"

Celia fluttered and rolled her eyes before giving Wynona a wry look. "Have you seen his muscles?"

Wynona pinched the bridge of her nose. She knew there was no way her sister was serious about the minotaur. He wouldn't have enough magic for her family to approve of. But apparently, that didn't stop Celia from having fun. "Okay, so Zysus and you were...together," Wynona clarified. "And the night of the ritual? You said you weren't there on time."

Celia huffed and folded her arms over her chest. "Obviously, Indigo wasn't killed that night," she argued. "Why do you need to know?"

"Because the night of the storm is when this all started," Wynona shot back. "Every piece of information could be a clue as to piecing together what really happened."

Violet chittered quietly and nuzzled Wynona's neck. She reached up and pet the soft fur. The tiny rodent always knew how to soothe Wynona.

"I was meeting someone," Celia finally admitted.

Wynona paused. "A man?"

"I guess you could call him that," her sister hedged.

"You were in the woods," Wynona whispered. Her eyes shot open wide. "Were you meeting a shifter?"

Celia just glanced up, but didn't answer.

"Just how many men are you dating?" Wynona asked in exasperation.

Celia huffed and turned on her hip so she wasn't facing Wynona. "It's not like you'd understand," Celia grumbled.

Wynona bit back her retort and thought on her sister's words. She was positive there was something to be learned from her sister's behavior, but right now, Wynona already had too much on her mind with the murder. Maybe after this was all over, she would psychoanalyze Celia's problems, but not until then.

"Okay, can I have his name please?" Wynona asked.

Celia pinched her lush lips together into a thin, white line. "Trace."

"Does he have a last name?"

Celia shrugged. "Probably."

Wynona closed her eyes and counted to ten. Her sister seriously needed help. "Could you find him again if I needed to speak to him?"

This time Celia gave a decisive nod.

"Okay, well at least there's that," Wynona murmured. Her eyes lost focus as she began to think. "You were in the forest during the storm, only arriving in time for the light gathering. You were at home during the murder." She turned back to her sister. "What happened between you and Chief Ligurio?"

Celia threw up her hands. "What is this? Dissect Celia's love life day?"

Wynona shook her head. "No. But we need to be able to work with him if we're going to maintain your innocence, and I think you and I both know, right now he's not your biggest fan." She refrained from saying that trying to blast him with a spell hadn't helped at all, but Wynona hoped her sister was already aware of that.

"We dated for a couple of months," Celia said, making a face. "But when we had a differing opinion, I broke up with him."

Wynona blinked. "That's it? There's no way that's it."

"We weren't a good match to begin with," Celia said snarkily. "Mom and Dad thought the chief of police would be nice to have in our pocket, so they're the ones who suggested I get to know him."

Wynona's jaw dropped. "What?"

"At first it was kind of fun," Celia said softly, her mind apparently tracing back to the beginning of the relationship. "I'd never dated a vampire before."

"You like him."

Celia's head snapped up. "No, I don't. He's a pig-headed jerk who refuses to see the world in anything but black and white."

"Does he know that our parents put you up to it?"

Celia deflated. "I think he figured it out by the end."

"No wonder he hates our family," Wynona muttered. "What did you two argue about?"

Celia picked at the tablecloth. "I don't even remember. It was something political that Dad asked me to push him on."

"Oh, Celia," Wynona said, sinking into the closest chair. "How awful."

Celia sniffed and straightened. She pushed her silky hair over her shoulder. "It didn't matter. Dad wasn't pleased, of course, but it's not like they would have let me marry a vampire anyway. He was just a means to an end."

Wynona didn't comment. She heard exactly what her sister was saying in those words and it had nothing to do with what came out of her mouth. Their parents were truly horrible. "Back to the topic at hand," Wynona said, giving Celia a reprieve. "The fact that you have an alibi is good, but now I'd like to know about the other women in the coven. You said any of them could have wanted to harm Indigo." Wynona tilted her head. "Anyone in particular? Anyone who has made threats in the past?"

Celia shook her head. "Not that I can think of." She shrugged. "I mean, we all know that Mother will replace us with a snap of her fingers if we step out of line, so I don't think any of them would actually murder anybody."

"What about her husband?" Wynona pressed. "I think it's odd that he's been in the human world for so long. I mean, I get that it's a bit of a commute, but according to Callista, he's gone for weeks on end. What exactly does he do? I heard it was something political."

Celia shrugged. "I have no idea. I've only met him once."

"And did they seem happy together?"

Celia gave her sister a look. "Aren't all married couples in public?"

Wynona shook her head. She could understand the jaded view, and maybe Wynona had time to read one too many fairy tales as a child, but she was certain that not all marriages were as terrible as her parents' or, apparently, Indigo's. Surely there had to be some couples who were blissfully happy in their choice of companion. Especially the ones who had found their soulmates.

Wynona would never admit it out loud, but she had a deeply hidden desire to find that part of her. A soulmate was rare, but not unheard of. As a witch, she wasn't the greatest candidate for having one, since it was more of a shifter thing, but sometimes...

"Are you telling me that Niam doesn't know his wife is dead yet?" Celia asked, interrupting Wynona's wandering thoughts.

Wynona shook her head. "Not that I'm aware of," she said softly. "No one can get a hold of him."

"Spells and hexes," Celia murmured, rubbing her forehead. "What a mess."

"Exactly," Wynona agreed. She glanced at the clock, then jumped to her feet. "Shoot. I open in twenty minutes and need to finish getting ready."

Celia pursed her lips but stood up. "I can take a hint," she snapped.

The mood swings were giving Wynona a headache. Wynona had decided it must be a witch thing, since all the ones she had been interacting with were the same way. She'd definitely be brewing herself a strong cup of lavender and mint after Celia left. "Thank you for understanding," Wynona said, following her sister to the door.

Celia scowled, but didn't speak, pulling the front door open, only to stop when she nearly tripped on Prim. "Excuse me," Celia said in a tone that was anything but polite.

Prim put her nose in the air, slipped past Celia and replied, "You're excused." She kept her back to Celia and grinned wildly at Wynona, who had to bite back laughter at Prim's behavior.

Growling, Celia stormed out, slamming the door behind her.

"Whew!" Prim said, wiping her forehead dramatically. "That was quite the performance." She narrowed her pink eyes and gave Wynona a once-over. "I can smell the gossip," she said. "What did I miss?"

Wynona smiled and shook her head. She couldn't share everything Celia had just said, but she could share some. And boy, would Prim be gloating for weeks. "Come on back," Wynona said, indicating the dining area. "I need to ready the kettles and I'll tell you what I can."

Prim rubbed her hands together. "This is going to be good."

Wynona shook her head. She wished that were true. The gossip might be good, but progress on the murder was not. In fact, now that Wynona had a deeper picture of the story, she was more confused than ever.

CHAPTER 18

Wynona was grateful that Rascal wasn't at the station this evening. He'd been on an earlier shift and had been home when she'd texted, which made her job a lot easier. She needed to share the pertinent information she had received from Celia, but Wynona did not, under any circumstances, want to share it when Chief Ligurio had any chance of hearing it.

Wynona parked her Vespa on the street, unstrapped her helmet and locked it on the scooter. The building was quieter than normal tonight. Usually an abundance of small children, many of them shifters, were racing around outside in a mass of chaotic fun. "It's probably too late for that," Wynona muttered to herself as she pulled open the building door.

It only took a few moments to arrive on Rascal's floor and Wynona kept a careful watch on Mrs. Reyna's door as she hurried over to knock on Rascal's. In the future, Wynona wanted to have a good, sit down chat with the older woman and find out everything she knew about Wynona's grandmother. But right now a murder needed to be solved and Wynona didn't quite have the time necessary to dedicate to a one on one.

Rascal pulled open the door and grinned, stepping aside to let Wynona come in. "Can I get you something to drink?" he asked as he pushed the door closed.

Wynona nodded. "Water would be great, thank you."

Rascal complied and was soon back with a cold ice water and a can of soda. He handed Wynona hers and indicated the couch and chairs. "Have a seat and give me the rundown."

Wynona did her best not to notice how attractive Rascal's messy hair was. He always looked like he hadn't shaved in a couple of days and the stubble on his jaw only defined the angles of his face, highlighting his masculine beauty. She knew that if she looked into his golden eyes, she would find them sparkling with humor, and that only served to keep her pulse moving at a much faster rate than it should have been.

Rascal frowned and seemed to concentrate. He closed his eyes and took a deep breath before opening them. "Are you okay? Your heart rate sounds...nervous."

Wynona's eyes widened and she nearly dropped her glass. "Excuse me?"

Rascal scratched the back of his head sheepishly. "I can, uh, hear your heartbeat. And it's moving pretty fast."

Wynona slapped her forehead. "You've got to be kidding me," she muttered. She almost turned around and left. This was beyond embarrassing.

"Hey, it's alright. Running away from Mama Lina can make anyone out of breath." He fell back onto the couch, lazily reclining and inviting her to do the same.

Wynona knew her cheeks were a fiery red and there was nothing she could do about that, but she could pretend his implication that she'd been running from Mrs. Reyna was true. That was one little white lie she felt she could get behind. "One of these days, I won't run from her," Wynona said as she eased into a chair. She didn't dare sit closer to Rascal after that fiasco. "I'd like to talk to her about Granny."

"But not until the case is solved," Rascal offered.

Wynona nodded sadly. "Yeah. I kind of hate having this hanging over my head."

He nodded, complete understanding in his gaze. "I get it."

His words of waiting until the case was over before they went out to dinner came back to Wynona's mind. Yes…there were many things pending on the solving of Indigo's murder, and it was serving to motivate Wynona to get it figured out.

"So…" He took a drink. "Tell me about the chat with your sister."

Wynona scrunched up her nose. "I'm not sure I'd call it a chat," she muttered. "It was more like war."

Rascal chuckled. "I can imagine. She doesn't seem like the easiest person to get along with."

Wynona rolled her eyes. "Understatement. But she's better than my mom."

Rascal leaned forward, elbows on his knees as he looked sadly at her. "I'm sorry you had such a rough childhood. If I'd known, I would have broken you free ages ago."

Wynona laughed and tucked a stray piece of hair behind her ear. "No…it's okay. If I had been raised differently, I wouldn't be who I am now, and though I'm far from perfect, I'm not upset about it either."

His eyes flashed with warmth. "I feel the same way."

Oooh, that heat hit her face so hard Wynona almost had to fan herself to keep from swooning. This man certainly knew how to push all her buttons…in a good way. Dropping his intense stare, she played with the condensation on her glass. "Celia has an alibi for both the night of the storm and the night of the murder."

Rascal frowned. "She was with the coven the night of the storm. I thought we already knew about that alibi."

Wynona shook her head. "Celia has been lying…at least about part of the night." She leaned in. "And I think it all has to do with Chief Ligurio."

Rascal's eyes widened. "You can't be serious?"

She nodded slowly. "I am. I think Celia is still in love with him."

Rascal shook his head adamantly. "She's got a funny way of showing it."

"Well, it gets even weirder," Wynona stated. "Celia wasn't with the coven the whole time during the storm. She was late."

Dark eyebrows shot up high on Rascal's forehead. "No one told us that."

"I think they're all protecting each other," Wynona said with wonder. "Which is odd since Celia was very adamant that the women in the coven aren't friends. She said they're basically in a never-ending competition. If one of them fails, it only serves to make the others look good."

Rascal pushed a hand through his already messy hair, making it stand up on end. "Sounds like a lovely group."

Wynona snorted. "You can say that again." She sighed. "Despite that, Celia couldn't quite think of anyone that would actually hurt Indigo. She seemed to think that the wrath of their mother was enough to keep them in line."

Rascal tapped his knee. "I wish we could get a hold of her husband. He's been gone for two weeks, but isn't expected back for another two."

"Celia wasn't sure what he did for a living," Wynona hedged.

Rascal grinned. "Fishing for more information, Wy?"

She made a face and folded her arms over her chest. "Can you blame me? With Callista out of the way, we both know your boss is going to be after Celia again."

"She did lie to him," Rascal pointed out. "It sounds like he has good reason to suspect her."

Wynona nodded. "I get it, but he's still wrong. And she had an alibi for the night of the murder."

"Which is?"

Wynona hesitated, but finally knew she was going to have to admit the truth if they were going to find a way to keep Celia out of it. "She was...with my family's butler."

Rascal raised a single eyebrow. "With?"

Wynona nodded meaningfully. "With."

He closed his eyes and chuckled. "And why was she missing the night of the storm?"

"Same thing," Wynona said.

"The butler?"

"No, that time it was a shifter."

"Wow...your sister..." He cut himself off and cleared his throat. "Nevermind."

"Oh, don't worry," Wynona assured him. "It wasn't anything I wasn't already thinking." She frowned. "Which is exactly why I think Celia's still in love with Chief Ligurio."

"She's dating every eligible man in Hex Haven because she's in love with the chief?"

"Yep."

Rascal stared. "Maybe I'm too much of a man, but I don't get it."

Wynona waved a hand dismissively in the air. "That actually doesn't matter right now. I came to share that with you so that you could help me come up with another list of suspects. Callista is free, Celia has an alibi, the husband is in the human world... Who's left?"

Rascal took a long pull of his soda. "That's a good question." He leaned forward again. "You said the coven was more of a competition than a family. Perhaps someone was desperate enough to kill, even if Celia thinks otherwise. Any idea where Indigo was in the lineup?"

"Apparently, the middle," Wynona responded. "It would be an odd position for someone to be after."

He nodded thoughtfully. "True. Usually people aim for the top." He paused in thought. "Perhaps that's exactly what the murderer wanted us to think though. Maybe they're looking at a long term gain, as opposed to shooting straight up."

Wynona tapped her nails against the glass. "Maybe, but something about that just seems off. Plus, could a weaker witch really catch a stronger one off guard to that degree? She would have to be quite talented to hide a hex potion so that Indigo didn't know what it was."

Rascal growled. "We've got to be missing something."

"I agree, but what?"

He shook his head. "I'm not sure." Another low rumble vibrated through his throat and Wynona felt an answering flutter in her stomach.

She had only seen Rascal in his wolf form once, but he was a beautiful creature. Multiple shades of brown all running together in perfect harmony. It appeared that frustration helped bring the animal to the surface and Wynona found herself wishing she could see him again.

"I keep coming back to the husband, but if he's anywhere in Hex Haven, we can't find him." Rascal took another long drink.

Wynona shook herself from her weird thoughts and came back to the matter at hand. "Their marriage was obviously difficult, but why kill? Would he have a motive for it? Why not just divorce? Especially since he'd apparently already found reasons to stay away from home. It seems really extreme to have her murdered."

"You'd be surprised at the excuses people give for murder," Rascal muttered.

A short, but hard shiver ran down Wynona's spine. From the first case she'd help solve, she knew his words were true. People killed for all sorts of reasons, and some of them were so flimsy it made Wynona sick to think about.

"The only thought I have is to interrogate the coven again, but this time one on one," Wynona mused. "Last time they banded together in order to protect one of their own."

"Which contradicts Celia's story of competition," he said.

Wynona nodded. "I know."

Rascal cleared his throat. "Have you considered the fact that Celia might be..." He trailed off and rubbed the back of his neck, obviously uncomfortable with the topic he'd brought up.

"That she might be lying to me?" Wynona stated bluntly.

Rascal nodded. "I'm sorry, Wy. But it's my job to consider every angle."

Her anger deflated. "I know," she said softly. "And I understand. She's been skirting the truth from the beginning, and that makes her suspicious. Plus, it's not like a servant couldn't be bribed or paid in order to lie about an alibi." Wynona shook her head. "I don't like my sister, but I also don't believe her to be a murderer. And what would Celia gain? There's no motive for her to kill Indigo."

Rascal nodded and didn't say anything else on the topic, though Wynona assumed it was out of respect for her, not because he was really ready to let it go. She knew Celia looked suspicious, but the idea of her killing Indigo just made no sense. Not unless it was an accident, and if it was, why work so hard to cover it up? Especially with the power the Le Doux family had, an accidental death would be swept under the rug faster than Wynona could brew a cup of tea. Magic and political power went a long way in hiding unwanted indiscretions.

Rascal slapped his knees. "I can tell the chief to call in the coven again. You're right that speaking to them one on one might help us determine where to go next. Until something else appears, we're kind of at a dead end."

Wynona nodded. "Good. If Chief Ligurio allows, I'd love to sit and listen."

Rascal grinned. "I can't make promises, but I think he's starting to realize you're more help than he wants to admit."

Wynona's smile broadened. "He didn't look too pleased at Callista's release to have to ask me those questions, did he?"

His low chuckle resonated through the room. "Nope. But a bit of humbling never hurt anybody." He stood up and began walking. "I'm starved. Want something?"

Wynona shook her head. "No, thank you. I really should get back. I left Violet at the shop and I still need to make a few tinctures tonight for a party I have coming in tomorrow."

A flash of disappointment went across Rascal's face, but he quickly covered it with his usual carefree smile. "Next time then."

Wynona knew exactly how he felt. She didn't really want to leave, but duty called. Hers and his. In fact, it was duty keeping them from that dinner he'd promised, and Wynona was quickly growing heartily sick of it. "Next time," she said with a nod.

Rascal walked around her and held the door open like a gentleman. "Tell Vi hello for me."

Wynona paused in the doorway and laughed. "It won't be the same. You know she adores you."

He winked. "The feeling's mutual. Next time I'm in, I'll have to cuddle her for a bit."

Wynona shook her head. "A mouse and a wolf. It's an odd pairing."

Rascal's hand came up and his knuckles grazed her jawline. "She's part of you," he said softly. "We were bound to get along."

Despite the buzzing on her skin from his touch, Wynona frowned. "She's part of me? What do you mean?"

He shrugged. "Can you deny there's a connection there?"

"Well, no, but I figured it was because I fed her all the time."

Rascal tapped her nose. "I think it's more than that, but only time will tell."

She huffed and put her hands on her hips. "What do you know that I don't?"

"Nothing...yet," Rascal assured her. "Just speaking in hunches."

"Okay," Wynona said, giving him the stink eye. "But after this case..."

Rascal laughed. "Of course. After this case."

She gave him a small smile. "Night."

"I'll text," he assured her. "We'll probably try to set up the interviews as soon as possible."

"Sounds good. Thank you." Forcing herself to turn and move, Wynona slipped into the hallway and down to the elevator. Rascal's presence was much too warm and comforting for her peace of mind. She wanted to bask in his presence and never leave, and that wouldn't do at all. They'd never even managed to go on a date, for heaven's sake!

"You gotta figure out this case," Wynona reminded herself as she strapped on her helmet. "Solve the case, get the shifter. Easy peasy, lemon squeazy."

CHAPTER 19

"There you go," Wynona said sweetly, setting the tiny tea cup and saucer in front of the pixie. "I added a touch of cinnamon with the apple blossoms. I think you'll love it."

"Oooh, thank you," Jubilee said with a small clap of her hands. "Your tea house has become my favorite!"

Wynona beamed. "I'm so glad," she gushed, putting a hand over her chest. She had been open long enough that she was starting to get regular customers, and Jubilee was one of them. The pixie came in several times a month, often with her book club friends, and was very friendly and generous with her praise. "My bakers have been working on some new recipes," Wynona offered. "Have you tried the blueberry tarts yet?"

Jubilee shook her head, her grey-streaked, green hair nearly falling out of its bun. "No, but it sounds wonderful." She leaned in. "Where do they get their berries from? Are they fresh?"

Wynona tapped her bottom lip. "I'm not sure where they purchase their produce, but they're definitely fresh. A friend of mine couldn't stop eating them the other day."

"I'll definitely try one," Jubilee said with a smile. "You've never steered me wrong yet."

"I'll grab a tray from the kitchen," Wynona promised. "Be back soon." She meandered away from the corner where she had set up several smaller tables for her patrons who weren't the size of a regular human. It had proven to be a brilliant move as the clientele it was geared towards had flocked in since day one, overly excited for a place to sit that was just for them.

When she felt more secure financially, Wynona already had plans to start a small patio at the back of the building in order to accommodate larger customers. Trolls, minotaurs and other larger than average creatures barely fit into her front room and would surely be more comfortable out in the open, as well as in chairs built to better hold their bulk.

"Lusgu?" Wynona called as she walked into the kitchen.

A grunt was her only response.

"Would you mind grabbing the mop? We have a spill in the private dining room."

The brownie appeared out of the corner's shadows, though Wynona wasn't quite sure what he was doing there. He seemed to come from that area a lot and Wynona couldn't find out where exactly he was hiding. She had walked into the corner several times, only to find a complete wall and corner, just like expected. But somehow, Lusgu melted into the area and appeared when called.

With a snap of his dirty fingers, the mop followed him out the door.

"Please choose kindness," Wynona called after him. She sighed and shook her head, knowing she'd have to follow him to smooth things over after he was done. The brownie didn't seem to care what others thought or if he drove away Wynona's customers, as long as the mess was cleaned up.

Grabbing the smallest of her trays, she began to fill it with tiny plates and then pulled out the pastries and a knife. Kyoz and Gnuq didn't make different-sized pastries, so Wynona had to cut the regular sizes into smaller ones for her pint sized tea drinkers like Jubilee.

She hummed while she worked, only jumping slightly when her back pocket buzzed. Setting down the knife, she pulled out her phone and tapped the screen for the text.

Niam is back. You might want to be here.

She froze. "Niam..." Wynona's mind churned. "The husband!"

"Husband," a gravelly voice scoffed.

Wynona spun to see Lusgu reentering the kitchen.

"Marriage is messy business," he grumbled, shaking his head. "It will be messy, messy, messy."

Wynona grinned. "Good thing I'm not married then, huh?"

Lusgu gave her a glare before shuffling past, heading straight back to his corner.

As soon as he wasn't looking at her anymore, Wynona went back to her phone. Glancing at the screen, she realized she still had an hour until she closed the shop. "Shoot," she muttered.

How long will he be there? I need an hour.

Wynona bit her lip as she waited for Rascal to respond.

I'll save you a seat.

She let out the breath she had unconsciously been holding. Stuffing the phone in her back pocket, she quickly finished up her work with the tray, then rushed to take it out to her customer. Usually Wynona loved working the last hour of the day because many of the ladies enjoyed lingering and chatting, but tonight Wynona needed them gone on time. She had a mystery to solve.

The sign on the door was turned at ten after the hour and Wynona didn't even bother to clean up. She knew Lusgu would handle it just fine, though she felt a small twinge of guilt. Usually Wynona liked to help so her janitor didn't feel like he was being taken advantage of, but today she had more important matters.

The wind whipped her face as she pushed her Vespa through the streets of Hex Haven, trying to hurry without truly breaking any laws. Luckily at that time of the evening, the police station parking lot wasn't full, so Wynona was easily able to find a spot and lock up the scooter.

Her legs moved quickly as she rushed up the steps and into the lobby.

"Wynona!" Officer Amaris Nightshade cried as Wynona approached the front desk.

"Ra-Officer Strongclaw is waiting for me," Wynona said breathlessly. One of these days she was going to have to start exercising. Apparently, crushing tea leaves didn't give her much of a cardio experience.

Amaris tilted her head toward the back. "Go on. You know the way."

Wynona ignored the heat in her cheeks and nodded her thanks before walking toward Rascal's office. Just as she came up to it, ready to knock, the door opened and Wynona squealed slightly, barely managing to avoid running into Rascal's broad chest. "Oh my goodness." Wynona gasped.

Rascal grinned. "Shoot. I should have waited an extra second."

She gave him a look, putting her hands on her hips, which only made laughter rumble out of Rascal's chest.

"Come on," he said, through his chuckles. "Chief was just getting started."

"Whew," Wynona said. "I was worried I had missed the whole thing."

Rascal shook his head. "Nope. Things have been a little chaotic around here this afternoon and we're just now getting around to speaking to Mr. Stocker."

"I'm assuming he knows at this point that his wife is dead," Wynona said softly as they navigated the hallway.

Rascal nodded. "Yeah. I was the lucky dog chosen to tell him, but it turned out he already knew."

"How?" Wynona asked, pausing for a second outside the interview room.

"He read it in yesterday's ghost report," Rascal explained. "That's why he came home in the first place."

Before Wynona could respond, Rascal opened the door and ushered her in. "I'm here, Chief," Rascal said, following Wynona in. He nodded to his boss, then led Wynona to the same seat in the back corner she had occupied when they'd been interviewing Callista.

"As I was saying," Chief Ligurio snapped, his red eyes flashing over his shoulder.

Wynona gave him her best smile and almost laughed when the police chief rolled his eyes.

"I'd like to hear your story from the beginning. Where were you on the night of the storm, a week ago?"

Niam Stocker was a lean, handsome warlock. His medium brown hair was cut short on the sides and just long enough on top to style in elegant waves that accented his masculine facial structure. A goatee graced his face and was obviously well groomed and kept trimmed on a regular basis.

Wynona narrowed her eyes as she studied the man. His posture was off with the rest of his look. His shoulders were slumped and weariness was etched in every line on his face. It was a look that Wynona felt fit the situation, considering the man's wife had just been murdered.

What did not fit the situation, however, was the clean cut of his suit. There were no wrinkles, no sign that he had come home in a hurry after reading about his wife's death. His hair was combed and his eyes clear, rather than red rimmed.

Her suspicion that he had been involved in the murder jumped up a notch.

"I was in the human world," Niam said in a low tone. He sighed. "I'm a liaison between President Le Doux and the President of the United States."

Wynona stiffened. How in the world did she not know this? Although she wasn't involved in her family's politics, Wynona was still very much aware of the people in various positions of her parents' employ. Parties, networking and other business had always been done at the castle, and Wynona knew the faces and names all too well... She'd just never met any of them face to face.

Rascal touched her shoulder and Wynona looked up. Seeing the question in his eyes, she subtly shook her head. He huffed quietly, then turned back to the front.

"I've been in Washington DC for a couple of weeks," Niam continued, "but had gotten my work done early, so I began to plan to come home when the report came through my desk." He shook his head. "I just...can't believe she's gone."

"Our department tried to reach you multiple times," Chief Ligurio said. "Why is it you were able to get a ghost report, but our calls were unanswered?"

Niam shook his head. "My cell phone doesn't work in the human world," Niam explained. "When I cross the barrier, I'm always flooded with messages and missed calls, but there's nothing I can do about it. I use a work phone while I'm there. It's built on a secure line so I can get in touch with President Le Doux, but no one else has access to the number." His brown eyes dropped to his lap. "Indigo used to complain a lot about the amount of time I was out of reach." His face started to crumple. "I guess now it really doesn't matter."

Wynona had to turn away when it looked like he might cry. This was more the reaction she had expected to see of a married man who had just experienced loss. Seeing it first hand, however, made her feel like she was intruding on something intimate. Grown men didn't usually show that much emotion in public, and it sent sympathy coursing through Wynona's system.

"While I'm sorry for your loss," Chief Ligurio stated, his voice a little less harsh than before, "I still need a few answers."

Wynona glanced back up to see Niam nod. "Of course. Anything I can do to help catch her killer."

"What do you know about hex poisoning?"

Niam scrubbed his face. "It's a horrible way to die," he offered. "If Indigo drank one, she either was forced to or the other person was skilled enough to hide it."

Wynona made a mental note to ask Rascal if there had been any signs of trauma on the body. She had been too caught up in the black poison lines to see if there were bruisings that would indicate a struggle.

"And is your magic level high enough for something like that?" Chief Ligurio continued.

Niam sputtered. "Of course it is, but how could you be suggesting that I had anything to do with my wife's death?" Gone was the grieving man from a moment before, and in his place was an angry warlock. Brown eyes flashed, but there was no sign of magic. Either Niam was very much in control or Mr. Black Hole at the door had struck again.

Chief Ligurio leaned back in his seat, folding his arms over his chest, looking for all the world as if he wasn't the slightest bit intimidated by the angry husband. "I've heard multiple times that you didn't have a very good marriage," he pressed. "You were gone for long periods of time, your wife spent the whole time you were home complaining... Seems to me that it might be an easy thing to simply get rid of her if only to save yourself the headache."

Wynona's eyes widened at the chief's crude suggestion.

Rascal's warm hand landed on her shoulder and gave her a light squeeze before disappearing.

She forced herself to relax. The chief more than likely had a plan for what he was doing. Maybe antagonizing Mr. Stocker would bring out some bits of information the warlock wouldn't share otherwise.

"How dare you suggest such a thing," Niam growled. His face turned a startling shade of red. "My wife and I might not have gotten along all the time, but I still loved her, and she loved me. We had planned to take a month-long trip in a few weeks in order to try and put our relationship back in order." He tilted his head to the side, raising his eyebrows in a challenging manner. "Is that what a man who was planning to kill his wife would do?"

Chief Ligurio snorted, but otherwise didn't reply. He leaned forward and checked through his notes. "Don't leave town again, Mr. Stocker. Until your wife's killer is caught, I might need to speak to you."

Niam stood. "You might have to take that up with President Le Doux."

Chief Ligurio leaned back again and smiled, but there was nothing friendly or warm about it. "The president has no power when a murder investigation is ongoing. Stay put."

Niam's nostrils flared, but he nodded before storming out of the room.

Officer Skymaw followed, along with the rest of the officers, until it was just the chief, Rascal and Wynona left.

Chief Ligurio spun his seat so he was facing her and Rascal. "Thoughts?"

Wynona glanced up at Rascal, who looked back and waited. "I'm not sure," she hedged.

A thick black eyebrow rose on the chief's forehead. "I thought you always had an opinion, Ms. Le Doux. Whatever could have happened to bring us to this momentous occasion?"

Wynona ignored his sarcasm. She found it better not to indulge him. "I do wonder about his timing though," she murmured.

"Timing?"

"Yes, the timing of him coming home," Wynona explained. "Doesn't it seem odd to you that a man who has a reputation for being gone for long periods of time just *happened* to get done early with his assignment?" She splayed her hands to the side. "No one has ever mentioned that he ever got done early at times."

"But he was still gone during the actual crime," Chief Ligurio argued. "Whether his timing is suspicious or not, he wasn't here."

"Have you checked his story?"

"Not yet, but we will." The chief turned and picked up his laptop and other notes. "If you think of anything useful...let me know." Without any other type of acknowledgement, he left the room.

Wynona's jaw was slack as she looked up at Rascal. "He really is softening."

Rascal ran a hand through his hair. "I never thought I'd see the day." He winked. "But tread lightly. Who knows how long it'll last."

She laughed a little and stood. "I better get back. I haven't fed Violet this evening, and I left Lusgu with a mountain of dishes."

"Oh, I'll bet Ole Lu just loved it."

Wynona shook her head. "You two need to learn to get along. It's like dealing with toddlers when you're together."

"I can't help it, I'm so irresistible," Rascal complained, putting a hand on his chest in a teasing manner "Lusgu just can't handle my magnetic personality."

Wynona rolled her eyes. "And at that, I'm out of here."

Rascal put a hand on her back. "Thanks for coming. I'll walk you to the door."

Wynona accepted his chivalrous act and said goodbye a few moments later, though she would have loved to have stayed in his presence awhile longer. But duty called and her mind was spinning with Niam's story.

Just like when she'd listened to Callista, Wynona was sure something wasn't quite right. She just couldn't quite put her finger on it. "This calls for a cup of matcha," Wynona said softly as she strapped on her helmet. A little boost to help clear her mind might just go a long way tonight.

CHAPTER 20

"Sunflowers are great listeners, you know," Prim said as she passed behind Wynona.

Wynona sighed and spritzed the flowers with her spray bottle. "I'm sure they are, but right now I need answers, not just a listener."

Prim bounced on her toes. "In that case, I would suggest you talk to me, because I just might have both."

Wynona frowned and turned to her friend. "What?"

Pink eyes were sparkling with delight as Prim placed her hands on the work table in the middle of the greenhouse. "I might or might not have gotten my hair done yesterday."

Wynona's eyebrows went up. That bit of information explained the sparkly look to Prim's pink do. She must have gotten a fresh glitter job. "And just what was the topic of conversation among Hex Haven's best gossipers?"

"Ha, ha," Prim said sarcastically before shaking her head. "But not a chance. You share first, then I'll give you the details."

Wynona groaned. "Prim. This isn't a game."

"Nope, you're right." Prim's voice was more serious. "It's a murder, and news of it is all over the city right now, so you might as well have a good brainstorming session with me."

Wynona hesitated, then nodded. "You're right. I'll do better if I talk it all out loud."

Prim did a little dance and plopped herself on a barstool at her work table. "Spill."

Wynona walked over and set her bottle down. "So, you know Callista was released."

Prim nodded. "Yep." She frowned. "But the ghost report was sketchy on the details."

"She was in jail during the time Indigo was actually killed."

"Oh, right," Prim said. "The sisters had faked the whole thing because Niam was gone so much."

"Yeah..." Wynona huffed. "I just...struggle with that story. I mean, I get that Callista was behind bars during the murder and obviously, murdering a sister is beyond extreme, but I just can't seem to understand their faking a death story. It seems so senseless."

Prim played with a few fallen petals, their colors glowing under her magical touch. "It is pretty extreme, but women have always done stupid things when it comes to getting a man's attention. I mean, think of pantyhose." Prim made a face. "Can you imagine going that far just to draw a guy's attention to your legs?"

Wynona laughed. "You're ridiculous."

"I'm totally serious!" Prim argued. "In fact, I would argue that most of women's clothes that are meant to make us look good are conspiracies run by groups of men."

"Says the fairy who loves ruffled dresses and bows," Wynona pointed out.

"Who wouldn't like to dress like a five-year-old?" Prim said, acting offended. "It frees my inner child and the flowers love that."

"I'll bet they do," Wynona agreed. She shifted to the side, sitting on her own stool, and put her elbow on the table so she could rest her chin on her fist.

Prim frowned. "Maybe that's why I struggle to get a date..." she mused.

"Prim, you're perfect the way you are," Wynona inserted. "Don't change for anything."

Prim preened. "Well, as long as you think that, and we both know you're never wrong, so..."

Wynona laughed and straightened. "But seriously. The whole thing is just bizarre."

"Agreed. But move on. Callista was under police care. She's not the killer. Who else are the police looking at?"

"No one in particular," Wynona admitted. "But they're checking Niam's alibi, and of course, Chief Ligurio would love nothing more than to pin the whole thing on Celia's shoulders out of spite."

Prim hesitated before a smile plastered across her face. "And we all know she didn't do it, right?"

Wynona's eyebrows pulled together. "How about you try telling me what you really think?"

"What?" Prim opened her eyes wide so she looked completely innocent. It was very well done, letting Wynona know her friend had practiced it many times.

"The truth," Wynona demanded. "You think Celia is guilty?"

Prim's cheeks colored and it wasn't the best match for her hair. "How can you tell?"

Wynona pointed at the petals. The soft pink pieces had curled up and dried into death husks.

Prim grumbled and swept the debris to the floor. "Sometimes magic is a nuisance."

Wynona bit her tongue, though she understood Prim's meaning. Still, when a person wasn't given the choice about whether or not to have magic, it was hard to be patient with those who complained about it.

A loud squeak caught their attention and Wynona looked over to see Violet racing across the floor. The mouse stopped halfway to turn back and scold someone very loudly, before sauntering, yes *sauntering*, over to Wynona's feet.

Wynona waited, doing her best to keep from laughing as she waited for Violet to climb her leg and come join them on the table. "What was that all about?" Wynona asked.

Violet sniffed and began to smooth her fur with her hands.

"Oooh," Prim said softly.

Wynona looked at Prim, who nodded toward the corner. When she looked, Wynona just managed to catch the tail of another mouse, this one a more normal brown color, as it disappeared behind a flower pot. She turned to Violet. "Did you meet a friend?"

Violet rolled her eyes and went back to grooming.

"The least you could have done was be nice," Wynona said. "That might be kind of awkward next time we visit."

Violet put her hands on her hips and chittered angrily.

Wynona put up her hands. "I'm just saying! Alienating anyone who eats a bite of your snack is going to leave you with no one to talk to pretty quickly."

Violet grumbled some more.

"He's a mouse," Wynona said. "That's what they do." She shook her head and smiled. "You've just gotten spoiled because I feed you all the time."

Violet huffed and turned in a circle until her face was buried, then promptly went to sleep.

Wynona laughed softly and looked back at Prim, who was sitting in shock. "What?" Wynona asked, jerking her head around to see what Prim was so upset about.

Prim gathered herself and studied both Wynona and Violet. "You're acting like she's..." Prim trailed off and shook her head. "Nevermind. I'm sure I'm just imagining things."

Wynona waited for her friend to explain, but apparently Prim didn't want to share her thoughts.

"Back to suspects." Prim snapped her mouth shut after she said that, but Wynona didn't miss it.

"You think Celia is guilty, don't you?" Wynona asked softly.

Prim couldn't seem to meet her friend's eyes as she drew a random pattern on the work table. "Not necessarily," Prim hedged.

"Then what?"

Prim didn't answer right away, but eventually she let out a long breath and her shoulders fell. "I don't know, Nona. It's just that…" Prim glanced up from under her eyelashes. "It's not like your family has a reputation for being on the right side of the law all the time."

The words hurt, but Wynona understood them. "I know," she admitted. "They've definitely skirted the legal line a few times, but murder?" Wynona shook her head. "Celia wouldn't murder anyone."

"Are you sure?" Prim asked. "Like, really, really sure?" She leaned forward and reached across the table to grab Wynona's hands. "Your sister is an entitled witch who thinks the world is at her fingertips," Prim said. "She doesn't ask, she simply takes, and Dearest Mumsy and Daddy make sure there are no repercussions."

Wynona slowly slid her hands away from Prim. There was truth in her words, but also a reminder that Wynona had never been loved or favored enough to receive the same treatment.

Violet, as if sensing Wynona's distress, stirred and quickly climbed up Wynona's arm until the mouse was nuzzling just under her chin.

Wynona couldn't help but smile and reach up to pet her little friend. "Thanks," Wynona murmured.

"I'm sorry," Prim said and her tone said she was sincere.

Wynona paused to notice the vines behind Prim starting to stretch in the fairy's direction. It seemed that they were coming to their master's comfort just as Violet had come to Wynona's.

"I wasn't trying to hurt you, though I knew it probably would," Prim continued, not noticing when leaves began to curl up her shoulders and into her hair. "But as your friend, I felt it needed to be said. There might be a good reason that Chief Ligurio still has your sister in his sights."

Wynona almost told Prim about the whole planned romance fiasco, but bit it back at the last second. That was personal information that really didn't relate to the case itself, just the relationship between the chief and Wynona's family.

"I understand," Wynona said, giving Prim a small smile. "In fact, Rascal asked me the same thing yesterday."

Prim whistled under her breath. "Brave man, especially for one who's trying to date you." She paused. "Speaking of, when exactly is that going to happen?"

"He only asked me out a few days ago," Wynona reminded Prim. "And we've sort of been busy solving a murder in the meantime."

Prim rolled her eyes and grumbled, but otherwise let it be.

"But back to Celia." Wynona took a deep breath. "I understand why you and Rascal are suspicious, and I wouldn't ever try to say my sister and I have a good relationship, but I truly don't think she's guilty."

Prim nodded. "I won't bring it up again."

Wynona shrugged. "It's fine. Her suspicious behavior is exactly what pulled me into this case in the first place. It makes sense that you're wondering if she's involved." Wynona straightened in her seat. "Now. You said you had news?"

Prim's eyes lit up. "Oh, yeah! I almost forgot!" The vines started to retreat and go back to their individual corners and pots.

Wynona found herself watching in fascination. Prim's powers were wonderfully strong, just like some of the people Wynona had read about in books while she was growing up. Reading about such powers and seeing them first hand, however, were two very different things and it was a beautiful thing to watch.

"Okay, so my stylist said the nail imp told *her*, that Gendyl, the dragon shifter who owns the gas station...?"

Wynona nodded, letting Prim know she knew who Gendyl was and silently urging her to continue. Most of Hex Haven was positive the elderly shifter refused to retire simply because she would lose her spot at the front of the gossip chain if she wasn't in the convenience store every day.

"Apparently, Gendyl swore she saw someone who looked exactly like Niam Stocker come inside to pay for a fill up with cash."

Wynona frowned. "That's it?"

Prim gave her friend a look. "Can't you see how weird that is? Who in the world pays with cash anymore? And you just said yourself that Niam wasn't a suspect because he was on a work trip during the murder."

Wynona slumped. "But Gendyl's eyesight is almost nonexistent," Wynona argued. "It could have been any teenager with blond hair who stepped inside, and Gendyl would think it was Niam."

Prim groaned. "I know. But still...the situation is suspicious."

Wynona brushed it from her mind. The source of the information made it completely useless. Gendyl was a nosy, but sweet older woman, but trusting anything that involved her eyesight would never be considered viable evidence. Wynona glanced at the clock. "Ah, geez, Prim. I gotta run. I haven't set the tables yet."

Prim hopped off her stool. "Okay, but I still need to be kept up to date on what you do next."

Wynona nodded. "I know, but I'm at a little bit of a loss."

"You really don't think Niam was in town?" Prim sounded almost disappointed.

Wynona shrugged. "I don't know. The police are checking out his story, so it should be easy to figure out. But mostly, I just don't trust Gendyl's eyesight."

"I know, but Niam is pretty distinctive," Prim said as she walked Wynona to the door.

Wynona paused at the threshold. "Did you know that Niam worked for my dad?"

Prim scrunched up her nose. "He's some kind of go between, right? I don't know what he really does."

Wynona sighed. It appeared that she was the only one who was completely out of the loop. The library she made good use of growing up did nothing for helping her know who held office in current times. "He's a liaison between my parents and the President of the United States."

Prim snapped her fingers and a sparkle of pink floated through the air. "Oh, yeah. I think I knew that."

Holding back a sigh, Wynona turned back to the door and pulled it open. "I don't really have any other leads to follow, so maybe I'll take Gendyl's story to Rascal and see what he thinks."

Prim's happy smile was enough to make Wynona promise to follow through with her idea. The fairy absolutely loved being of help in Wynona's investigating.

"I need to go handle the tea house, then I'll get a hold of Rascal."

Prim preened. "Yay! Let me know what he says!"

"Okay," Wynona said with a soft laugh. She put a hand up to double check that Violet was stable on her shoulder. "Okay, gotta run. See ya!"

Prim waved enthusiastically until the door shut between them.

Wynona didn't speak as she walked to her scooter and started for home. "Do you think it's a viable lead?" she asked Violet.

Violet looked up from the basket she rode in and chittered.

"Okay," Wynona said. "It's not like it's going to cost us anything to follow it through." She paused. "Hopefully, Niam doesn't get too angry though. Maybe we'll make sure Rascal goes with us."

Violet squeaked her agreement and the two fell silent for the rest of the trip home.

The quiet suited Wynona just fine, as her mind was going over and over how things would change if Niam really had been in town. The more she thought about it, the more the idea took root. She had thought something about his timing had been off anyway, so technically, she probably shouldn't dismiss Gendyl's story quite so quickly.

But if he was lying, did that make him the murderer?

"Not necessarily," Wynona whispered to herself.

Violet looked up.

"Sorry." Wynona parked the scooter and pulled off her helmet. "I was talking to myself," she told Violet as she lifted up the creature and headed inside. "For now, let's just focus on work. We can work out the rest later."

CHAPTER 21

"Thanks for meeting me," Wynona said to Rascal later that afternoon. Her clientele had been slower than normal, so Wynona had taken the opportunity to close up shop and give a little extra time to solving this case.

The lack of progress was starting to drive her crazy and she couldn't help but feel a little worried that everyone, even her friends, were so easily pointing the finger at Celia. Not that Wynona blamed them. She was simply worried that if it continued, Celia would be taken into custody and their parents would create a scene, making life miserable for the public in general.

Rascal grinned. "Nice to see you out before dark," he said.

Wynona rolled her eyes. "Yeah. Despite the fact that today was slow, I'm starting to think I should hire a server. I just can't keep up all on my own, and I haven't taken a true day off in months."

Rascal nodded. "You have been working pretty hard."

"Agreed." Wynona looked up at the Stocker home. It was a decently grand estate. Not quite a mansion or the castle that Wynona had grown up in, but it was definitely nothing to sniff at. "I'm starting to wonder why every time I've gotten involved in a case, I always end up speaking to people in fancy houses. Do the poor never commit crimes?"

Rascal chuckled. "I think it says more about your social circle than anything else."

"You mean my family's social circle," Wynona grumbled. Her friends were definitely not at the top of the economic food chain, and that suited Wynona just fine.

"Ready?" Rascal asked, his hand paused above the door.

Wynona nodded, her hand straying up to pet Violet, who was tucked into the crook of her neck, as usual. The mouse was starting to accompany Wynona more and more on her trips to town. There was something about it that just seemed natural to have her nearby. Not to mention, once in a while, Violet had had an insight that had been crucial to whatever Wyona was working on.

Rascal knocked in a bold manner and stood back with his hands on his hips. He looked dashing in his uniform yet slightly intimidating at the same time. The width of his shoulders and the serious look on his face made Wynona glad she was on his side and not going up against him in a dark alley.

The door opened without the slightest hint of a squeak and Niam stood in the doorway. "Deputy Chief Strongclaw." He looked at Wynona. "And I believe you're Ms. Le Doux. What can I do for you today?"

"We have a few questions for you," Rascal said in a low tone. "Would you mind if we came in?"

Niam's eyes narrowed and he looked his two visitors over before finally nodding and stepping back. "Of course. Anything to help the people working on my wife's murder."

"Niam?" a soft voice called from farther in after he closed the door. "Who was it?"

Wynona looked farther into the house to see Callista emerging from a room. The witch stopped in her tracks, looking shocked.

"Oh. Wynona." Callista's blue eyes flittered to Rascal. "Deputy Chief Strongclaw." She frowned. "What are you doing here?" Distrust fairly dripped from Callista as she watched the visitors with caution.

"There are a few questions we'd like to clear up," Wynona said with a pleasant smile. She walked forward and wrapped her arm around Callista. "I didn't realize you would be here. If I'd known,

I would have brought you some of my latest blend. It's got passion fruit essence mixed with lemon peel and ginger."

Callista's demeanor had softened the longer Wynona spoke. "That sounds interesting."

"Oh, it's wonderful. Slightly fruity, mixed with the kick from the ginger. It's a great way to start the morning." Wynona looked into the room Callista had stepped out of. "Do you mind if we sit in there? These questions might take a little bit of time."

Callista waved an arm in that direction. "Of course. Forgive me." She backed out of Wynona's hold. "I'll grab drinks if you'd like to sit down."

Wynona didn't really need a drink, but she let Callista go anyway. It gave the nervous witch something to do and let Wynona and Rascal have a minute or two with Niam alone.

"Ms. Le Doux," Niam said, waiting at the sitting room door for her to enter.

Wynona smiled graciously and walked in, settling gently on a pure white couch. The room was dominated by the color, or lack thereof, and it made Wynona nervous to touch anything. A nuzzling at her neck let her know Violet could feel her anxiety. Wynona relaxed slightly at her friend's touch.

Rascal sat next to her, giving Wynona a weird look. His phone was in his hand as if he had been looking at it, but before Wynona could ask what was going on, Niam gathered their attention.

"Now..." he started. "I don't mean to be rude, but I do have other things to do. What's this about?"

Wynona waited, but Rascal didn't speak right away, giving her the floor. "I wanted to ask about your alibi again," Wynona said, jumping straight to the heart of the matter. Niam didn't seem the type to enjoy small talk, especially when he seemed very keen on getting them out of the house.

The warlock crossed one leg over the other and rested his arms on the back of the couch he occupied. "What about it? I thought it was very clear," he said testily.

Wynona smiled, pretending she didn't understand his setdown. "You said you got done with work early?"

He nodded.

"How often does that happen?"

Niam scowled. "What does it matter?"

Wynona tapped her fingernails on her knee. "It matters because I find it odd that you have such a reputation for being gone very long periods of times, and yet the one time there's a problem, you just *happen* to be on your way when you find out about your wife's murder."

Red flashed through Niam's eyes and Wynona leaned back, realizing his magic was surfacing.

"Perhaps I was anxious to see my wife," Niam said stoically. "I told you we were trying to work things out. Spending less time away from home was a way to work out our problems."

"But that wasn't it, was it?" Rascal interrupted.

Wynona looked over, not sure where he was going with this.

"Excuse me?" Niam scoffed.

"Because you weren't in Washington DC when your wife died...were you?"

A gasp from the doorway sounded right before a loud crash of breaking dishes. All the heads in the room looked over to see Callista standing with a tray at her feet and broken pottery littering the floor. "What are they talking about?" she whispered to Niam, her eyes pleading with her former brother-in-law. "You said you were gone!"

Niam stood and put his hands up. "Callista, just listen for a moment, hm?" He looked at the floor and sighed. With a wave of his hand, the mess rose in the air and Niam sent it out of the room.

Wynona could only assume it found its way to the garbage, since Niam paid no more attention to it once it was out of sight. His power was impressive if he could work magic without needing to see it. It was no wonder he worked for her father.

Niam held out his arms and Callista fell into them. He held her close as he guided her to the couch and gently settled her against a cushion.

Wynona did her best to keep a straight face as she watched the two. They seemed a little too close for a brother and sister-in-law. Callista had certainly mentioned the rumors said Niam was stepping out on his wife. Could it have been with Callista herself?

Niam finally sat down next to Callista and leaned forward onto his knees, rubbing his temples. "You're right," he said with a weary sigh. "I wasn't in DC when the news came through."

Rascal tucked his phone away and straightened in his seat. "Why don't you tell us the true story this time?"

Wynona was slightly hurt that Rascal obviously knew something she didn't. Why hadn't he shared his information with her? She had asked him to meet her at the Stockers' because she had a hunch and a possible rumor. But Rascal seemed to have more information and she felt shut out that he hadn't shared it with her.

"I was only halfway through my assignment when I got a strange call," Niam started.

"Hold on." Rascal held up his hand. "A call? You said your phone didn't work in the human world."

"It doesn't," Niam defended. "I was telling the truth about that. The only contact I had with Hex Haven was through the president's line."

"So the call came from President Le Doux?" Rascal's eyes darted to Wynona before settling back on Niam.

Wynona listened carefully. What did her father have to do with any of this?

Niam shook his head. "That's just it," he said. "It wasn't the president. In fact, I'm not even sure who it was." He sighed and pushed a hand through his hair, messing up his perfectly styled hairdo. "It was a female voice, and before you ask, no, it wasn't Indigo. I'd know her voice anywhere. But still, the voice said that Indigo had faked her own death, and was hiding at the Hexmoon Inn."

Wynona frowned and looked at Callista, who had slumped on the couch as if she didn't have the energy to sit upright. "Who else knew about your plan?" Wynona asked the witch.

Callista began to tremble as she shook her head. "No one! At least not that I knew!" Her face crumpled. "I'm sure one of the other witches in the coven could have overheard us planning, but I thought we were so careful! We didn't want anyone to get in trouble, which is why I was supposed to take the blame."

Niam handed Callista a handkerchief and she leaned into his shoulder while dabbing her eyes.

Wynona studied the couple. Callista looked like she would fall apart at any second, while Niam was frustrated but unmoved by the tears. It was an odd combination if they were seeing each other behind Indigo's back.

"So you got a call and..." Rascal urged.

"And I came rushing home," Niam said. He stood from the couch, forcing Callista to shift away, and began to pace. The tips of his fingers were slightly glittered with red as he clenched and unclenched his fists. "I rushed to the inn and confronted Indigo about the situation." He shook his head and stopped to face Wynona and Rascal. "At first she was angry that I knew what she'd done, but then she and I had a long overdue talk. Indigo was always a stubborn one. She felt like I wasn't giving her enough time, that my work meant more than she did."

"Excuse my interruption," Wynona said, "but why didn't Indigo go with you on your business trips?"

Niam's eyes darted to Callista and back. "She had things she felt needed her attention at home."

Wynona nodded, though she felt there was more to the story. Violet stirred, making Wynona think that her hunch was correct.

"At the end, I think we both got a little clarity from the situation and..." Niam stuffed his hands in his pockets and shrugged. "I ended up spending the next two nights with her. But when I woke up on the second day, she was gone."

Callista let out a broken sob and Niam hung his head.

"Come on," he said to her, walking back to the couch. "Why don't you go lie down for a while?"

Callista let him lead her from the room where Wynona watched him hand her off to a woman in a uniform. Callista looked back over her shoulder as they walked, but ultimately allowed the woman to take her away.

Niam messed up his hair again as he came back into the sitting room. "Sorry," he said. "Calli is really sensitive. Indigo and I had to be really careful around her or we'd set her off all the time."

"What kinds of things set her off?" Rascal asked.

Niam shrugged. "She doesn't like talk of violence or even keeping up with current events. I made sure not to share anything about my work when Calli was in the area because she hated politics. She really struggles with people in general. We only have a small household staff in order to keep from overwhelming her, and Indigo and I often had to make sure not to touch or act like a couple because Callista felt like we were ganging up on her when we did."

Wynona shook her head. "I'm lost. Why does Callista even live with you? And how did she manage to get into the Sisters of Eternity if she requires so much help?" The coven was extremely exclusive. It didn't make sense that they would take in a witch who was weak or mentally struggling in any sense of the word.

Niam fell back on the couch, his head resting on the back cushions. "Indigo's parents had struggled with Calli for years and had finally had their fill. They were kicking her out when Indigo stepped in. We were newly married and still getting to know each other, but I was trying to be supportive." He tilted his head just enough to look at them. "She's...different, but a good person at heart. Indigo came to rely on her and as long as Callista had a direct purpose, she did pretty well. The coven thing was Indigo's idea. Despite being terrified of almost everything, Callista actually is a pretty talented witch. I've seen some of her powers over the years, and she was as good or better than Indigo."

He sat up. "Don't tell Callista I said that," he whispered. "She worshiped her sister and it would set her off if she thought she had usurped Indigo in any way."

"While all of this is fascinating," Rascal said, "I need to know where you really were when Indigo was killed."

Niam nodded. "I know. Sorry." He sighed. "I was asleep in the hotel." He shook his head. "I had worked hard not to be seen by anyone, so I can't offer you a witness. I wasn't supposed to be in town yet, and not knowing why Indigo had faked her death, I made sure to come back as incognito as possible."

"Why didn't you say so when we found her body?"

Niam scowled. "I knew it would get back to President Le Doux," he grumbled, his eyes moving to Wynona. "I'm supposed to have his permission before travelling and I hadn't finished my assignment. I didn't want him to know I was in town, and I was afraid if the police knew I had spent the night with Indigo, they would blame me for her murder." Niam's eyes went back to Rascal. "I couldn't win either way," he stated. "But when news of her murder came out, I knew I had a way to get out from being in trouble from the president. Even he couldn't blame me for coming home when my wife was killed."

"And you didn't hear anything the morning she was killed?"

Niam shook his head. "No. She likes to get up early and catch the sunrise. It's something she's done since she was a teenager." A small smile played on his face. "Says the morning magic keeps her looking young." His eyes glazed over for a moment before Niam cleared his throat and focused. "So it's not uncommon for me to wake up to an empty bed. It was when she didn't come back that I began to get worried."

Rascal put a hand on Wynona's back. "I know Chief Ligurio already said this, but don't leave town, Mr. Stocker." He rose and took Wynona with him.

Niam nodded wearily. "Got it." He stood and walked them to the door. "I really am sorry," he said softly. "I realize I shouldn't have lied."

Wynona didn't bother to answer. There really was nothing to say about it. The man had made a couple of terrible errors, but if her own significant other had been killed, Wynona wasn't sure exactly how she would behave. "Thank you for your time," she said softly as she and Rascal headed outside.

Rascal led her to her scooter and waited while she got her helmet on. "Can we meet at the shop?" he asked.

Violet squeaked her approval and Wynona couldn't help but smile. "Sounds like a plan."

"Good." Rascal ran a knuckle down her cheek. "I'm thinking we have a few things to discuss."

"I couldn't agree more." Wynona pressed the start button and pulled away from the house. It wasn't a place she had any desire to return to. Despite the clean, white interior, the place felt haunted in multiple ways and Wynona wanted away from the heavy sorrow that penetrated the home.

She set her determination once again that she would see this case through. Both Callista and Niam deserved closure in this matter. But even with the latest confession, Wynona was still lost as to who would want to kill Indigo. Hopefully she, Rascal and Violet could set some things straight over a nice cup of ginger and lemon peel.

CHAPTER 22

"Is good Ole Lu hanging around?" Rascal asked as they came inside the shop from the back entrance.

Wynona glanced around the kitchen. "I don't see him, but that doesn't mean much. I'm pretty sure he lives here at this point, though I can't prove it."

Rascal frowned. "What does that mean?"

Wynona shrugged and picked up a kettle to fill with water. "He seems to emerge from that corner over there." She tilted her chin in the direction of the darkened spot. "I've tried going over there but I can't find anything out of the ordinary. But I swear that he just...appears."

Rascal frowned and walked over while Wynona put the kettle on the stove. He knocked on the wall, going higher, then lower. "I don't see anything out of the ordinary."

"Told you," Wynona said.

Violet chittered and ran down Wynona's arm, then leg, only to scurry to the corner and promptly disappear.

"Violet!" Wynona cried. She rushed over and dropped to all fours, searching everything she could touch. "Where is she?"

Rascal tugged on Wynona's shoulders. "Hey, hey, she's gonna be just fine," he said.

"How do you know that?" Wynona cried. Tears were stinging her eyes. The little creature had come to mean a lot to Wynona in a very short amount of time.

"There's obviously some kind of magic going on here that you and I don't understand," he said, rubbing her arms. The movement should have been soothing, but Wynona's anxiety was too strong for it to help.

"Exactly! We don't know where she is or if she's okay!" Purple sparks began to float through the air and Wynona blinked rapidly, backing up when they became stronger. "Granny?" Wynona whispered.

Rascal began to growl. "What's going on?"

Wynona's whole body began to shake as the sparks turned into tiny bolts of lightning that randomly began striking the wall. "I'm not sure," she said, reaching out to clutch his arm. The sparks grew even stronger and Wynona ducked her head to the side. "Granny, stop it!"

"Your grandmother is doing this?" Rascal shouted, pulling Wynona into his chest and turning them so that he was protecting her from the chaos.

"I think so!"

"Prohibere!"

The gravelly tone, mixed with the sudden silence, caught everyone's attention and Wynona peeked over her and Rascal's shoulder to see Lusgu standing in the corner, hands on his hips and a deep scowl on his face. "Lusgu" Wynona said breathlessly. "Where exactly did you come from?"

A squeaking noise caught everyone's attention and Wynona's eyes widened when she caught something purple in Lusgu's hair.

"Vi!"

The mouse ran down the brownie's side and straight up Rascal's, until she was perched on his shoulder.

"Don't scare me like that!" Wynona scolded.

Rascal picked up the mouse and curled her into his chest. "Hey, sweetheart," he cooed. "I think maybe you've been holding out on us."

Violet began having a conversation with Rascal, but Wynona tuned it out. She was suddenly very aware of the fact that Lusgu was still watching them, and she grew afraid that he would throw something at Rascal. "Thank you for retrieving her," Wynona said, stepping forward just enough to put a barrier between the two men.

Lusgu was still glaring, but after a moment, Wynona realized it was at her, not Rascal. "Should have told you from the start," he grumbled.

Wynona blinked. "Excuse me? Told me what?"

The brownie shook his head and turned around. "Secrets never did any good," he continued. "A body can't even relax without being disturbed." He waved a finger in a circle.

Wynona gasped and stepped back slightly when Lusgu's body disappeared right into the wall. She also jumped approximately a foot off the ground when the whistle went off on the kettle. She almost tripped as she ran over to grab it in order to stop the noise. Her nerves couldn't take it right now. "Did you see that?" she stammered.

Rascal slowly backed away from the corner. "How well do you know your janitor?" he asked, never taking his eyes from the corner.

"We've been working together for months," Wynona said. "You know that. But I haven't really bothered to dig into his background. The agency cleared him and he was good at his job, so I didn't do anything more."

Rascal kept his eye on the corner, but led Wynona out to the sitting room.

"What are you thinking?" she whispered, even knowing it was ridiculous to do so.

"I don't know yet," Rascal murmured. He finally shook his head. "It's probably nothing."

Violet's scolding caught their attention.

"Sorry," Rascal said, easing his hold and setting her on the table. "I wasn't paying attention."

Violet began to groom herself, turning her back on Rascal, but instead of being offended, he chuckled.

"I think you messed up her look," Wynona said with a smile. She felt much lighter now that they were out of the kitchen and away from the magic, both Lusgu's and her grandmother's. Granny's magic had come and helped save Wynona several times, but there was no danger in this instance. And the magic nearly did more harm than good. It made Wynona wary of having her grandmother's ghost hang around, though without magic of her own, Wynona had no way of contacting her grandmother to discourage the situation.

Forcing herself to focus on what she *could* do, Wynona set down the kettle, then rushed to grab a couple of her antique cups. She picked one with a branch design for Rascal and a calla lily for herself.

"I've got something new for you," Wynona said with a smile as she came back to the table. "I tried mixing your normal rosemary with ginger and I was pleasantly surprised by it." She handed him a tea infuser full of the mixture. "See what you think."

Rascal grinned and let his fingers slide along her hand when he took the offering. "Thanks," he said.

Wynona's overactive blush immediately shot up her neck and into her cheeks. "You're welcome," she said in as calm a tone as possible, though she knew she wasn't fooling anybody. His hearing was much too good to hide her racing heart and there was no way he'd miss the breathiness of her voice either. "So," she said, dunking her own infuser. "Thoughts on Niam and Callista?"

Rascal frowned into his cup. "I don't think I had realized how much Callista struggled...emotionally, I mean."

Wynona nodded. "I know. I thought she was quite normal, though a bit overly dramatic when we first spoke to her. It's been a bit of a shock to discover she actually has some issues that require help. I guess it explains how she was so easily convinced to help Indigo go through with the fake death situation. It sounds like she worshiped the ground her sister walked on. Especially since their parents had basically kicked Callista out." Wynona pinched her lips together.

"I know that look," Rascal said, leaning back with an easy grin. "Spill it."

Wynona smiled in return. "I don't know...I just...this whole case has me kind of mixed up, I suppose," Wynona began. "I'm confused at the relationships we're seeing." She leaned forward. "Did Niam and Callista's relationship seem odd to you?"

Rascal huffed a sarcastic laugh. "I suppose you could say that." He raised an eyebrow. "I have a couple of brothers and I don't really see myself getting cozy with their wives."

"Me neither," Wynona murmured. "But...Niam also seemed sincere when he spoke about Indigo. I think he did love her, even if their relationship was difficult." Wynona's shoulders sagged. "I mean, I'm sure most relationships have rough moments, especially if your wife is taking care of an ill sister."

"Coming from a man's perspective, that would've been hard for me," Rascal admitted. "When I get married, I don't want to share my wife with her sister, especially when we're first married."

Wynona made sure she was looking anywhere but at Rascal. They hadn't even managed to go on a first date yet, but speaking of marriage made her heart do a little flip. She reminded herself to slow down and remember he was talking about the case. This had nothing to do with them whatsoever. "I can imagine," Wynona murmured in order to move the conversation forward.

"So, you don't think Niam could have killed his wife?"

Wynona looked up. "You think he did it?"

Rascal frowned and scratched the back of his head. "I'm not sure. But I'm struggling to find other suspects." His voice grew quiet at the end and his eyes didn't quite meet Wynona's.

She knew exactly who he was thinking of, though Rascal didn't mention the name. "Celia didn't do it," Wynona whispered.

Rascal nodded. "I know."

Wynona shook her head and set down her cup. "But you think she's guilty. Even Prim mentioned it the other day." Wynona leaned back. "Why is she at the top of everyone's list? Being a spoiled brat doesn't make her a murderer!"

Rascal put a placating hand in the air, but Wynona was too worked up to listen to him.

"Your chief is just bitter because my family got involved in his love life, and you know what? He's right," Wynona said quickly. "They shouldn't have done that. My dad should have minded his own business and not tried to make his daughter date the chief of police just so that they had an advantage with the law. It was dirty and manipulative and all sorts of wrong, but again...it doesn't make any of them murderers!"

"Wy," Rascal said loudly in order to be heard over her rant. "I know you want to defend your family, but are you even aware of how many times they've broken the law in the past?"

Wynona rolled her eyes. "Are you telling me they're different from any other political family with too much power?"

"Why are you so set on defending them?" Rascal argued. "According to your own testimony, they treated you horribly."

"Because despite how terrible they are, despite how much I don't want to go home for dinner or join in on family celebrations, despite how many years I spent wishing they would notice me...they're still my family," Wynona said. Her voice had gotten thick and soft, and she was blinking back tears. "And they're the only family I've got."

"Wy," Rascal groaned. His frustration dissolved and he rubbed his forehead. "I'm sorry," he said, his sad, golden eyes meeting hers. "You're right. They're family and I won't argue about it anymore." He stood and walked over until he was next to her chair before kneeling down and taking her hand. "I trust you," he said softly. "If you say your sister didn't do it, then I'll believe it too."

"I don't want you to believe it just because I said so," Wynona pouted.

Rascal chuckled. "Man, you're stubborn."

Wynona finally broke through her anger enough to laugh softly as well. "Yeah, well, when Saffron Le Doux is the person who raises you, you learn a thing or two about surviving. If I wasn't stubborn, I definitely wouldn't have made it."

He brought her hand to his lips and kissed her palm. "And I will be forever grateful for that. I'll even be grateful for Granny's light show in the kitchen, despite the fact that it scared me out of my fur."

Wynona smiled and relaxed. "I'm sorry I yelled."

Rascal kissed her hand one more time, then stood. "I'm sorry I gave you trouble about it." He slowly walked back to his seat and Wynona felt cold from the loss of his touch.

Violet whimpered and stood on her hind legs, staring at Wynona.

Wynona forced a smile and held out her hand. Violet rushed up her arm and quickly nuzzled into Wynona's hair. "I'm fine," Wynona assured her friend. "I'm sorry I worried you."

Violet laid herself against Wynona's neck, wrapped her tail around as well and settled in, obviously not wanting to lose contact for a while.

"I feel like I have a mouse necklace," Wynona quipped.

"You sort of do," Rascal teased. "Next time you should try matching it to your outfit."

Wynona's laughter broke the last of the tension in the room. "So tell me why you think Niam might be guilty."

Rascal shrugged. "I'm not sure. The guy just lied to us so easily before. Why couldn't he be lying now?"

Wynona nodded sagely. "That's a definite possibility, but not the vibe I got. I felt like he was telling the truth."

"But?" Rascal pressed. "You don't sound like that's all you felt."

Wynona shook her head. "Just the relationship thing again. It bugs me." She couldn't quite place her finger on the problem. It really didn't affect her, nor did it affect the case, but something about it was off. Niam had an alibi, weak as it was, and Wynona was sure that if they dug, they could find a hotel maid or front desk clerk who could corroborate his story.

"I probably need to check with the hotel staff," Rascal said, as if reading Wynona's thoughts. "We'll need to see if anyone saw Niam around."

"Gendyl told the ladies at the Curl and Die that she saw him," Wynona offered. "That's why I wanted to go talk to him in the first place."

"Gendyl? The half-blind dragon shifter?" Rascal asked with a laugh.

Wynona smiled. "I know, but I promised Prim I'd check into it, and it looks like it was a good thing."

Rascal nodded. "I'll give you that. I'll send someone around to take her statement."

"Thank you," Wynona said as she finished her cup of tea. "Did you like the new flavor?"

Rascal looked at his empty cup, then grinned sheepishly at Wynona. "Probably a little too well. I was never a tea drinker until I met you." His eyes were warm enough to let her know it wasn't just because she was good at creating tea that he kept drinking it.

That blush came crawling back up her skin. "Glad I could introduce you to the finer things in life," Wynona flirted.

Rascal chuckled, a low, delicious sound that said he highly approved of her actions. He leaned forward. "We haven't really gotten a chance to cash in on that promise," he began.

Wynona felt her heart rate skyrocket. "True."

"I know I said we probably needed to finish the case first, but...with it taking as long as it is, I'm not sure I want to—" There was a buzzing sound that cut off his words and Wynona wanted to scream in frustration. "Hang on," Rascal muttered as he checked his phone. "Deputy Chief Strongclaw." His face grew serious and after a second, those enticing eyes shot up to Wynona's. "Uh-huh," he said, never looking away.

Wynona felt her speeding pulse change from anticipation to fear. What she wouldn't give for the ability to hear what was being said.

"Got it." He glanced at the wall clock. "We'll be there in a few minutes. Do not proceed without me, do you understand? Do *not* proceed without me." Rascal waited a beat, then hung up the phone. "We have to go," he said, jumping up from the table.

Wynona frowned, but stood and began to gather dishes.

"Leave them," Rascal ordered. He softened when Wynona jerked at his words. "Please let Lusgu handle it this time. You're not going to want to waste any time."

"What's going on?" Wynona asked, coming over to his side. "You're scaring me."

Rascal ran a hand through his hair. "They got a tip and ended up finding some important evidence out in the field where Indigo's body was found."

Wynona put a hand on her churning stomach. "And just who does it indicate was involved?"

For his part, Rascal really did look sorry when he said, "Celia."

CHAPTER 23

Wynona was sure her fingers were going to be broken before the night was out. She couldn't stop wringing them together as Rascal drove the two of them out to the field. The police were still searching the area and Wynona was extremely grateful they had gotten the call before her sister was actually arrested. "Did they say what they found?" Wynona asked, her eyes glued to the windshield.

Rascal sighed. "No. But we're almost there." He glanced her way. "I'm really sorry, Wy. I wanted her to be innocent...for your sake."

"Thanks," Wynona whispered. She forced her hands apart and clenched her fists. The knuckles were aching, but she needed to be doing something! This case had been a nightmare from the beginning, and now the worst possible scenario was coming true.

Wynona wasn't sure whether to curse or to cry. She had spent her energy and risked her reputation defending Celia, and now it looked as if it might be in vain. Wynona could only hope that the police were wrong. That maybe their evidence wasn't as strong as they thought, because no matter what they found or what anyone said, Wynona still couldn't see her sister as a murderer.

Violet squeaked softly and wrapped herself further into Wynona's dark locks.

Wynona sighed. She hadn't wanted to bring Violet along, worried about the chances of them losing each other in the wide open field, but Violet had been insistent and eventually Wynona couldn't argue any more. "I know," Wynona whispered back. "It doesn't make sense, does it?"

Violet chittered.

"Maybe they're wrong," Rascal offered as he put the truck in park. "We both know Chief Ligurio isn't exactly a fan of your family, especially not of Celia. Maybe he's jumping the gun with this evidence."

"Let's hope so," Wynona said, jumping down from the passenger side. She wasn't exactly short, but she also wasn't exactly tall. Wynona considered herself a fairly average sized woman, but Rascal's truck was obviously not built for the average. It took a bit of work to get in or out of it.

"Here we go," Rascal said as he walked around to her side and offered his hand.

Wynona took the offering without hesitation. Right now she needed all the support she could get. She didn't even care if the chief saw them.

"Deputy Chief Stronclaw," an officer said as they drew closer. His deep, gravelly voice caught Wynona's attention and she looked up, realizing it was the ogre officer she had seen from a distance during the case about Chef Droxon.

Seeing the large creature up close was more than a little intimidating. His face looked like it was made out of stone and Wynona was positive that if the man had been wearing short sleeves, his bulging muscles would have looked the same.

"Oozog," Rascal said curtly. He had gone into officer mode, other than the fact that he was still holding Wynona's hand. "Where's the chief?"

Officer Oozog pointed to a group a little way into the field. "They're searching for more pieces of the bracelet," the officer said. "The chief has all the creatures with good night vision working on it."

Rascal nodded and pulled Wynona along. "Thanks," he threw back over his shoulder.

Wynona scrambled to keep up with Rascal's long strides. "Bracelet?" she asked. "People probably lose jewelry out here all the time, since hikers come through here. How in the world can they be sure anything they find is pertinent to the case or that it belongs to Celia?"

Rascal didn't answer as they were coming up on the men, though Wynona knew he didn't truly have an answer for her anyway. She had mostly been speaking out loud.

"Deputy Chief." The officers all began their greetings as Wynona and Rascal passed by them.

Chief Ligurio stood up and whipped around, having heard Rascal's name being whispered. "Strongclaw!"

Rascal nodded and walked up to his chief's side. "Chief. Catch me up."

Chief Ligurio's red eyes were glowing in the semi-darkness as they darted down to their combined hands, then back up to Rascal. "We got an anonymous tip that brought us back out here."

"What did they say?" Wynona interrupted.

Chief Ligurio frowned, then sighed, as if he understood why Wynona was so anxious. "They said they were hiking the area and saw several beads during their walk. It struck them as unusual, so they didn't pick them up, simply called it in since it was near where the media said Indigo's body was found."

Wynona pinched her lips together. "That seems a little convenient," she muttered.

Rascal squeezed her hand, but didn't turn to her. "Can we see what you've found?"

Chief Ligurio reached into his pocket and pulled out a small plastic bag. Inside were two pieces of dark stone.

Wynona squinted and leaned in closer. The daylight was quickly disappearing and she was struggling to see what type of bead it was.

"Hang on," Rascal said. He let go of her hand and fumbled around until a light shone from his phone, illuminating the stones.

Wynona's eyes widened as she saw the dark green color. She knew those beads. They had been clanging against her tabletop just a couple of days ago.

"What is it?" Chief Ligurio demanded.

"What makes you think these belong to Celia?" Wynona asked, though her raspy voice more than likely gave away her concern. "They could be from anything."

The chief nodded slowly. "Which is why we're still out here," he said, watching Wynona carefully. "The tip said they'd seen the stones before and implicated your sister."

Wynona scowled and folded her arms over her chest. "And you don't find that suspicious? It sounds a little too easy."

Chief Ligurio sighed and tucked the baggie back in his shirt pocket. "Ms. Le Doux, despite what you might believe, I'm not the bad guy here. But a woman is dead and we're running out of leads."

"What about Niam Stocker?" Rascal asked. "I sent you a message about what Wynona and I discovered."

Chief Ligurio nodded. "We called the hotel and no less than three workers can confirm they saw him. Not to mention the security cameras show that he hadn't left his room during the timeframe of the murder."

"Did you see Indigo?" Wynona asked quickly.

Chief Ligurio nodded. "Yes. She was spotted on video leaving the premises before sunrise, but once she walked out the front doors, we lost her."

A sinking feeling began to build in Wynona's stomach. Something was niggling at her. "What about Indigo's shoes?" Wynona asked. "Her body didn't have shoes. What was she wearing in the video?"

The chief paused. "I'll admit I didn't focus on her shoes, but I seem to recall some sandals."

"So she had to have known her attacker," Wynona whispered to herself. She rubbed her forehead. A nasty headache was starting to pulse behind her temples.

"They didn't have video on the outside of the hotel?" Rascal inserted.

Wynona looked up in time to see the chief shake his head. "They have a ward on the outside, but not inside. Hence the video."

Rascal blew out a breath and nodded. "Got it." He looked to Wynona, as if asking what she wanted to do.

Violet squeaked softly and Wynona paused to listen.

"Can we see where the body was again?"

Chief Ligurio narrowed his eyes at Wynona's shoulder, but ultimately nodded and turned to lead the way.

"What did Violet say?" Rascal asked as they walked.

Wynona shook her head. "I'm not sure, but I'm pretty sure this is where she wanted to go."

Violet chittered a little louder and Rascal's ear twitched in the mouse's direction. "Ah...good point."

Wynona almost stumbled. "What did you catch? Can you really understand her?"

Rascal shrugged. "Just the jist of it. You speak to her like you understand. What do you hear?"

"I mostly get feelings and just indulge them," Wynona said. "Since she usually responds, I figure I'm not too far off."

"Here," Chief Ligurio interrupted.

Violet scrambled down Wynona's shoulder and leg, then began darting around the flattened patch of grass.

Wynona's anxiety went up a notch. She didn't want Violet to get lost. But instead of interrupting, Wynona forced herself to trust in her tiny friend and began walking around the spot herself. "Can I borrow your flashlight?" she asked Rascal.

He handed her his cell phone and she turned it on, shining it on the scene.

A delicate shudder ran up Wynona's spine as she considered what exactly they were looking at. The body's imprint was still slightly visible if one knew what they were looking for, and Wynona hoped that Indigo wasn't vindictive enough to want to stick around and haunt her scene of death. The last thing Wynona needed was for a vengeful spirit to come and scare the living daylights out of her when she had no magic in order to protect herself or anyone else.

Her eyes stayed glued to the ground as she slowly walked the perimeter. Violet paused and began to squeak. Wynona shifted until she could see what her mouse was staring at. She squatted down to get a closer look. "I don't see..." Her voice trailed off as Wynona realized what Violet was trying to show her.

"What?" Rascal demanded from over Wynona's shoulder.

"See this?" Wynona gently ran her fingers over the grass. "See how it's bent?"

Rascal and Chief Ligurio stepped up closer. "She was dragged," the chief snapped. "Or at least partially. The grass isn't all the way down, so there must have been some magic involved in carrying the body."

Wynona nodded. "It looks that way." She frowned. "Which way were Indigo's feet?"

Chief Ligurio pointed to the area closest to the bent grass. "Her feet were closest to where you are now."

"Why would someone with magic drag the body low enough to the ground to leave a trail though?" Rascal asked, scratching behind his ear. "It seems odd."

Wynona nodded in agreement as Violet began making noise again.

Violet darted from side to side and then suddenly took off into the grass.

"Vi!" Wynona cried, rushing after her friend.

"Hang on," Rascal called. With a small groan, he hunched over and a burst of fur dove after the mouse.

Wynona was frozen for a split second as she tried to process what she'd just seen.

Chief Ligurio cursed. "Dang wolf," he grumbled before following the chase.

Wynona forced her feet in motion and tried her best to keep up, but all the other supernaturals left her quickly in the dust. By the time she caught up to the group, she was breathing so heavily she could barely see straight. If she could speak to whoever cursed her as a baby, Wynona definitely had a few choice words for them at the moment. "Did you find something?" she asked between pants.

Rascal laid down in his wolf form and whined.

Wynona frowned as she watched Violet scramble up to burrow into the fur on his head. "What is it?" she asked Chief Ligurio, since he was the only one who could actually speak to her.

Chief Ligurio cleared his throat and stepped to the side. "For what it's worth, I'm sorry," he said. Without waiting for her response, he stepped off and began shouting orders in the radio on his shoulder.

Wynona's entire body began to tremble and she once again turned on Rascal's flashlight. There in the grass lay a white sandal. Only a few feet away, in the direction of where they had just come from, was the second one, but the first held Wynona's attention the most, since there were other pieces with it.

Several jade beads were scattered around the area, along with a wire that was more than likely the inside of the bracelet itself. A single gold bead stood out from the rest and Wynona couldn't help but notice the initials carved into the gold.

Even without the letters, however, there was no denying it at this point. Wynona knew that her sister had a jade bracelet. But she hadn't been wearing it the other day when she and Celia talked at the shop. The jade one was a piece Celia had received many years ago for her birthday. The gold bead was certainly distinctive and even in the dark was clearly read.

Tears pricked Wynona's vision. "It's Celia's," she whispered.

Rascal stood up and padded over, rubbing up against her thigh.

Wynona sunk her hand into his fur and let the soft strands soothe her, but it was difficult. She wanted to scream and rage that none of this was fair. Someone had to be setting her sister up, but the evidence was right in front of her. How could she continue to affirm Celia's innocence with so many red flags screaming otherwise?

Violet ran up Wynona's arm and began to nuzzle her neck.

"I'll be alright," Wynona said woodenly. She didn't let go of Rascal. His strength and warmth were an absolute necessity at the moment, but she did try to calm Violet's agitation. "It'll all work out." The words were meaningless, but they gave her something to focus on.

"Strongclaw," Chief Ligurio said, coming back to the group. "Go change and get back here. I want this wrapped up tonight."

Rascal's glowing eyes looked up at Wynona and she reluctantly let go and stepped back. "Thank you," she said softly.

With a slow nod, he trotted into the woods and came back only moments later, back in his human form. "Do you want me to take you home before we get too deep into this?" he asked her in an aside.

Wynona shook her head. "No. I think I want to be there."

His eyebrows went up. "You sure?"

Wynona nodded. "Yes. I need to hear it from her."

He sighed and pushed a hand through his hair, but nodded. "Okay. Hang tight. We need to bag this all up, and then a few of us will go pick her up."

A Le Doux family reunion was on the horizon and Wynona was anything but happy about it.

CHAPTER 24

Wynona was going to throw up. Rascal was giving her worried glances as they pulled up to her family's castle, placed imperiously at the top of a small hill. As a child, Wynona had always assumed it was so the people in the home had a pretty view. The older she got, the more she realized it was a power play. The president's home stood taller than everyone else's and was set apart in a way that couldn't be missed.

Memories of loneliness and being rejected a thousand and one times wouldn't stop playing on a loop inside her head. Even Violet's nuzzling and whimpers weren't enough to pull Wynona from her dark place.

Squeezing her eyes shut, she forced away outside stimuli and began to focus on breathing normally. She was an adult. She could do this. She ran a successful business. She had friends. She wasn't alone. She had the right to leave this place any time she wanted.

"Wy?"

A warm hand caressed her cheek, waking Wynona from her downward spiral, and she cracked open one eye to see Rascal frowning as he cupped her cheek. "Are you going to be okay? You don't have to come in."

His thumb rubbed back and forth on her cheekbone and the warmth it created slowly helped relax her muscles. "I know," she whispered, then cleared her throat. "I need to though. Celia asked for my help and I failed her. I need to own up to that."

Rascal shook his head. "You don't owe her anything," he argued.

Wynona gave him a sad smile, relaxing even further into his touch. "You're right, but my greatest goal in life is to be the exact opposite of my family. They might not hold any loyalty to me, but I refuse to be like that."

Rascal's eyes flashed a bright gold and he slowly leaned in a couple of inches before pulling back and dropping his hand. Shaking his head, the glow in his eyes went away, though his voice was still slightly growly when he spoke again. "Let's go," he said.

Wynona watched him climb down from the driver's seat before heading in her direction. She sighed in disappointment. "We need to have that first date," Wynona whispered to Violet as she unbuckled. "I don't know how much more of this push and pull I can take."

Violet grumbled her agreement as they jumped out of the truck.

Rascal took her hand and together they caught up with Chief Ligurio and a couple other officers, including Officer Skymaw, their resident black hole.

Wynona would never admit it out loud, but she was extremely grateful for the man's presence. Her family wasn't going to be happy about them arresting Celia, and their powerful magic was their greatest weapon.

"This is your only warning," Chief Ligurio stated, his eyes snapping to Wynona's.

Wynona took a deep breath, dropped Rascal's hand and straightened her shoulders. "I'm fine."

A flash of emotion passed through the vampire's eyes before he nodded curtly and turned to knock on the massive door.

It took less than two seconds for the slab of stone to be pulled back. Zysus's broad chest filled the doorway. The minotaur's black eyes widened. "Chief Ligurio," he said in a low tone. Zysus looked over the crowd of officers. "What brings you here today?"

"I need to speak to Celia Le Doux," the chief said calmly, as if this wasn't an official call, but something more social.

Zysus scowled. "She isn't receiving visitors at this time."

"You'll get her and then you and one of my officers will have a chat as well," Chief Ligurio said in a steely tone. Gone was the nonchalant attitude. "This is official police business, and unless you want to be found guilty of obstruction of justice, I suggest you do your job."

The two creatures glared at each other, each refusing to give ground. If no one did anything, Wynona was sure blood would be shed.

She pressed a hand to her stomach and forced her feet into action. When she brushed past Rascal, she ignored his low growl and stepped between the chief and Zysus. "Hello, Zysus."

The minotaur's face softened only infinitesimally, but it was enough. "Ms. Wynona." His nostrils flared. "You're here with them as well?"

Wynona nodded, locking her knees to keep them from trembling. She could feel the chief's anger pulsing against her back, and with Zysus's giant body in front of her, there was nowhere to go but forward. "We need to see Celia. And she doesn't get to refuse this time."

Zysus brought his head down to Wynona's level, a puff of air blowing her hair from her face.

"Careful," Rascal growled, stepping up to Wynona's side.

"Please," Wynona said, ignoring the butler's disdain. "It's important."

Another puff from his bull-shaped nostrils blasted her face before Zysus rose to his full height once more. "I'll tell the president your wishes."

The granite door slammed into place and the entire group of officers shifted uneasily.

"One of these days you're going to get yourself killed if you keep doing that," Chief Ligurio grumbled.

Wynona knew exactly what he meant. That was the second time she'd stepped in between him and an angry paranormal, though both times had been people from her family, or in this case a family employee, and Wynona felt she had a responsibility. The chief was only trying to do his job. She couldn't let him get hurt on her watch. "Maybe one of these days my family will stop threatening you," she quipped back with a lightness she didn't feel.

Chief Ligurio's eyes widened before he barked out a sarcastic laugh. "My nearly immortal life might be over before that ever happens."

Wynona sighed, then relaxed when Rascal took her hand again. "It might," she agreed. "But at least it won't be because someone I share blood with did something stupid."

The door opened again and Wynona turned back to face it, preparing for the worst. Her preparation was not in vain when she came in contact with a woman who looked exactly like her, only a few years older.

"I didn't believe it," Marcella Le Doux, Wynona's mother, drawled. She cocked a hip in an enticing manner and flung her perfectly styled, black hair over her shoulder. "The prodigal daughter has come home."

"I'm here to get Celia," Wynona said, putting her chin in the air. She wasn't alone this time and didn't want her mom to think she was weak.

"Celia doesn't need to go anywhere with you," Marcella hissed, losing some of her pretend casualness. "If you think you can fill her head with thoughts of independence and abandoning her family, then you might as well go back to the hole from which you crawled. The only reason we've left you alone is because we all knew you would fail and eventually come crawling." Marcella smirked. "I'm looking forward to the day. But until then, you won't take my useful daughter from me."

The words were consistent slaps to the face. They hurt far worse than a knife to the heart or any other weapon a person could implement. They were personal and directed solely toward Wynona in an effort to try and break her. And it was working, though Wynona didn't show it. She had perfected the ability to hide her emotions, a necessary skill after thirty years of living with the woman in front of her.

Cold hands gripped her upper arms and Wynona found herself tucked behind a growling, half-shifted wolf and a livid vampire.

"Madam Le Doux," Chief Ligurio said in a tone so icy it felt as if the temperature of the night had dropped. "Your daughter, Celia Le Doux, is under arrest for the murder of Indigo Stocker. You will bring Celia to us of your own accord, or I will instruct my men to use force, and we will drag her out by her hair if necessary."

The next moment was one that Wynona would never forget. For the first time ever, Marcella Le Doux had been caught off guard. Her mouth gaped open and for a few seconds, no sound came out. But when her black eyebrows began to furrow, Wynona knew they were in trouble.

"How DARE you!" the witch screeched. Her hands came up, shaped like claws as she began to make intricate signs in the air.

Wynona opened her mouth to shout a warning, but nothing happened. A small grunt caught her attention and she turned to see Officer Skymaw looking pale and sweaty, but otherwise unharmed.

Chief Ligurio glanced back at his officer, who nodded, then he faced Marcella again. "This is your last warning before I come in."

"Chief Ligurio." A male voice came from behind Wynona's mother. When the dark head of her father appeared, Wynona felt her anger begin to build. She just wanted this over with. "Officers," President Le Doux said congenially. He gently pushed his livid wife to the side. "I hear you're looking for my daughter." His smile was so perfect that Wynona was sure he used a spell to keep it in place. "Why don't you all come in and we'll talk this out. I have no doubt it's one big misunderstanding."

"One minute," Chief Ligurio warned, his eyes back on Marcella.

President Le Doux frowned. "Are you giving me ultimatums?" he asked, a smile still in place even as he tilted his head consideringly. "That's a little above your pay grade, isn't it, Chief?"

"Harboring a fugitive is above yours," Chief Ligurio shot back. "You're now down to thirty seconds before I force my way in."

"Do you really think I don't have wards in place to keep you from doing just that?"

"Do *you* really think I haven't brought provisions for such an occasion?"

President Le Doux's smile finally faded and he took the time to truly study the group, his eyes flaring when he spotted Officer Skymaw, then stopping completely on Wynona. "I see," her father murmured. "Not enough to just leave us, now you have to try and take us down?" He shook his head and tsked his tongue. "Chief Ligurio, I'm now more certain than ever that this is all a case of misguided jealousy." His eyes were on the chief as he waved a hand at Wynona. "She can't help who she is, really, but having one's powers bound certainly can and does affect a creature's mind. You really can't believe anything that comes out of her mouth. She's no better than a human."

"Zero," Chief Ligurio ground out. With a tilt of his head, the officers all began to move forward, but a high pitched shout stopped them once more.

"I'm here!" Celia shouted, pushing her way in front of her parents.

"Celia, get back inside," President Le Doux snapped.

Celia shook her head. "No. We don't need a fight." Turning on the charm, Celia faced her father and patted his chest. "How would it look in the ghost report if there was a siege at the president's house?"

Marcella wailed. "You can't let them take her!" she screamed.

President Le Doux held up a hand and surprisingly, his wife quieted. "Celia, as usual," he said with a sneer in Wynona's direction, "is correct. We'll handle this exactly according to the law." More gently than he had handled his wife, the president pushed his daughter toward Chief Ligurio. "Celia will cooperate fully," he said, emphasizing the last word. "We will handle hiring her attorney, and everything in the media will show our goodwill and reconciliation. However, when this is all proven to be a mistake, don't think I won't take great personal pleasure in ruining every bit of your precious reputation, Chief Ligurio."

There was a threatening message in those words and Wynona knew it had something to do with the relationship her father had tried to push between Celia and the chief.

Ignoring the threat, or at least appearing to, Chief Ligurio stepped aside to allow his officers to thread Celia's wrists behind her back as one began to read her the charge and her rights.

Now that it was finally time to go, Wynona found her legs locked in position and she struggled to move. It was only then that she realized she was still holding Rascal's hand and it was far softer than normal. She glanced down to see that he was covered in fur. Apparently, he had stayed in his partial shift during the entire confrontation.

"Come on," he lisped softly through his elongated teeth, pulling just enough to help move her weight forward.

"She would find a dog," Marcella muttered behind them.

Wynona almost came to a stop, her desire to protect Rascal much stronger than her sense of self preservation, but Rascal let go of her hand and put his hand on her back.

"Not worth it," he whispered. "You're far better than they'll ever be."

Wynona couldn't help the small feeling of satisfaction, however, when Violet squeaked and screeched as loud as a mouse could, shaking her fist back at the house while they walked away. Sometimes a little show of anger felt pretty darn good.

They walked past the squad car where Celia was being loaded inside and Wynona couldn't help but glance over.

Celia's dark blue eyes were glued to her sister. "I didn't do it," Celia whispered, but the message was clear.

Wynona hesitated, not sure where to put her loyalties. She had fought so hard, but this kind of evidence was hard to ignore. Still...there was something in her sister's eyes that looked almost...vulnerable. Scared. Worried. It wasn't the look of a killer. Not knowing what else to do, Wynona nodded at her sister, then picked up her pace and got inside Rascal's truck.

"Are you ready for me to drop you at home?" Rascal asked before closing her door.

Wynona shook her head. "No." She looked at Rascal and reached out to run her fingers through his hair. "She needs me."

Sighing, Rascal shook his head in understanding. He might not agree, but Wynona knew he wouldn't argue. Her heart flip-flopped yet again as she watched him walk to his own seat in the truck. They needed to get this case cleared up and out of the way. Wynona was tired of dwelling on her past. She wanted to look forward to the future, and she desperately hoped it had a lot to do with the man climbing behind the wheel.

CHAPTER 25

The police station was abuzz with activity as Wynona followed Rascal down the hall toward the interrogation rooms. Her heart felt as if it would pound out of her chest, knowing her sister was inside and being accused of murder. Wynona still felt as if she were in shock over the whole thing. The evidence was right in front of her, but she struggled to come to grips with it. And when Celia had whispered she was innocent, Wynona wanted so badly to believe her. And therein lay the problem. She *wanted* to believe Celia. But everything said Wynona *shouldn't* believe her.

Rascal opened the door and ushered Wynona inside, only stopping when they reached their corner in the back of the room. Rascal took his officer stance, with his legs wide and his arms folded over his chest in a way that emphasized his physique. Normally, Wynona thoroughly enjoyed the display of strength, but right now she couldn't appreciate it.

Celia was sitting across from Chief Ligurio at the desk and she looked far more contrite than normal. Her white skin was pale and her hair was pulled back into a ponytail. Her clothes were impeccably tailored as usual, but tonight there were wrinkles and smudges on them that Wynona had never seen before.

Officer Skymaw's place at the door explained the less than immaculate appearance, since Celia's normal magic wasn't able to help her at the moment.

"Why am I here?" Celia asked, her weariness evident in her voice. "Despite what you think, I didn't kill anyone."

Chief Ligurio didn't answer right away and the silence made Wynona extra anxious.

Wynona shifted in her seat, growing more and more uncomfortable. This couldn't be right. It just couldn't! Celia was spoiled and entitled, but she had no reason to kill anyone! What could she have possibly gained from Indigo's death?

"Deverell," Celia said in a low tone. "If this is about us—" Celia quickly closed her mouth when the chief's head snapped toward her.

"Ms. Le Doux," he said, emphasizing the formal address. "You are here because you are being charged with murder. Any...relationship, or other situation that might have happened between us in the past, has absolutely no bearing on this case. I would ask that you refrain from hinting otherwise."

Celia's cheeks colored and she looked anywhere but at the chief.

Wynona pinched her lips together. She knew from her own experience that Chief Ligurio was fairly grumpy, but he didn't have to be so mean.

Violet huffed and sat down on Wynona's shoulder angrily.

Wynona nodded her agreement. She didn't like how this was starting out either.

"Do you recognize this?" Chief Ligurio held out the bag with all the jade beads in it.

Celia leaned a little closer. What little color was in her cheeks completely faded. She reached for the bag. "Where did you find this?"

The chief pulled it back. "Is it or isn't it yours?"

"Yes, it's mine," Celia snapped. "But you already knew that or I wouldn't be here. And again, I'll ask where you found it."

"Scattered on the trail near Indigo Stocker's body."

Celia's mouth gaped. "W-what?"

"When did you last see the bracelet?" Chief Ligurio asked casually as if he hadn't just dropped a bomb in the room.

"Yesterday," Celia stammered. She grabbed her ponytail and began twisting it. "I wore it to a meeting for the coven and later that afternoon, I realized it was gone."

"Who was at the meeting?" the chief asked, typing away on his computer.

"Everyone," Celia said, then sighed. She slumped in her seat. "Everyone but Indigo, that is. We were discussing names to fill her position in the sisterhood."

Wynona's eyebrows went up. They certainly didn't waste time, which affirmed Celia's statement that it was more of a competition than a family.

"Do you believe someone took it from you?" Chief Ligurio pressed.

Celia shrugged. "How should I know? I was wearing it! It wouldn't have been easy to get it away from my wrist without my noticing. At least not without a spell, and if someone used a spell, we should have been able to feel it in the room."

Wynona held back her disappointment. Celia was right. Taking the bracelet would have been near to impossible. Unless she had taken it off for any reason, it wouldn't have been feasible to slip it off a wrist without being noticed.

"Can anyone corroborate your story that you were wearing it yesterday?"

Celia shrugged. "I don't know. You can certainly ask. But I don't walk out of our meetings having memorized all the other women's jewelry."

"Why don't I tell you what I think really happened," Chief Ligurio said, folding his hands on top of the desk.

Celia glared but didn't speak.

"I think you decided that Indigo was a threat to you and your place at the top of the coven."

Celia's lips pinched into a tight, white line.

"I think you overheard Indigo and Callista talking about their plan to fake Indigo's death in order to get her husband's attention, and I think you decided to use it to your advantage." The chief leaned across the desk. "I also think that you met her outside of the hotel the second morning she was there. Apparently, you knew about her morning sunrise ritual and joined her. But instead of going through with the ritual, you tricked her into drinking something laced with a liquid hex."

"You're wrong," Celia said through gritted teeth. Her face was turning red again and her hands were clenched into fists on her lap.

"I think Indigo struggled with you as she died, which caused the broken bracelet, which you didn't notice at the time because you were too concerned about hiding the body. You used magic to drag the body through the grass until you deposited her at the foot of the hill, knowing she would be difficult to find, and that to any general passerby, it would look like an accident."

"No!" Celia shouted.

"I also think you paid your butler to say the two of you were together the night of the murder and that during your time away during the lightning ceremony, you were using the added power that night to create the hex you needed in order to kill Indigo."

"How can you say that?" Celia screamed. "I didn't kill her! I had no reason to kill her!"

Wynona bit back tears. Chief Ligurio's scenario made more sense than she wanted to admit. Suddenly, Celia's blue eyes snapped to Wynona.

"I didn't do it," Celia whispered thickly with a shake of her head. "You know that, Wynona. I know you do."

Wynona didn't speak. She wasn't sure what to say. She wanted to believe, desperately, but how could she fight such solid evidence?

"You have to believe me!" Celia shouted at her sister.

Wynona jerked back a little at the vitriol in her sister's tone.

"Hello, Chief," a tall elf in an expensive suit said a little too pleasantly as he walked into the room without knocking. "My name is Ailmar Bizana, defense attorney. You wouldn't be interrogating my client without her counsel present, would you?"

Chief Ligurio leaned back in his seat. "Your client has yet to ask for counsel. I'm well within my rights."

The man tsked his tongue and set his briefcase on the desk. "Was she ever given the opportunity to?" His smile was more shark-like than friendly. "I'm sure you're aware of what family Ms. Celia belongs to, Chief. Surely you don't want to risk your job by stepping out of bounds unnecessarily?"

"Her family has nothing to do with this," Chief Ligurio hissed. He stood from his seat and even from behind, and Wynona could read the rage all over his body. "Our president isn't above the law," Chief Ligurio said in a dark tone. "And neither is his family. So, go ahead, take your client and find some way to work around the murder charge on her head, but hear me now..." The chief pointed a long, white finger at the lawyer. "If they think their money or power are going to get rid of this, they can think again. I can't be bought, and I won't allow our justice system to be bought either. We do things according to the law in my precinct and I don't make exceptions for anyone."

Celia had gone back to being pale and tears tracked down her cheeks while she watched the police chief argue with her lawyer. "Deverell," she whispered.

"That's Chief Ligurio to you," he growled. Slamming his laptop and gathering his notes, the chief stormed toward the door. "You can use this room," he called over his shoulder. "I'll be in my office putting together the case against her."

Wynona stood on shaky legs, but she hurried to follow the line of officers leaving the room.

"Wynona?"

She froze at the threshold and slowly turned back.

"I know it doesn't mean much," Celia said with a sniff. "But I promise I didn't do it." Celia wiped at her tears, but more replaced them, and Wynona noticed her sister wasn't wearing any of her usual jewelry.

"When did you last wear the bracelet?" Wynona couldn't help but ask. There had to have been half a dozen on Celia's wrist when they'd talked at the tea shop.

"Exactly what I already said. Yesterday," Celia insisted. "It's true."

"Not another word," Mr. Bizana said, frowning at Celia. He turned to glare at Wynona. "Unless you have something important to say, might I suggest you follow your police buddies and leave? We need to do serious work here and your kind won't be helpful."

Wynona swallowed the angry words on her tongue. She was so tired of always being judged for her lack of magic. *Her kind.* As if she were a different species simply because she had been cursed.

Clenching her fists, she turned and slammed the door behind her. Ooooh...she was mad enough she could spit, but Violet seemed to have taken on the task herself, since the tiny mouse was hissing and squeaking enough to bring down the house.

"Shhh..." Wynona said, reaching to her shoulder to pick up her friend. She cupped the mouse in one hand and petted her with the other. "It's alright," she crooned. "The jerk doesn't have anything to do with us."

Violet squeaked out a few more choice words before huffing and then resettling her fur.

Wynona sighed. "My sentiments exactly." She put Vi back on her shoulder and turned to walk down the hall, but was cut short. "Callista!"

Callista jerked her head toward Wynona, her light blue eyes widening in surprise. "What are you doing here?" she asked softly, walking away from where Niam was speaking to an officer.

Or...maybe arguing was a better word. The warlock seemed quite agitated.

"I've been helping Ra-Deputy Chief Strongclaw," Wynona explained, catching herself from being too familiar with Rascal in public. He did have a reputation to maintain, after all. "Plus, they brought in Celia and I thought she could use the support."

It hadn't been lost on Wynona that although her parents had sent a lawyer, they hadn't bothered to come down themselves. They had put on a good performance at the door, but neither of them was willing to put in the time or energy to come down and actually support their daughter. Even their magical daughter.

Knowing Celia wasn't treated much better than herself didn't help Wynona feel better. In fact, it only made her feel worse. Perhaps she shouldn't have judged her sister quite so harshly over the years.

"I can understand," Callista said with a sad smile. "It's hard to watch our loved ones choose paths that are wrong."

Wynona frowned, but nodded. "Yes, I suppose so."

"It must have come as such a shock to find out Celia killed Indigo."

Wynona jerked back a little. "How did you hear that?"

Callista's cheeks turned red and she ducked her head, making Wynona feel bad for snapping. This woman wasn't well and she didn't need Wynona hurting her feelings. "The ghost reporters have already spread it across town," Callista said quietly.

Wynona sighed and pinched the bridge of her nose. "I'm sorry, Callista. I shouldn't have snapped. I just didn't expect the news to spread so fast."

Callista nodded, but still didn't meet Wynona's gaze. "I understand. I wouldn't want word to get out about my sister either."

Wynona refrained from explaining that she thought her sister was innocent. She didn't have any reason for the argument other than her internal gut instinct, and it wasn't worth arguing over at the moment. "Is that why you and Niam came down?"

Callista glanced over her shoulder, her hands wringing together hard enough to break one of her long nails. "Yes. He wanted to speak to Celia. Find out why she did it."

Wynona winced at how tightly Callista was twisting her knuckles. It looked painful, but the woman appeared unaffected. "Celia hasn't been found guilty yet," Wynona couldn't help but point out. "I think you and Niam probably need to wait until a judge and jury have their say."

Callista's smile was anything but pleasant. Her bottom lip trembled and she looked like she would have a nervous breakdown at any moment. "I understand."

"Here." Wynona gently put her hand on Callista's upper back. "Why don't I walk you back to Niam? He can take you home."

Callista nodded jerkily. "Thank you," she whispered. She kept her face down as if afraid to meet the eyes of any of the officers. It made Wynona feel terrible for the ordeal the ill woman was obviously going through.

"Don't worry," Wynona soothed. "Everyone is here to help." She looked up and smiled. "And here's Niam."

Niam glanced toward the women and frowned when he saw Callista, before sighing. "Come on, Calli. Let's go home." He held his hand out and Callista practically lunged for it, her wide skirts flying behind her with the movement.

Wynona winced a little at the witch's neediness. It seemed so overly dramatic, but still...Callista obviously felt safe with her brother-in-law and that was most important.

"I'm...sorry about your sister," Niam said woodenly as Wynona continued to watch them.

Wynona struggled to hold his gaze, but somehow found the courage when Violet huffed quietly in her ear. "Thank you for that, but until she's proven guilty, I'm still holding out hope."

Niam looked confused. "I thought they said she was being charged with murder."

"And even though you're very nice," Callista inserted softly, "it had to be your sister."

Wynona's eyebrows furrowed together. "Why do you say that?"

"It's not like there was any other way for the bracelet to get there. Indigo would have never been caught dead with jade jewelry. She always wore sapphires." Callista looked up at Niam with wide eyes, very similar in color to her sister's. "She told me you once said how much you enjoyed when her accessories matched her eyes, so that's what she always wore."

Niam's countenance fell a little more and Wynona knew it was time to let the grieving people go.

She walked over and rested her hand on Callista's. "I'm sure we'll get it all figured out." Wynona glanced down to see there was a bit of slickness on her finger. Pulling back, she realized it was a slight smear of blood. But it wasn't hers. "Oh, you got hurt!" She picked up Callista's hand and studied the cut across her finger. One of the witch's long nails had obviously done damage during the hand wringing and Wynona's guilt ratcheted up a notch. "You might want to put a bandage on that."

Callista pulled her hand back and leaned into Niam's shoulder. "Of course. Thank you."

Wynona watched the two of them walk away. Niam was treating Callista like a fragile, delicate doll and Wynona couldn't blame him. It was still odd that the witch lived with her sister's widower, but Wynona couldn't help but be surprised at the kindness and respect Niam showed. None of his actions gave any indication that he thought of Callista as more than a friend, which put to rest the theory that they were having an affair. But taking care of Callista even after Indigo's death just seemed so...above and beyond, especially for a man who had struggled with his wife to begin with. And what would happen if Niam decided to marry again?

Wynona shook her head. It didn't matter. That was something Niam and Callista would have to address if or when the time ever came. Wynona had enough problems of her own to deal with at the moment, and the first one would be to talk to Chief Ligurio.

Wynona started to walk, then paused and turned toward Rascal's office instead. She might need the shifter's interference to keep from getting her neck torn in two if the chief hadn't calmed down from his encounter with the lawyer.

Hopefully, the chief wasn't hungry at the moment, but was in the mood to listen, because Wynona just couldn't get rid of the nagging feeling that things were not quite what they seemed.

CHAPTER 26

"Deputy Chief Strongclaw?" Wynona called out as she knocked and opened his door simultaneously. She glanced around the frame and smiled when she spotted him at his desk on the phone.

"Uh-huh," Rascal said with a nod. He waved her in. "Right. Well, that's good to know. Thank you."

Wynona walked in quietly and sat down in a metal seat opposite Rascal. It definitely wasn't built for someone to sit and linger comfortably. She shifted until she found a spot that didn't hurt too badly.

"Can you send the whole list over?" Rascal paused. "I realize you have privacy clauses, but this is a police investigation," he argued. "That'll be enough. Thank you." He hung up the phone and paused for a second before sighing. "Sorry," he said, making a sheepish face. "I didn't mean to leave you on your own after the interview. You had stopped to talk to Celia, and Chief was hounding me about getting a couple of phone calls taken care of."

Wynona waved off his apology. "I was fine. Thanks." She nodded toward his phone. "I take it that was the work you were supposed to handle?"

Rascal nodded and leaned his elbows onto the desk. "Yeah. I was asking for a full list of the coven members at that meeting Celia mentioned. Mrs. Murik did confirm Celia was there, but didn't remember if she was wearing a bracelet or not."

Wynona sighed and nodded. "That'll be a hard one to prove, I think."

"Much harder than just taking the evidence at face value," Rascal admitted.

Wynona squished her lips to the side as she considered her next move. Somehow, she needed to convince Rascal and then the chief that they were missing something, even though Wynona had nothing to prove that, other than the unsettled feeling in her gut.

"What's going on in that head of yours?" Rascal asked with a smirk. He tilted his head to the side. "You're thinking so loud I can hardly hear Violet snoring."

Wynona laughed softly and tucked a piece of hair behind her ear, revealing a napping Violet. "She was tuckered out."

"Understandably," Rascal said. He raised his eyebrows. "But that didn't answer my question."

Wynona made a face. "I don't think Celia did it." She held up a hand to stop his argument. "I saw the evidence. I understand the trail leads directly to her. But I still can't get past the feeling that we're missing something there, somewhere along the line, some clue that will prove her innocence and give us the real killer."

Rascal sighed and leaned back in his chair. "I don't know what to tell you, Wy. I'm sorry about how it all turned out, but everything we have points to her. We even have her admitting that she lied to us in the beginning. She lied about where she was during the storm. She's been difficult and belligerent every time we speak to her. She was in the coven with Indigo, and it's not that hard to believe that Indigo was threatening Celia's position in the group." He spread his hands to the side. "And now we have her bracelet at the scene of the crime. What more do you want?"

Wynona shook her head. "I don't know. I just know that it doesn't feel right."

"I can't imagine it would. We are talking about your sister, after all."

"It's not just that," Wynona began. "It all seems a little too easy, don't you think?"

Rascal scoffed. "You think the last week has been easy?" He whistled low. "I'd hate to see your definition of difficult."

She gave him an unimpressed glare. "That's not what I meant. Don't you think some random hiker calling in about the bracelet is a little too convenient? And how come we didn't see the trail in the grass the first night?"

Rascal gathered a bunch of papers from his desk and stood up. "Come on," he said in a resigned tone.

"What? Where are we going?" Wynona stood, careful not to knock Violet off her shoulder.

"To Chief Ligurio's office. We might as well hash this out together," Rascal said with a tired grin. "Besides, I'm not the one you need to convince anyway. The chief is calling the shots on this one."

Wynona stepped up to where Rascal waited at the door and rested her hand against his chest. "Thank you," she said sincerely. "For being willing to hear me out."

The gold in his eyes began a low burn as he looked at her. "Anytime," he said in a husky tone. "But you can show me your gratitude this Sunday at seven."

Wynona frowned. "Why then?"

"Because whether or not this case is solved, we're going to dinner," Rascal stated firmly. "I'm tired of letting dead bodies get in our way."

Wynona smiled and tapped her finger against his uniform. "So I get to spend time with someone who's not an officer?"

Rascal slowly nodded. "On that night, at that time, it'll just be Rascal Strongclaw and his beautiful date. No case, no evidence collection..." His eyes darted to her shoulder. "And I'm afraid, no extra company."

"Violet will be mad," Wynona sang out as she pulled open the door to the hallway.

"She'll understand," Rascal shot back. He tilted his head down the hall. "It's Chief who's going to be mad."

Wynona scrunched up her nose. "I have to admit it worries me a little."

"Don't worry," Rascal whispered. "The big bad wolf will protect you from the big bad vamp."

Wynona shook her head and smiled. "He'll hear you."

"He did hear you," a voice snapped, drawing their attention.

Wynona felt her cheeks color, but she straightened her shoulders. She was learning well with the police chief that weakness wasn't tolerated well. "Chief Ligurio, I'd like to speak to you, if you have time, please." Politeness also helped.

Red eyes rolled toward the ceiling before the vampire disappeared back into his office. "Don't just stand out there," he shouted.

Rascal winked at Wynona and they headed inside.

"Thank you," Wynona said as she sat down on the opposite side of the desk.

"A complete list is on its way," Rascal added, dropping the file of papers onto Chief Ligurio's desk.

The chief glanced at the paper before coming back to Wynona. "Let me guess. You think your sister is innocent."

"She is," Wynona said without preamble. She folded her hands neatly in her lap and sat up straight.

"I have evidence that says otherwise."

"I know," Wynona said softly. "I've seen and heard it all. But I still don't believe it."

The chief hung his head for a second before punching a button on his phone. "Blood coffee, now."

Wynona raised an eyebrow. "That headache back?"

Chief Ligurio scowled.

"Would you like me to add some herbs to help you feel better?" she continued.

The police chief growled slightly. "Do you go around fixing the headaches of every person you meet?"

Wynona smiled and stood, walking back to the cupboard where the chief kept a few supplies. "No. Just rude vampires who are so stressed they don't eat as often as they should."

"If we're going to spend time going over my domestic habits, you might as well walk right back out that door," Chief Ligurio snapped.

Wynona found the tea packets she wanted and walked back to her seat. "Here. Sprinkle this in and it'll help."

The scowl never changed, but the chief grabbed them from her. "Now, you were going to convince the big bad vamp that your sister is innocent."

Wynona held back a wince at his quoting her and Rascal's conversation. Too many of these officers had enhanced hearing. Secrets must be terribly hard to keep at the station.

"Chief?"

The whole room waited a moment while Officer Nightshade brought in a steaming cup and left it on the chief's desk.

"Thank you, Amaris!" Wynona called out as the officer left.

"Ms. Le Doux," Chief Ligurio said, bringing her attention back. "I don't have all night."

"Right." Wynona nodded. "I just have a very strong feeling that we've missed something significant," she began. "I find the fact that we didn't find the shoes or the bracelet a little odd. Your officers searched a good distance from the body," she said.

"Obviously not far enough," Chief Ligurio said before taking a sip.

"And how did a hiker just happen to know the bracelet belonged to my sister?" Wynona pressed. "There are nearly fifteen thousand creatures in Hex Haven. Don't you think the odds of that are slim to none?"

"The odds might be slim, but there are still odds." The chief sounded bored with their conversation, but Wynona wasn't willing to give up yet.

"Celia had an alibi!"

"One which she could very well have paid for." Chief Ligurio's tone had grown dark at the reminder of Celia's confession. "I realize you helped us previously on a difficult case, Ms. Le Doux, but that doesn't make you an expert. I've listened to you because you have had good instincts and because, unlike the rest of your family, I don't believe you have an agenda." He shook his head. "But you're still an inexperienced, magicless witch, who runs a tea shop. You're hardly qualified to handle a murder investigation."

His words, though said without his usual sharpness, still dug deep into Wynona's chest as well as if he had used a knife to send them.

"Too far, Chief," Rascal growled.

Wynona could hear Rascal's breathing as it became heavy and more animal-like than normal. She put up her hand and did her best to smile over her shoulder at Rascal, though the sentiment was strained. "No. He's right," she forced out. "I'm not really qualified to be here." She stood, her knees slightly shaky from the feeling of betrayal. The movement woke Violet, who snorted and then began to chatter, unhappy with the situation.

"Ms. Le Doux," the chief began.

"No..." Wynona shook her head, her smile failing, though she tried hard to keep it up. "I already admitted you're right. I'll just head home now."

"Wy!"

Wynona didn't blame Rascal for the situation, but at the moment, she was too close to tears to speak to him, so she ignored his call and hurried toward the door. Before she could get there, however, Officer Nightshade poked her head back in.

"Chief?" she looked around uncertainly, obviously reading the tension of the room. "Uh...the coroner dropped off Mrs. Stocker's things." Amaris held up a plastic bag.

"Bring it here," Chief Ligurio said on a sigh.

Wynona paused at the door when Rascal's warm hand landed on her arm. "Don't go like this," he whispered, though they both knew everyone else in the room could hear everything.

Wynona looked up at him. "It's okay," she said softly. "You can call me when you're done, okay? I'll probably be at the shop..." Her eyes drifted to the chief. "Where I belong."

Chief Ligurio poured the contents of the bag on his desk, not paying any attention to Wynona's single barb. Several pieces of blue jewelry fell onto the desk. "This is all of it?" he asked.

"She didn't have anything else with her," Amaris replied. "This is just what she was wearing. It's all been tested and now needs to be given back to Mr. Stocker."

"Wy?"

Wynona slowly walked to the desk, her eyes focused on the jewelry. She couldn't seem to look away. Something was churning and she just knew she was on the verge of a breakthrough. She could feel it.

Wynona picked up a single earring. It was a sapphire set in silver. All the jewelry was blue, just like Callista had said it would be.

"Ms. Le Doux, what are you doing?" Chief Ligurio asked sharply.

Wynona held the stone up to the light. She barely noticed Violet humming a sort of purring sound and wrapping herself around Wynona's neck. The noise of the office was soon drowned out and Wynona lost herself in the translucence of the gem.

Purple spots began to enter the edge of Wynona's vision, but she still felt frozen to the spot. There was something here, something about the sapphire...

"Wynona!"

Rascal's shout and grip on her upper arms finally pulled Wynona from her daze. She sucked in a huge breath, not having realized she wasn't breathing.

"Oh my goodness." She gasped, putting a hand on her chest, where her heart was racing painfully. "I'm so sorry."

"What was that?" Chief Ligurio demanded.

Wynona looked over to see that the chief was standing and Amaris looked as if she'd seen a ghost, which was saying something for an already pale vampire. "I know who did it," Wynona whispered.

"You what?" Rascal shouted.

"Are you crazy?" Chief Ligurio growled.

Wynona closed her eyes and shook her head, organizing her thoughts after the moment of weirdness. There was no time to dwell on what had just happened. Wynona needed to act quickly. But first...

"Chief. I need to see Celia."

"I thought you said she was innocent," Chief Ligurio argued.

"She is," Wynona said with a much stronger surety than before. This time she wasn't just hoping, she actually knew. "But I need to ask her something. And if all goes well, then I need to set a trap for a killer." She rushed to the door, ignoring the shouts of the others in the room.

They could follow if they wanted, but Wynona wasn't going to be stopped. Her sister and her dating life depended on her getting this right.

CHAPTER 27

"Are you sure about this?" Rascal asked as he parked the truck outside the Thornheart mansion.

Wynona nodded. "Yes. The best way to get a confession is for us to throw out a line and hope our killer picks it up."

"I'm not very excited about you being the bait though," Rascal grumbled.

Wynona smiled at his pouty voice. She reached over and patted his hand. "I'll have you waiting in the wings to protect me. It'll be just fine."

Rascal growled softly in his throat, but didn't argue with her. "Fine. Let's get this over with. If I never have to deal with a group of conniving, vengeful witches again, it'll be too soon."

Wynona sighed and nodded. She couldn't blame him for his frustration. The Sisters of Eternity coven hadn't exactly been very helpful during the investigation, and the more Wynona and the police dug, the more they realized that Celia's description of a competition market, rather than a sisterhood, was true. These women wanted power, and they were using each other to get it.

And yes, Wynona completely understood what that said about her sister. Celia was far from being a good person, but in the end, she definitely wasn't a murderer. For one of the sisters, however, that title was a little too appropriate.

Rascal put his hands around Wynona's waist and lifted her down from the truck. She'd been so caught up in her thoughts that she had forgotten to climb down before he reached her side.

"Thank you," she said breathlessly, enjoying the feel of his large hands spanning her waist.

Rascal grinned roguishly. "Anytime."

Wynona laughed. "You like that word."

"Only in conjunction with you," he quipped. "Come on." His golden eyes went to the mansion. "This place gives me the creeps. In and out."

Wynona nodded and together they walked up the driveway. They were parked near the bottom, since the concrete was filled with the cars from the members of the coven. By the time they got to the door, Wynona was near panting. "I have got to start exercising," she grumbled, wiping at her forehead.

Rascal chuckled, then knocked firmly.

Wynona had almost forgotten the Thornhearts had a zombie butler, when the dead man opened the door.

"How may I help you?" he asked stoically.

"The coven is expecting us," Rascal said in an official tone.

The yellow eyes of the butler went from Rascal to Wynona, then back. "Right this way, please." Slowly, the man stepped back, swinging the massive door wide and allowing Rascal and Wynona to step out of the heat.

"Thank you," Wynona said with a small smile. Truth was, the butler sort of frightened her. He was the first zombie Wynona had ever met, and seeing a dead person walking and talking solely from magic was a little on the creepy side.

Rascal must have noticed her anxiety because in the next moment, his warm hand landed on her back and Wynona automatically relaxed into his touch. She really needed to get this case over with so they could go out to dinner. Wynona definitely wanted more from the police officer than their current circumstances would allow.

"Deputy Chief Strongclaw and Ms. Wynona Le Doux," the butler announced in the threshold of the same sitting room as before.

Wynona's eyebrows shot up. She hadn't actually told the butler her whole name, though anyone who paid attention could tell she was a Le Doux. She made a mental note to figure out how he knew who she was.

"Wynona," Madam Murik said coldly. Her blue eyes flashed to Rascal. "And Deputy Chief." She folded her arms over her chest. "We're all here, just as you asked us to be, all except for the one you've got locked behind bars," the older woman said testily.

Rascal put his hands on his hips and spread his legs in a wider stance. "Thank you for your cooperation, Madam Murik," he replied with a tight smile. "We're still working on the case and right now, Ms. Celia Le Doux is being held for her own safety." He continued past the gasps. "When we feel the danger has passed, we will be more than happy to return her to your circle."

"Danger?" Madam Murik dropped her arms and walked away from the other women a few steps. "What are you talking about? What danger? I thought she was being held on murder charges."

Wynona stepped forward, knowing this was her cue to take over. "She was...at first," Wynona explained. "But some new information has come to light that has caused all of us, myself and the police included, to rethink the situation."

"Why are you here?" Adel Thornheart walked away from a plush chair where Callista was sitting with her head tilted into the soft corner.

The pale colored witch appeared as if she were sleeping and Wynona felt a tug of sympathy concerning the dark rings under Callista's eyes. Now was not the time for such emotions, but it was difficult not to feel them. She turned back to Adel. "We have reason to believe the killer is still loose and that they are specifically targeting this coven," Wynona stated bluntly.

Adel stopped short, her dark eyes widening. "What are you saying?" she asked, her hand rising to her throat. "Someone is trying to kill us?"

Wynona nodded, making sure to keep eye contact. "We believe so, yes."

Madam Murik walked up beside Adel, her eyes narrowed suspiciously. "What do you have to do with all this, Wynona? Why are you involved?"

"I'm involved because my sister asked me to be."

A witch in the back corner that Wynona didn't know scoffed. "Celia would never have asked a cursed witch, sister or not, for help."

Wynona bit back a rude response.

Madam Murik tsked her tongue, her eyes still on Wynona. "Watch your words, Ariya. Things are not always what they seem."

Wynona frowned and almost stepped back. Did Madam Murik know that this was all a farce? A plan to pull out the real killer? Surely the woman couldn't read minds. Even the most powerful magic user was unable to do that.

A sudden thought hit Wynona and she had to work hard to school her emotions on her face. Perhaps Madam Murik could sense intentions. It could be done if one practiced enough. At least according to the books Wynona had read.

She clenched and unclenched her hands, doing her best to remain impassive, but it was difficult. "Celia and I don't always get along, but she knew that I had helped the police once before, when a murder happened at my tea shop." Wynona turned to face the disbelieving Ariya head on. "When the evidence began to mount, Celia asked if I would help clear her name. Now I'm trying to do that as well as keep her safe."

"By doing what exactly?" Madam Murik asked, her white eyebrows rising on her forehead.

"By warning all of you to be careful," Wynona said, dropping her voice to sound more urgent. "The precinct doesn't have the creature-power to put a guard on each of you, which means you need to be extra vigilant." She looked over her shoulder at Rascal, who nodded his affirmation.

"What should we be looking for?" another witch asked. The brunette stepped up near Adel. "The reports said Indigo was killed by hex poisoning. What happened with Celia? Was there an attempt on her life?"

Wynona shook her head. "Not quite. As many of you might have heard, Celia was taken into custody on suspicion of Indigo's murder. But like I mentioned earlier, new evidence actually suggests that Celia is a victim and that her life might have been endangered rather than her being the criminal."

"You still haven't told us what this evidence is," Adel snapped. "How are we supposed to know how to protect ourselves if we don't know what to look for?"

"When Celia's bracelet was found near the place Indigo's body was discovered, it was run through forensics," Wynona said carefully. "There was poison on it."

"But Indigo was poisoned," Adel argued, folding her arms defensively. "Wouldn't it make sense for some of it to have gotten on Celia?"

"It wasn't the same poison."

The room went still.

"So you now believe someone is trying to poison all of us?" The brunette's voice shook slightly. She looked to her coven mother. "What should we do?"

Madam Murik tilted her head, but her eyes never left Wynona. "I believe we should follow what Ms. Le Doux suggests. Be careful." Madam Murik tilted her head up. "Tell me, Deputy Chief." Her eyes moved to Rascal. "How long do you expect it to take to catch this villain?"

Wynona forced her breathing to stay normal. It was harder than it should have been, but something inside her core was telling her

Madam Murik knew more than she should. It would ruin everything if the coven mother figured out their plan.

"We hope to have the actual murderer in custody tomorrow morning," he said simply.

"So quickly?" Madam Murik nodded. "Then you must have an idea of who it is?"

Rascal shook his head. "Not exactly, but we do believe we know where to find evidence of that." He glanced at Wynona before going back to the crowd. "We've set up a time with the hotel tomorrow to search the room that Indigo was staying in. Ms. Le Doux is not only here because of her sister, but because of her expertise in herbs and poisons. She'll accompany us tomorrow and hopefully within that room we'll be able to find what we're looking for."

"What could possibly be in the room?" Adel asked, her brow furrowed in confusion.

"While Celia's poison was attempted from skin contact," Rascal clarified, "Indigo's was ingested. We believe we'll be able to find the container of whatever she ate or drank. There could be fingerprints, or there could be other evidence our forensics team can piece together in order to find our culprit."

Several of the women in the room began to murmur and gather closer together. It was obvious that the scenario had them on edge.

"And you're not going tonight?"

Rascal shook his head. "The janitorial team needed time to find the correct garbage from her room and they've promised to have it ready for us as we search tomorrow."

Adel wrapped her arms around the brunette at her side. "Well, for all our sakes, we hope you find what you're looking for."

Wynona nodded. "Thank you," she said. Moving slowly through the women, Wynona approached Callista, who still looked sleepy. "Callista? I have something for you."

The blonde witch blinked several times then straightened and cleared her throat. "I'm sorry. I guess I haven't been sleeping well lately." She yawned and shook her head as if to clear her mind. "What can I do for you?"

Wynona smiled softly. "Nothing. I just thought you might like to have Indigo's jewelry." She held out the plastic bag from the police station. "They were brought back from forensics while I was still there and I figured you would appreciate having them back."

Gingerly, Callista took the bag, her eyes growing misty. "Thank you," she whispered thickly. Her eyes came up to Wynona. "I'll treasure these."

Wynona nodded and stood straight again before walking back to Rascal's side. "Thank you for taking the time to meet with us this evening," she said, looking each witch in the eye. "We'll let you know what we find out."

Rascal once again put his hand on her back, guiding Wynona out of the house. She was grateful for his touch, as it kept her grounded from all the lying she had just done. She hated fudging the truth, but in times like this, there seemed little else she could do.

"Do you think they bought it?" Rascal asked as they sat in the truck and buckled their seatbelts.

Wynona stared at the mansion, waiting to see if any type of intuition would hit, but she felt empty inside. "I sure hope so," she finally whispered back. "It's the best shot we have."

CHAPTER 28

Wynona's heart kept jumping at every little sound as she waited in the dark dining area of the tea house. The only light on was in her office and Wynona had made sure to sit in a corner where it couldn't touch her. Rascal hadn't been very happy that she'd wanted to be left alone, not when their suspect could react in a violent way to their trap.

It had taken both Wynona and Violet to convince the wolf shifter that things would go better if he left. In fact, Wynona had been pleasantly surprised at Violet's ability to communicate and persuade the wolf to take their side.

"Alright," he'd growled finally, giving Wynona a resigned look. "I'll leave, but if you think that we're not finishing this case together, then you better think again." He'd glared at Violet, then Wynona, then stormed out of the tea shop with a tangible anger in his wake.

Trembling fingers picked up the hot cup of lavender, and Wynona took a sip, doing her best to calm her nerves. Waiting was the worst, but it was their only choice. She had left the bread crumbs, and if the murderer was as intelligent as Wynona thought, then they would be arriving soon.

The only problem was, they would more than likely be coming in order to kill Wynona.

The squeak of a hinge caught Wynona's attention and she stiffened. Very carefully, she set her mug down and made sure not to move. Her eyes widened and she strained to see in the dark. Soon her efforts were rewarded.

The kitchen door slowly swung open and a black silhouette crept out, carefully placing the swinging door back in place.

Wynona felt a drop of sweat trickle down her spine, but she forced herself to stay still. She needed to be sure. Any common thief could have come in at the wrong time, completely ruining her plan.

The shadow fumbled for a moment before a small light broke the dark. Wynona winced and hoped that the intruder didn't shine it in her direction. If she moved, it would be sure to attract attention, but she couldn't let the suspect shine the light on her either.

Her breath left her chest when the light slowly began to work its way over the room. There was no way to hide! And without the element of surprise on her side, Wynona felt certain she would have a hard time containing the situation.

A scuttling sound caught Wynona's attention and that of the intruder, as the person swung the flashlight to the other side of the room, following the sound.

Wynona forced herself to hold still when she heard Violet squeak and more scratching of feet against the hardwood floors.

The intruder muttered, then faced the flashlight forward and began walking toward the hallway that led to the offices.

Wynona took a second after they had disappeared to let her eyes close and her breath slowly release from her lungs. That had been far too close. Slowly, she forced her shaky limbs into movement and began to walk toward the hall herself. Wynona plastered herself against the wall, barely peeking around the corner to make sure her suspect was in place.

Her office door was slowly opened and a black clad arm appeared in the light. The slim fingers wiggled and blue sparks flew from the tips.

Wynona flipped the switch at the end of the hall, illuminating her guest. "Looking for someone, Callista?"

Callista visibly startled, her wide eyes clashing with Wynona's. "Wynona! Oh my goodness! There you are!" An awkward smile tugged at her pale lips. "I was looking for you, and I couldn't find any of the light switches."

Wynona folded her arms over her chest. "Come now, Callista. We both know why you're here. Let's not play games."

The startled, weak persona fell to the ground in an invisible heap as Callista straightened and her smile became much more smug and calculated. "I suppose we do," she said in a sultry voice. "It's nice to be able to get rid of the idiot facade once in a while."

Wynona hoped her erratic pulse wasn't visible from the end of the hallway. Her heart was beating painfully against her chest and she feared she wouldn't be able to keep her body under control if this drew out too long. "Was he really worth it?" Wynona asked, allowing a hint of derision into her tone.

Callista's blonde brows shot up high. "Haven't you seen him?" she asked before sighing dramatically. "He's magnificent." The words were practically purred and they created a churning sensation in Wynona's stomach.

"He was your sister's husband," Wynona argued. "Most people would say that makes him off limits."

Callista laughed harshly and waved a hand through the air, blue speckles floating to the ground. "Theirs was a political marriage," she explained. "They weren't in love with each other."

"Then why not help them seek divorce? Why kill her?"

Callista's face hardened. "Because my perfect, younger sister decided she wanted to make her marriage work. Ha!" Callista rolled her eyes. "The little tramp actually thought someone like Niam Stocker might see something more than a pretty but weak witch." She made a face and spoke with a high tone. "I need to shock him...make him see me...and then I'll be able to confess that I love him." Callista groaned after her little performance. "Like Niam was stupid enough to fall for that."

"I don't know…" Wynona hedged. "He came back when you called and they did spend a couple of days together."

"You figured out I was the caller. I'm impressed." Callista's face grew red. "That moment, however, was exactly when I knew I needed to finish what I had started. Men," she spat. "They've always had a hard time looking past a pretty face. It's what makes them so pliable."

"But Niam wasn't pliable, was he?" Wynona pressed. "Even with Indigo gone, he hasn't given you what you're looking for, has he?"

The red cheeks grew deeper and the speckles of magic began to drop more heavily. "He'll learn," Callista said in a dark tone. "He'll learn to see what I'm truly capable of. Right now he sees a damaged witch because it was the only way I could stay close to him. But with Indigo gone and my secret dying with you…" She smiled cruelly. "I have all the hope in the world that he'll come to his senses."

Wynona backed up at the look in Callista's eyes. The witch was absolutely planning her death at the moment, and Wynona needed a few more pieces of information before she ran for her life.

"I have to ask though," Callista said softly, striding easily down the hall.

Wynona scurried backward, putting several tables and chairs between them.

"How did you know?" Callista stopped at the entrance to the hallway. "You were my biggest supporter in getting free the first time. What tipped you off that I was the actual murderer?"

"A few different things," Wynona said. She nervously tapped the chair in front of her. She needed to think of a way to hide when the time came. Perhaps her shop hadn't been the best meeting place.

"Since we seem to be having a sweet little tete a tete," Callista sneered, "why don't you share?" She tilted her head and considered Wynona. "You're magicless, which means you couldn't have used any spells to help you. Just how did you do it?"

Wynona swallowed and slowly put a hand behind her back. "I have to admit that letting yourself get caught over the fake murder threw me off," Wynona said. She felt the tip of her phone in her back pocket.

"That was rather brilliant," Callista said with a laugh. "But then something changed." She propped one hand up by the elbow. "Your gift of Indigo's jewelry with one jade piece was pretty clever. I'm guessing it means you don't have any back up coming, or else you wouldn't have given it to me so underhandedly." Sharp sparks began to shoot about two inches from Callista's fingers. They were only a warning, but it was enough to leave Wynona's knees shaking. "Tell me where I went wrong."

What had she been thinking, having this show down here? "The sapphires were the last piece of the puzzle," Wynona said, gently lifting her phone from her pocket. One button, one button was all she needed in order to have the entire police station come barging in. "Your relationship with Niam kept my attention for a long time." Wynona pinched her lips together, as if in thought. "You were a little too close for a brother and sister-in-law. And my first big clue came when Deputy Chief Strongclaw and I were speaking to the two of you at the house, though I didn't recognize its significance until later."

"Which was?"

It was easy to see that Callista was growing tired of Wynona wasting time. Wynona needed to get her emergency button pushed and then she'd be able to rest easy, knowing Callista wouldn't be able to hurt her by the time the cavalry arrived. "The way Niam was able to use a spell without seeing it."

Callista huffed, then grinned. "Neat little trick, isn't it?"

Wynona nodded. "I'd never seen it done, but I'm guessing you learned it from him."

The other witch looked particularly pleased with herself. "Not only did I learn it from watching him, but I perfected it in a way others can't even imagine." She laughed. "I'm actually quite fascinated with that little brain of yours. It would be fun to see what else you figured out, but..." She sighed as if in regret. "I'm afraid I've been here too long." She pointed long fingers at Wynona. "Time to be done with these games. I'll be sure to let Niam know you said hello."

Wynona hit the floor so hard, she was sure she'd broken something. A spell shot over her head and she covered her head from the pieces of her wall that rained down. "Crud, crud, crud," she muttered, scrambling for her phone, which was under her body.

"Come now, Wynona," Callista taunted. "I promise to make this quick. You'll never know what hit you."

From under the table, Wynona could see her pursuer coming closer. Wynona climbed to all fours, moving opposite Callista's steps. Wynona just needed a few more seconds...

"What is that?" Callista muttered. "You again? Stupid mouse, I should have...AH!"

Wynona gasped and jumped to her feet, the phone slipping from her fingers in her haste. "Violet!"

Callista was clawing at her clothes, magic shooting every which direction, making Wynona duck yet again.

"VIOLET!" Wynona screamed louder.

A purple blur shot across the floor and Wynona felt the small body leap onto her neck and scurry down the back of her shirt.

"Are you okay?" Wynona asked with a sob. She couldn't help the display of emotion, too worried about her tiny friend to stay quiet.

Before Violet had a chance to answer, Callista stepped around from the edge of the table and stood over Wynona with a triumphant look on her face. "No more distractions," she sneered. "I've got a warlock to take care of." She once again held out her hand.

Wynona's vision grew blurry with a purple haze and she could actually feel the power gathering in Callista's hand. This witch was far more powerful than anyone had ever given her credit for. Hiding it had all been part of the game.

Knowing there was nothing more she could do, Wynona covered her head and screamed when she felt the release of the hex.

"HOW ARE YOU DOING THAT?" Callista shouted, her magic pulsing forth in large spurts.

Wynona felt as if her body were being pelted by rocks, but other than bruises, nothing else seemed wrong with her. She cracked open her eyes at Callista's screams of rage, but could barely see the other witch. A purple bubble surrounded Wynona, fending off the magic spells rapidly spewing from Callista's hands. With each hit, Wynona physically felt the jolt, her body starting to grow weak with aching.

"Granny?" she whispered, but no one answered.

Violet appeared on Wynona's shoulder and put a paw to Wynona's cheek.

When Wynona glanced down, she realized Violet was glowing as well. Her eyes bulged with realization. "This isn't Granny...is it?" Wynona whispered.

Violet shook her head slowly.

Suddenly the bubble burst and Wynona felt herself collapse to the ground. She was in too much shock and pain to comprehend what was going on around her for a few seconds, but after blinking rapidly and shaking her head, she recognized the shouts of a dozen men and women, all of whom were finally there to save her.

"Ms. Le Doux," Chief Ligurio said with a frown. He reached down to help her up.

"It's about time," Wynona huffed, rising on sore legs. She winced. There were bruises all over her body and she felt as if she could sleep for a week.

"My apologies," the chief said. He clasped his hands behind his back and looked over the room. "There was a brownie keeping us from coming in." Chief Ligurio's red eyes landed on her. "Said something about it not being time yet."

Wynona's jaw dropped. "What?" she screeched, then winced and groaned. "Sorry." She rubbed her neck. "I think I'm still in a bit of shock."

"Wy!" Rascal's large body completely engulfed Wynona. The hug was so tight that she could barely breathe, but the feel of him was better than oxygen.

Allowing herself to melt, Wynona enjoyed Rascal's support and concern.

"Never again," he growled. "You don't get to play bait anymore."

Wynona leaned back and raised her eyebrows. "Is that so?"

"That's so." His teeth were still a little longer than normal, his eyes glowing like amber jewels, and his hair was standing straight up, letting Wynona know he had recently shifted.

She gave him a tired smile. "Despite what it looks like, I don't really plan to make a habit out of this, but..." She leaned up on tiptoe until they were almost nose to nose. "I will always help those I care about no matter the cost."

His arms tightened around her back and a small smile played on his lips. "Then I'll just hope no one you care about is ever caught up in this kind of thing again. Two murders in a few months is enough, don't you think?"

Wynona came back to her feet and rested her head against his chest. "More than enough."

CHAPTER 29

Callista sat in her seat in the interrogation room looking much less vulnerable and weak than she had the last time they'd all spent time together in the room.

Chief Ligurio sat in his usual seat, his computer in front of him and a steaming drink to his left.

Wynona had opted to stand this time, not willing to let go of Rascal's comfort quite yet. His hand was on her lower back, keeping their touch away from prying eyes, but helping Wynona stay calm, and she was fairly certain Rascal's wolf side needed the contact as well.

"I don't have to answer anything," Callista sneered. Her hands were tied with the hag thread in front of her, but Officer Skymaw was also standing at the door.

It had been his presence in the dining room that had caused Wynona's bubble to burst and the magical attack to come to an abrupt stop. Wynona really did need to send the officer a thank you card. He'd saved her from the pain of a hex more than once at this point. A note was the least she could do.

"Would you like to walk us through it from the beginning?" Chief Ligurio asked, his hands neatly folded on the desk. "Or do I just get to make my own assumptions?"

Callista's nostrils flared in irritation, but she kept her mouth shut.

This had been going on for ten minutes and Wynona knew that if they didn't get a confession soon, Callista's lawyer would show up and it would all be over. Right now they only had Wynona's word against Callista's. They needed more.

"How about if I tell the story," she offered, stepping away from Rascal, though she didn't want to. Wynona sauntered to the desk and stood next to the chief. She looked down. "You can tell me if I get it wrong."

When Callista snorted, the chief's lips twitched and he nodded. Wynona's little game was going to drive Callista crazy. Hopefully enough to make her say something she shouldn't.

Wynona drew a random pattern on the desk. "I do believe that Callista was jealous of her sister." She paused, but Callista's only reaction was to turn red. "From the time Indigo and Niam were engaged, Callista began feigning mental illness as a way to stay close to the man she thought she was in love with." Wynona tilted her head and studied the livid witch across from her. "Callista has always been powerful, but I'm going to guess she was also a bit on the erratic side."

Bright blue eyes, blazing with hate, met Wynona's.

"Which is why her parents gave Indigo the marriage contract, rather than Callista." Wynona narrowed her eyes. "Indigo's desperation for some love in her marriage eventually gave Callista the chance she needed to set everything she'd been waiting for into motion."

"She didn't deserve him," Callista said through gritted teeth. "My stupid sister had no idea the prize she'd been given."

Wynona nodded, hiding her glee that Callista was starting to rise to the bait. "Be that as it may, you knew your parents would never allow a divorce, so in order to get what you wanted, you had to get your sister out of the way. I'm guessing that the first plan, the one about faking her death, was actually yours, not Indigo's."

A muscle in Callista's jaw began to tick. "That plan was ridiculous. Like anyone would ever fall for such a prank."

"Exactly," Wynona said, leaning onto the desk. "You put together a plan that was sure to fail and made positive you were the scapegoat. It was the only way to make sure there was no suspicion on you when the real murder occured."

"You can't prove any of this," Callista said in a cool tone. Her color had gone back to normal and she relaxed in her chair. "I was in prison when Indigo was murdered, if you recall."

"Oh, I know," Wynona said, slowly walking around the desk toward Callista. She heard Rascal give an angry huff, but Wynona ignored him. He was being protective, but in a room full of officers and no available magic, Wynona felt certain the contained witch could do little to her.

Violet nuzzled the back of Wynona's neck, giving her courage to keep going.

"But we already discussed that you learned a handy little trick from your brother in law," Wynona said. "Remember that?" She stood behind Callista and glanced at Rascal. He looked like he was barely containing his wolf, but Wynona smiled at him, hoping she could calm him down. "Niam showed us that he could do magic out of sight." Wynona leaned down near Callista's ear. "You didn't need to be at your sister's side to kill her."

Callista jerked, but then stilled. "Prisoners are kept from magic," she said, though her voice betrayed her nervousness. "The whole prison is bound."

Wynona nodded. "Except you had set up the hex in advance. You knew your sister spent every morning gathering magic at sunrise. You also knew she would take a water bottle with her." Wynona walked back around to Chief Ligurio's other side. She was grateful the vampire hadn't interfered yet, and it gave her hope he was coming to trust her just a little bit. "The hex you put in the water was set to react when the sun rose. Another nifty trick you learned from playing with light magic within the coven."

Callista's bottom lip began to tremble and she looked less and less sure of herself. "How did you know that?"

Wynona sighed. "It was the lightning storm. The spell you had used that night was the same kind. Wasn't it? The light from the lightning set it off so that Indigo could disappear at a specific moment in time, making your story more believable that the out of control nature magic was the cause of the problem."

Chief Ligurio's black eyebrows rose up and he glanced at Wynona.

She shrugged. "I read about it...once."

Callista slumped. "I was so careful." She sniffled. "Everything went perfectly."

"Until Niam came back," Wynona supplied when the other witch paused.

Callista began to cry in earnest.

"You were afraid he would drink the water you had stashed in Indigo's room. When you had called him about her deceit, you had assumed he and Indigo would fight and leave room for you to slip in." Wynona's voice dropped. "You hadn't planned on him staying the night."

"He should have come back to the house with me," Callista cried, holding her fisted hands against her chest. "He was supposed to be mine! I was supposed to comfort him!" Her eyes blazed behind her tears. "But Indigo always got everything. Just because she was more beautiful than I was, my parents used her to pull our family one more wrung up the political ladder." Her lips curled up in a sneer. "It didn't matter that I was the better witch. It didn't matter that I had been in love with Niam since we were kids." She pounded her chest. "I *had* to kill her! It was the only way to keep her from controlling the rest of my life! Don't you see?"

Wynona stepped back as Callista's screaming grew to epic proportions. Several officers rushed over and held onto the woman, finally escorting her out at the command of Chief Ligurio.

As the door shut, Wynona walked back to Rascal and collapsed against him. She felt him press a kiss to the top of her head.

"You okay?" His voice was gruff with concern.

She nodded. "Yeah. But I think I'm gonna need a vacation after this one."

He chuckled. "Only if you take me with you."

Wynona glanced up and smiled. "I can't say I'd argue with that."

Rascal's eyes were just starting to glow when the chief interrupted them.

"I have a few more questions, Ms. Le Doux."

She sighed and turned. Rascal held her hand as they walked up to the desk. They sat in a couple of extra chairs and waited for the chief to go on.

Chief Ligurio's red eyes were intimidating to say the least, but Wynona knew at this point that he wouldn't hurt her. He was definitely a case of "his bark is worse than his bite". She was slowly beginning to see what her sister found so fascinating.

"First of all...thank you."

Wynona's eyebrows shot up. She hadn't been expecting that.

"I pride myself on getting to the truth and in this case, almost put an innocent woman in prison. So I appreciate your tenacity in setting me straight."

Wynona smiled. "Of course."

"Second, I'm still stuck on a few things. I'll admit that I went along with your plan, not because I believed Ms. Umbra was guilty, but because..." The chief trailed off and cleared his throat.

He didn't need to say any more. Wynona knew he hadn't wanted Celia to be guilty any more than she did. But as an officer of the law, he wasn't willing to use his own prejudice as a reason to keep digging when it seemed like they had the case solved.

"The sapphires are what set me off," Wynona explained. "You see, Callista had already set up for us to find Indigo's body. It was her get out of jail card. But when things went sideways with Niam, Callista needed to give him more incentive to let her in." She straightened in her seat. "Niam had just spent a couple of days alone with his wife and instead of being grateful she was gone, he was now a grieving widower. Callista hadn't expected Naim to actually care. But when Deputy Chief Strongclaw and I interviewed the two of them, I kept feeling like something was off. At first I just thought it was the relationship between them. Why in the world was Callista still living with her sister's husband? It seemed strange. But later I realized it was the out of sight magic that was tickling my brain."

Wynona picked Violet up from her shoulder and held her to her chest, cuddling the tiny creature close. "Once I realized that magic could have been done without the culprit being there, I began to notice other clues as well."

"And how did the sapphires help with that?" Rascal asked.

Wynona smiled at him. "Callista told me that Indigo never wore jade. She always wore the color of her eyes. Sapphires. The body had shown no signs of a struggle. In fact, odds are that Indigo was dead before she could understand what had happened. So it didn't make sense for Celia's bracelet to have gotten broken during the murder. To be sure, I checked Celia's wrists. There were no scratch marks. Nothing that would indicate Indigo had tried to take the bracelet accidentally or not."

"Callista's cut," Rascal said in awe.

Wynona nodded. "Right. The day Callista mentioned the sapphires, I found a cut on her finger. I thought she'd done it herself because of her long nails, but she didn't. The metal wire of Celia's bracelet did it when Callista broke it out in the field."

"So Callista set up the beads later?" Chief Ligurio clarified.

"Uh-huh," Wynona said with an eager nod. "The fact is, Indigo's body wasn't moved. She died right where we found her."

"How did Callista get the bracelet?" Rascal wondered.

Wynona huffed. "It was during the coven meeting. When I was checking Celia's wrists, I asked her if she took it off at all and she admitted she went to the bathroom, taking off her jewelry when she washed her hands." Wynona's right eyebrow went up. "I'm fairly certain Callista used another of her out of sight magic tricks to steal it during that time."

"And the grass?"

"The grass was broken from Callista's robes," Wynona said with a shake of her head. "Your crew didn't miss a thing when they first inspected the scene of the crime. Callista planted the shoes and the beads later. It was those long dresses she always wears that broke down the grass, not a floating body."

Chief Ligurio leaned back in his seat with a heavy sigh. "That's quite the tale, Ms. Le Doux."

Wynona smiled. "I think we can go with Wynona at this point, don't you, Chief?"

His smile was slow, but eventually he nodded. "Alright...Wynona." His brows immediately furrowed. "But don't think that this means we're friends." He pointed a pen at her.

Wynona held up both hands in surrender. "Nope. I promise not to make assumptions."

The chief huffed and looked down at his computer. "It's late," he said. "Might as well get home."

Wynona yawned as she stood. "Thank you."

"I'll take you home." Rascal said, standing with her.

"You're pulling an all-nighter," Chief Ligurio snapped. "Come straight back here."

"On it," Rascal said, rolling his eyes playfully at Wynona.

She held back a laugh and let Rascal lead her out of the room and down the hall. Using her free hand, Wynona covered another yawn.

"Too bad you can't just add a little something to your tea to give you energy," Rascal teased as he helped her into the truck.

His joke made Wynona realize that she hadn't told him anything about the safety bubble thing during her fight with Callista. She opened her mouth to do just that, then snapped it shut and smiled.

"Perhaps a strong green tea in the morning will be just what I need," she said. She really should probably talk to somebody about her suspicions, but right now she didn't have the energy. Wynona had no idea what exactly was going on with her, but they'd already solved one big mystery tonight. Hers could wait.

Rascal paused before closing her door. "Are you still going to be good to go Sunday night?"

She frowned and tried to remember why Sunday was important. "Our date!" she cried before she could control her response.

Rascal gave her a look. "Should I be offended that you didn't remember?"

A blush crept up Wynona's neck and cheeks. "Actually, I've been looking forward to it all week, but what with having to fight an evil witch and all..." She made a face and Rascal chuckled.

"I guess that's a good enough reason," he said with a grin. "So?"

"I wouldn't miss it," Wynona whispered.

His eyes flashed the beautiful golden color she loved and he winked. "Perfect."

From the way his eyes roamed over her before he closed the door, Wynona knew his word had been much more than a response to her acceptance of the date. She could barely contain her smile as he drove her home, and even after walking inside and depositing Violet at her little cushy bed, Wynona knew sleep couldn't come fast enough. She had a wolf shifter to dream about.

CHAPTER 30

"I can't believe I always miss the good stuff," Prim pouted, folding her arms over her chest. "Maybe if I followed you around like a love-sick wolf, I'd get in on the action once in a while!"

Wynona rolled her eyes and fought to control her blush from the wolf comment. "Waking you up late at night in order to come watch me try and bait Callista Umbra was not exactly high on the priority list," Wynona said wryly.

"I know!" Prim threw her hands in the air. "That's the problem!"

Wynona laughed softly and finished with her hair. She looked over herself in the mirror and turned to Prim, striking a pose. "What do you think?"

"I think you could wear a burlap sack and those golden eyes wouldn't leave you for a second," Prim said with a snort.

Wynona gave her friend a look. "No. Really. Am I okay?"

"You're stunning and you know it," Prim offered. She shook her head. "I don't know how you pull off such dark colors so well. You're like a living Snow White, but with much better curves and hair."

Wynona choked on air and began to cough. "Is that supposed to be a compliment?" she asked through her gasps.

Prim shrugged. "I'd take it as one. Only I don't want to look like Snow White."

Wynona finally caught her breath and shook her head. "And just who would you like to resemble?"

Prim pursed her lips. "I don't know...there aren't a lot of fairy tales where the princess has pink hair."

"True." Wynona put her make up away, took one last look in the mirror and walked out of her bathroom.

Violet was sitting on the dining table, pouting and grumbling under her breath.

Wynona walked up. "It's a date," she explained for the thousandth time. "That means Rascal and I are supposed to get to know each other...alone!"

Violet sniffed and began grooming her fur, completely ignoring Wynona's explanation.

Wynona turned to Prim and shrugged. "What more can I do?"

"Let the mouse brood," Prim said with a wave of her hand.

Violet took offense to the comment and began chattering loudly and shaking her fisted paws in Prim's direction.

Prim stuck her tongue out at the rodent.

"Really?" Wynona asked the two. "What are we? Three?"

Prim grinned and bounced on her toes. "I'll never tell."

Wynona rolled her eyes. She pointed a finger at Violet. "I'm going on a date. I love you, but I think I've earned this time alone with Rascal, so you'll have to get used to it." She then turned to her snickering fairy friend. "And you can help by not making the situation worse."

Prim huffed. "Fine. But the mouse started it."

Violet went off again and Wynona groaned.

"You two are impossible." She grabbed her coat and checked the wall clock.

Just as the hour chimed, a knock came on the door.

"It's him!" Prim squealed in delight. She rose up on tiptoe as if trying to fly from the floor and put her fisted hands in front of her mouth. Some of the herb plants around the room began to tremble and dance, matching Prim's excitement.

Wynona wanted to join in the joyous shout, but her heart had suddenly decided to begin beating so hard she struggled to breathe. This was it. The night she had been waiting for.

Wynona didn't have a lot of experience with men, but she felt certain that her feelings for him were more than just a mere crush. She could feel his presence when he was in the room. His touch not only gave her butterflies, but soothed her worries at the same time. When he wasn't around, she wanted him to be, and when they were together, she found herself able to read his emotions better than any other person she'd ever known.

It was possible that her feelings were based on the fact that they had been through some dangerous situations together, but it didn't really seem that way. From the first time he'd winked at her, Rascal had been upending Wynona's world and she found herself looking forward to more of it. Much more of it.

"Well, go on!" Prim whispered loudly.

Wynona nodded, her nerves nearly making her knees buckle. She wiped her clammy hands on her skirt before finally finding the courage to open up the door. "Rascal," she breathed, at once delighted by his appearance.

His black, button up shirt brought out the brightness of his eyes, which were already glowing, and the way he'd rolled up the sleeves looked casual and cool all at the same time. His forearms were tan and strong and completely swoonworthy. His fitted jeans and motorcycle boots were the perfect finishing touch to his look and Wynona knew she'd be the envy of every woman they crossed tonight.

Rascal's eyes went down and then back up in a slow, lazy manner. He whistled low under his breath. "You look amazing," he said, his voice slightly gruff.

Wynona smiled and didn't even bother to fight the blush creeping up her neck. "Thank you," she said sincerely. "You look wonderful yourself."

"She better, after all that time in front of the mirror!"

Wynona closed her eyes and counted to ten. Prim was a lot of fun and Wynona's first real friend after escaping her family, but sometimes her uninhibited way of speaking was more than Wynona could handle.

Rascal chuckled. "It was well worth it," he said, holding out his hand.

Wynona smiled in relief and reached out to take his offer. His palm was warm and reassuring, absolutely perfect as she walked across the threshold with him.

"I'll have her back by midnight!" he playfully called into the cabin.

"Don't bother," Prim shot back. "I'm living vicariously through her, and midnight isn't nearly enough time for a good make-out session!"

"Oh my word, Prim," Wynona groaned. "Please, stop."

Prim just grinned and wiggled her fingers in farewell. "Have fun!"

"Please ignore her," Wynona muttered as Rascal walked her to the truck. "I've learned to only listen to about half of what comes out of her mouth."

"Actually, I appreciated her approval," Rascal said. He paused before opening the door for her. "And she's right."

"Right? About what?"

"Midnight isn't nearly enough time," he whispered, leaning in and caging her against the truck. His eyes glowed brighter than ever and Wynona found herself entranced by them. "I've been waiting a long time for this. Should we give her something to enjoy?"

Wynona opened her mouth to respond, but the only thing that came out was a sigh as he leaned in to nuzzle her neck.

Rascal's lips brushed along her skin, leaving watermelon sized goosebumps in his wake. He paused and took in a deep breath.

"Are you smelling me?" Wynona asked with a soft laugh.

"Yep." He leaned back, grinning wildly. "Does that bother you?"

She tilted her head at him. "Is it like...a wolf thing? I mean, you smell fantastic, like woods and fresh rain, but I don't usually lean in just to smell your skin."

He came down and met her nose to nose. "You should try it sometime. And yes, it's a wolf thing." He ran his nose along her jawline. "Smell is very important to us and yours is...intoxicating."

Wynona melted against the truck door as Rascal continued to kiss and nuzzle the sides of her face and neck. "Rascal," she whispered.

"Hmm?"

"Please." She wanted...no, *needed* him to stop kissing her everywhere but her mouth. The anticipation was going to make her explode if he didn't just put her out of her misery.

"Please?" She could feel Rascal's grin against her skin. "Are you asking me to kiss you properly, Ms. Le Doux?"

Growing tired of his games, though slightly amused by them, Wynona reached up and put her hands on either side of his face, bringing him around to face her. "Hugo Strongclaw, you're driving me crazy."

He jerked back. "You know my first name? How?"

She grinned and let her hand slip into the back of his hair. When his eyes flared and grew brighter, she guessed she was doing something right. "A woman has to have some secrets," she whispered. "But this woman is also getting impatient. If you want any chance of—"

Apparently, Rascal took her threat seriously because he didn't even let her finish her sentence before claiming her lips.

Wynona gasped slightly at the attack before settling into the all-too pleasurable sensation of Rascal's kiss. His large hand went around her waist, tugging her into his chest, and his other dove into her hair. It didn't matter that it had taken her nearly an hour to create the perfect wave. All Wynona wanted was more of Rascal Strongclaw.

His hold was firm, but still made her feel precious. He kissed her with confidence but was still being gentle enough to claim the title of gentleman. All in all, with each press of his lips, Wynona found her knees growing weaker and weaker.

But it was when he tilted her head to gain better access that Wynona felt something within her begin to shift and eventually burst.

She jerked back from Rascal with a loud gasp as purple lightning shot through the air around them.

Rascal immediately covered Wynona as if to protect her, but she pushed at his chest.

"It won't hurt us," she whispered.

"How can you be sure?" he growled, glancing over his shoulder at the display. "I don't think your grandma liked me kissing you." The disappointment in his voice was easily heard and Wynona knew she had kept her secret long enough.

"It's not my granny," she said.

Rascal whipped his head around to look at her. "Excuse me?"

She shrugged. "I'm not exactly sure what's going on, but I think we need to talk." The lights slowly came to a halt, until just a few sparks floated through the air. Rascal had backed away from her and Wynona held out her hand, catching one of the pieces of magic. It sizzled against her skin, but didn't hurt before absorbing into her palm.

"I think you're right," Rascal said in awe. His wide eyes moved from her hand to her face.

Wynona dropped his gaze, suddenly feeling awkward and out of place. She had just had the most gloriously intimate moment of her life, and now she found herself terrified that Rascal was going to run from the weirdness that was her life. "If you don't want to go out...I'll understand."

He reached out and put his knuckle under his chin, bringing her face up until they could see each other. Still holding her, his thumb caressed her jawline gently. "It's just another piece of the puzzle, Wy," he said in a low, rumbly tone. "I didn't ask you out because I only liked what I saw on the surface." He leaned in and kissed her forehead sweetly. "That's just a bonus."

Wynona sighed and smiled as he helped her into the truck. She had a lot to figure out about herself along with figuring things out with Rascal, but knowing he wasn't running screaming into the night made her feel cherished and warm all over. Perhaps with his expertise and her book knowledge, between the two of them, they could figure out what exactly was happening to her.

And if it took a few more mind blowing kiss experiments to come to any conclusions...well, Wynona decided she was definitely up for the challenge.

Ready for Wynona's next adventure?
Don't miss Le Doux Mysteries #3
"A Sip of Murder"

Third time's a charm...until someone commits murder.

With her sister back at the castle and the tea shop thriving, Wynona feels like her life is finally on track. The fact that a certain werewolf is hanging around an awful lot, only makes it all sweeter.

Until her best friend, Primrose, while pretending to be a vampire, becomes a suspect in a murder investigation.

Wynona's life is once again turned on its head as she navigates the world of Hex Haven's most passionate fangirls. The deeper she digs, the more confusing the evidence becomes, and the harder she must work to clear her friend's name.

With her own magic completely out of control, a burgeoning relationship distracting her, and a police chief with an eternal grudge against her family...Wynona isn't quite sure how she's going to pull this off. But for Primrose's sake, she has to try.

Get it at your favorite retailer!